T0103999

GOOD REEDE-ING

HOWARD REEDE-PELLING

Order this book online at www.trafford.com
or email orders@trafford.com

Most Trafford titles are also available at major online book retailers.

Print information available on the last page.

ISBN: 978-1-4907-6033-9 (sc)
ISBN: 978-1-4907-6032-2 (e)

Trafford rev. 01/28/2016

Trafford PUBLISHING® www.trafford.com
North America & international
toll-free: 1 888 232 4444 (USA & Canada)
fax: 812 355 4082

Contents

ABOUT THESE ENTRIES

These twenty two entries are a compilation of the author's own memories and experiences throughout his lifetime. The majority of the tales within are entirely fictional but many of the pieces are also true life. The reader will be able to differentiate between the two types of writing and the author is sure that both the fiction and the real life entries will be most enjoyable to peruse; for both are either enthralling or interesting.

There are many pages of history within including a rare insight into the wonderful area of bottle collecting. The author has detailed what is a remarkable history of the pottery world of a century or more past; this history may not be available to the average reader as it is mostly known only to bottle collectors. A MUST read for Ginger Beer Bottle Buffs.

ENJOY!

1 The Coach 1978

I remember him well my coach, I had no wish to swim. I hated the thought of being taught and that ugly bloke with the straggly hair that mum pushed me over to; was not my idea of a teacher. I just knew he would throw me in and snarl - 'Come on Ronald, move your arms, kick your feet, go-go-go!' For sure he would call me 'Ronald', I hated the name anyway. I didn't mind being called Ron like Dad does, or 'Pud' as Grandpa nicknamed me; but Ronald - ugh! I stood around with a curled lip and hatred in my eyes. Mum pushed again, saying.

"Go on Ronald, go to the man."

I had to do what mum said or she would thump me, not only here but again when we got home. I shuffled closer, the coach looked up from the youngster he was instructing - a fat little twit who poked his tongue out at me - I returned the compliment and the coach frowned.

"Come on you two, that is enough, behave or I will not bother with you!"

Ha! Little did he know that suited me fine, I turned to go, a hand firm upon my shoulder swung me about, and it was the coach his eyes seemed to smile as he asked my name, I told him as mum said I should, that it was Ronald.

"Okay Tiger, hop in the water here and hold the rail". He waited as I shuffled.

I was afraid, I wanted to go back to mum and get out of the place.

"Come on Pal, don't be frightened." He urged.

I hesitated still, he told me to sit on the edge and talk a bit. I did, we talked and slowly I began to realise this man was not an ogre, he really understood my fright; he was not 'pushy'.

The coach seemed to mesmerise me with all he said how I should take my time and trust him, how I need not hurry into the water if I did not want to. He kidded me into letting him hold me as I kicked my legs and got used to the water. His strong arms gave me confidence but I clung on desperately, still sure he would let me go - but no! I began to trust the man as he continually gently, quietly, confidently explained the reasons for what we were doing and how I should relax and enjoy the activities. His patience was heartening and before I knew what I was up to, he had me duck-diving of my own accord. By the time the lesson was over I was doing the 'fail safe' method of survival even though I still could not swim. My coach understood kids alright and most of the time he called me 'Tiger' or 'Pal', only once by name and then it was 'Ron'; yeah he is not really as bad as he looks. I loved my coach - well - I didn't really love him, I mean I liked him a lot and tried the best I could to please him. Mum said he is a good guy 'cause I was swimming the width of the pool after only a few lessons. It took time but he sure made a good swimmer of me and I looked forwards to my lessons after a shaky start. The coach is still going strong, he is a little older now and probably uglier too but I know he is no ogre. I have my son here today, he is only four. Damien is not as frightened as I was, little ones rarely are. The coach is looking over at Damien as I push him forwards. I wonder will the boy like the coach as I did. Sure, he will love him. Think I will wander over to the store for the paper and relax a bit, Damien is safe - he is with the coach!

The End

2 Susie-Pie 1978

She was very small for her age, most of the family called her 'Pixie' and to Grand dad she was 'Little bit'. I was just a friend of the family over a few years of association as swim instructor to her brothers. They were older by five and seven years. My favourite name for her was 'Susie-Pie', I don't know why but I called most little girls 'Susie-Pie. At five years of age the little girl only looked three and a cute little three at that. Her christened name was Larette but not a soul would dare call her by name, it was always a hard one for her to pronounce. I suppose it was mutual love at first sight between us. Like most people I could not resist the golden-haired blue eyed baby-doll and there must have been a twinkle in my eye or a chuckle in my heart that drew her to me, be that as it may, we had something between us and my visits to her home were always a rewarding experience. Susie-Pie was a very shy youngster by nature and in her dainty baby way would suppress a giggle and hide behind a door before letting it out. One first became aware of her presence by the feeling of being stared at and upon looking about, would catch bright blue eyes peeping over the arm of a chair behind which she would be hiding; the light flashing off her bright wavy locks that shimmered and cascaded about the dear pretty doll-like face. A button of a nose resting atop the padding on the arm of the chair and that steady wide-eyed gaze penetrating. If one stared back she would duck out of sight and pretend she was not there at all. I made friends with Susie-Pie on my first visit when I happened to find one of her dolls with the head unhooked from its elastic support and by fixing it, was rewarded by her snatching the doll, kissing my hand, and then diving out of sight behind a chair. Her mother, Karen, announced that I should be honoured to be so attended on my first visit, but as the visit lasted about an hour and I made a habit of catching Susie-Pie looking at me and smiling as I did, it became a regular game with us. It was not long before the cutie came near enough to touch me and eventually to sit upon my lap as her mother and I chatted about the boys' progress at swimming. She was like a wriggly bundle of nothing perched atop my knee, tiny fingers exploring all that was new to her. The pattern of my pullover, my watch band and the hairs upon my wrist; she would stroke them and peep at me out of the corner of her eye to see if I had noticed the affront. Susie-Pie, like most children, could not sit still for long and the next minute would see her slip off my knee and crawl after the cat or pester one of her brothers. It was a great moment for me when on one of my visits to her home, Susie-Pie came in from playing out in the garden and upon seeing me in the lounge-room, rushed over with arms outstretched and gave me the greatest little hug - just because I was there. It made me feel quite humble that the little one took to me so well and that I had her love and friendship - however - there was this feeling of being an interloper, an outsider who had pushed into the family circle and not wanting to upset these wonderful people, I realised that I must make my visits fewer; slowly detach myself. Obviously I was becoming too attached to someone else's child. I would still teach the boys swimming and possibly soon Susie-Pie too but for the moment I must quietly, inconspicuously ease my way out of her life. I am going to find it hard to see her less often but I love her so much I know I have to; the bright spot is the future, perhaps in five or six months when her parents bring her along for lessons with her brothers. Dear little Susie-Pie, I wish you were mine.

END.

3 Tracy 30/1/1978

"Yes Aunt Muriel, I'll come over now. Mum said to ring you first. Yes Aunt Muriel - about ten minutes!"

Tracy hung the receiver on its hook and left the telephone booth, making her way through the dark streets a little apprehensively, because of the late hour in which her mother made her go to stay with the aged Aunt Muriel. Her brother was supposed to keep the old lady company for the night but he was very late coming home. No doubt he would cop it when he did arrive but that did not help Tracy at all, she still had to spend the night at the large, rambling old mansion that housed only her mother's sister. As she carefully picked her way through the dark streets, endeavouring always to keep in the lit areas; she saw a very small person walking towards her in the distance. It was indistinct in the darkness but Tracy felt sure it was a tiny tot. Her heart thumped. What on earth would a toddler be doing out this late at night? It must have wandered off unnoticed, obviously! As they neared each other, Tracy could see it was indeed a small boy, possibly only two or two and a half years of age. He was wearing pyjamas and when they met, he said "Mummy!" Tracy shook the shoulder length brown hair out of her eyes as she knelt before the child.

"Well, you are a duffer, wandering off like that. Where does Mummy live?"

She took his hand and continued on her way, taking the child back the way he came. Each time they passed a house with an open gate, they stopped and Tracy asked, "Where is Mummy?" The little one would cry "Mummy" and point in various directions, but never through any of the gateways. As Tracy neared her Aunt's home, she realised that no good would come of her efforts as they may have already passed the lad's house, or else it could be in any one of the half score of streets they had crossed. She would dearly love to take him with her; no one would know she had him. Tracy knew she could easily sneak into her Aunt Muriel's house and keep him tucked away in one of the back rooms in her rambling building. Aunt Muriel never went into some of the rooms of her large home. But then, Aunt Muriel had reasonably good hearing and no doubt somewhere along the line the youngster would cry out and scream for his mum. It was a stupid thought really. Still, Tracy knew it would be a lovely opportunity to have a real live baby of her own. She yearned to bath and dress him up and hear the happy gurgles. At thirteen she was beginning to show signs of womanhood and dolls were fast becoming a thing of the past. Here was reality on an open plate. Tracy shook the feeling off. The tiny tot's welfare came first; its poor mother must be frantic for the return of her baby. Tracy began walking to the police station; it was only two blocks away. She carried the lad who was beginning to grizzle, as it had bare feet and no doubt would be feeling the cold. The headlights of a car temporarily blinded her as it turned the corner and bore down upon them. It appeared to be attempting to run them down. Tracy became frightened and rushed into the driveway of a house they were passing, in case the vehicle really was out of control. It screeched to a stop at the kerb. Two tall men came at Tracy from different directions, she screamed as they took the terrified boy from her and bundled her into the car. Upon seeing the blue light atop of the car, the sign and then hearing the siren, Tracy stopped her resistance and breathed a sigh of relief.

"Gee! You gave me a fright. I didn't know you were policemen, I was just taking the boy to the police station - I found him wandering!"

Her smiling explanation was brusquely "Harrumphed". At the police station, one of the men took her inside firmly gripping an arm, the other drove off; apparently to return the toddler to its home. The room Tracy was left in (after her name and address was entered in the log), was a typical office. A typewriter and telephones adorned the desk which had an array of books and papers upon it. A couple of decrepit old chairs and a bench along one wall were the only furniture apart from bookshelves attached to the wall. A uniformed policewoman entered, she greeted Tracy with a smile.

"Hello Tracy, I am Sergeant Dorkin - it is Tracy isn't it?" The girl nodded.

"Why am I here? I am supposed to be at Aunt Muriel's, she will be worried!"

The policewoman pointed to a chair.

"All in good time, I will ask the questions. Why did you take the child?"

Tracy sensed an undertone, it all seemed unreal.

"Huh? Well - there was no one else, I mean - he was lost. I tried to find his home but he couldn't tell me, so I was bringing him here!"

Sergeant Dorkin frowned as she pursed her lips.

"That is not very original Tracy, I want the truth. You do not seem to realise how serious it is to kidnap a child. You can not just take them from their parents like that! Now start from the beginning. How did you get past the dogs and into the nursery? It was locked from the inside!"

"But I didn't, I! --"

Sergeant Dorkin thumped the desk as she raised her voice.

"Tracy!" The frown deepened. "Don't deny it, you were caught with the child, you tried to hide it from the detectives - now no more beating about the bush. How did you get in?"

Tracy burst into tears as she blubbered.

"I found him wandering, truly. I did not kidnap him!"

She laid her head upon her arms on the desk and sobbed. A comforting arm was around her shoulders as Sergeant Dorkin soothed.

"Come, come Tracy, stop sniffling. I will be back in a minute."

Tracy could not understand how a simple trip to Aunt Muriel's place could end up with her at a police station, charged with kidnapping. She was not sure if she was charged or not. Tracy knew she did not kidnap the child but remembered the thought of it entered her head. How lucky she was that her common sense prevailed, although it did not seem to be doing any good. Here she was, accused of taking the boy whether she did or not. Aunt Muriel would be worried because she hadn't arrived. One consolation was that Aunt Muriel would not be able to ring her parents because there was no 'phone at Tracy's place. What a mess to be in, if she could only prove she was nowhere near the boy's house, Tracy was sure the police would let her go but then; she did not know where the little fellow lived. But how to prove that to the police? That minute Sergeant Dorkin was going to be had become a quarter of an hour, when suddenly the door burst open and her father rushed in.

"Tracy Dear!"

He opened his arms to her. She rushed into them and cuddled close to dad.

"They frightened me. I did not steal the boy Dad!"

"I know - I know, so do the police now, I have explained everything. They know it was not you because you were ringing Aunt Muriel at the time the boy went missing. It is all over Pet, will you still go to Aunt Muriel?"

Tracy nodded.

"Yes Dad, I'm all right now!"

Police woman Sergeant Dorkin waved a cheery goodbye as they left but Tracy was not impressed.

"I thought she was very rude the way she bullied me." Tracy informed her father.

"Oh, forget it dear, they were only doing their job. They have to find out the truth for the sake of the child. Was he a nice little fellow Tracy?"

"Yes, I would like to be able to look after him. It must be nice to have a baby brother Dad! Do you think I will ever be able to have one?"

Her father became startled. He coughed.

"Yes, well I - er - no, no I do not think that is possible dear. You see, mother and I think we already have enough family. I mean, you do have a younger sister and two older brothers that is plenty for us. Your time will come, have patience!"

When Tracy returned home the next morning, a strange car was parked in the driveway. Curious, she hurried inside. Her parents introduced her to the newcomers as Mister and

Missus Mayfold, but the youngster on the floor caught her attention most. It was the little lad of the previous night.

"Thank you dear." His mother was saying. "We are terribly sorry for your ordeal last night. Honestly, we thought Gerald was stolen, because he has never gone off like that before. We think he has learned how to unlock the nursery door and he just went walkabout. Thank you very much for taking care of him." She gave Tracy a kiss.

"Aw, I did not do much really; the police took him from me!"

"Never-the-less" Mister Mayfold said "You were doing the right thing taking him to the police station."

There was a lull in the conversation as Tracy sat on a pouffe' and Gerald climbed onto her knee.

"Well, you certainly get on well together, how would you like to baby-sit for us some nights. Do you think you could manage - do you want to?" Missus Mayfold asked.

Tracy beamed as she cuddled the child to her.

"Oh! Could I?"

She turned to her mother.

"May I Mum?"

"It has all been arranged. We only wished to know if you wanted to do it."

Tracy was elated. 'No doubt about it' She thought 'If you do the right thing, your wildest dreams can come true!'

The End.

4 Stevie 7/1/1978

"Gotcha! You little beauty. Stevie, look what I got!"

Paul leaned precariously outwards from the dim shadows of the Presbytery roof, his excited whisper almost a shout. Cupped firmly in his hands a pigeon attempted to flutter out of its predicament. The wiry fingers held firm as the youngster held aloft his prize, the better for his pal to see. Stevie answered his call with a stifled -.

"Shush you bloody idiot, do ya want the Father to hear us. Wotcha got?"

He scuffled around the corner of the veranda roof. Paul shoved his captive under the nose of the curious one.

"It's a Sandy, th' light one, you know - with the white markin's. I caught 'er right there."

He indicated with a nod the general direction; oblivious to the fact that the action was unnoticed by his pal who was attempting to study the bird; already being stuffed up Paul's jumper.

"Gee, you always were lucky, I couldn't get near one. Let's hold it a minute, I'll carry it down!"

Stevie reached out.

"No, bugger ya, I caught it so I take it, you get ya own!"

"Who is up there, what are you doing?"

A stentorian voice sounded from below. Two startled faces peered down for a second as a torchlight flashed across their features, then panic set in as the mischievous pair scurried towards the rear of the rooftop to make their escape. Father Trengrove could be most frightening at times and this certainly was one of those times. As he could be heard briskly walking around the side of the presbytery, the two lads were sliding down a plank onto the garage roof. By the time the Father had arrived by a more round-a-bout route, the lads were going hell-for-leather along the rear lane.

"Christ that was close!" Stevie puffed. "Do ya reckon he saw us? He got the torch right on me face!"

Paul shrugged, still clutching at the fluttering bird up his jumper.

"Dunno, think he must of but, I could see him pretty clear."

It was nine o'clock in the evening and the two eleven-year-olds were just a little nervous as they hurried through the park, keeping to the pathways where there was an occasional light. The park was a fun place in the daylight but at night it was scary. They crossed another road and then turned up a side street. Here was Paul's place. Hurrying around the side way, Stevie opened the door of the pigeon-coop as Paul shoved the bird in; it fluttered about in the unfamiliar surroundings and finally subsided in a corner. A chorus of dissent came from the other birds in the cage.

"Well, I am gonna sneak in now, see ya termorra Stevie!"

Paul began to move.

"Hey! Aren't you going to walk home with me?" Stevie was panicky.

"No way, I'm already home I'd only have to come back. You're on ya own, see ya!"

"Gee, some friend. Leave a fella stranded in the dark!"

Stevie was grumbling to himself as he made his way home with apprehensive steps. Each shadow held terror for Stevie. He was big and brave with his mates - but alone at night - he was just a frightened little boy. As the last few steps of the corner approached, Stevie breathed a sigh of relief; three more houses around that corner and he was home.

"Bloody hell!"

It was a small man, pale of complexion and beady-eyed. The boy walked straight into him in his haste. A bottle of wine the man had fell to the pavement and broke, spilling the liquid over them both. Stevie was aghast.

"Gosh, I'm sorry Mister, I - I couldn't help it."

"Little bastard of a kid." The weedy thin man snarled. "Cost me two dollars thirty that did. Why doncha look where you're going?"

The boy surveyed the broken mess.

"I couldn't help it!"

"You come chargin' 'round the corner." The man fastened his beady eyes on the boy. "You just better pay for it!"

Stevie was trembling.

"Ar gee! I ain't got any dough, how ya expect me to pay for it?"

The stranger put an arm around the boy's shoulders and edged him into the darkness near the fence, kidding to the youngster.

"Now look son, you broke my bottle worth over two dollars and you can't pay for it in cash. There may be another way you can pay me though."

Suspicion entered the boy's thoughts as he cautiously asked.

"How?"

The man got down on one knee and with a hand on the lad's buttocks, pulled him closer.

"It'll only take a few minutes; I just want to do somethin'."

He began to pull the boy's trousers zip-per undone.

"No, lemme go!"

Shocked, Stevie tried to pull away. The beady eyes blazed as the man held the youngster firmly, attempting to de-bag him. Desperation seized the frightened boy as he kicked with all his might at the man's shins, so far as he could, restricted by his sagging trousers. Suddenly released as the man grabbed his tortured legs, Stevie made off and stumbled around the corner flat on his face; tripped by his own pants. Before the man could grab him again he dragged them up and was inside his own home shouting for his parents. They were not at home. He bolted the back door and checked all the windows, then hid under his bed in the dark, scared and trembling; cold sweat dampened his forehead. Stevie had heard of these bad men, his parents had warned him about them and all of the boys at school spoke of them; however this was the first time Stevie had ever come into contact with one. He did not really know what the man intended to do, but he knew they were rude and he was frightened that he may have been killed. Gosh! Would he have something to tell the kids at school? None of them would be able to boast that a 'Poofter' had taken their pants off. Won't Paul be surprised? 'Serves him right' Stevie thought 'If he'd 'a walked home with me he might have been in on the fun - huh, fun?'

Stevie shuddered, it wasn't any fun, and Stevie was scared stiff. Perhaps it might not be a good idea to tell the kids, now he thought of it, they would probably make fun of him and call him names. Names like 'Poofter's little pet' and 'Hi Pansy.' Stevie would have a bad time with the other kids if they found out and it might not be a good idea to tell his parents either. For sure he would not be allowed out after dark again and no more pigeon chases with Paul. Stevie was not sure if he wanted to go out after dark now, anyhow. He could not hear the man prowling about, maybe he ran off too. The boy crept from under the bed and peered out of the window. There was no sign of the man. He pulled the blind down and arranged his clothing properly. Stevie was determined now that he should not tell anyone and was glad that his parents were still out. They thought he was in bed asleep when they left to go to the Pub for a few hours, but Stevie was still dressed lying under the bedclothes; because he and Paul had prearranged to sneak onto the church roof to catch pigeons.

"P'raps I had better be in bed when mum and dad do get home, or I'll have some explaining to do! Geez! I woulda copped it if they hada been home when I raced in before, I was supposed to be in bed asleep!" He muttered to himself, still edgy.

The lad climbed into bed but sleep would not come. The morning found Stevie at Paul's place; they were looking at the catch of the night before. Although still a little ruffled, the new addition to Paul's coop was a fine specimen. Stevie was not as enthusiastic as his little mate thought he would be. The shock of the night before was gnawing at the boy. Stevie knew he should report the matter but was afraid to do so. His mates would make fun of him and he would be punished by his parents for being out at night when he was supposed to be in bed. If he went to the police about it, for sure they would tell his dad. It was not the sort of thing one would discuss with the Sisters at school, so it was a problem. What to do? He could just forget it and hope he never met the man again, more than likely he would not; Stevie had never seen the man before and he expected not to see him again. Sure, if he did not say anything to anyone, no one would know about it - no! That is not true, Stevie had a Catholic upbringing and he knew God would know, furthermore he knew also that it should be reported to someone because the man might get another kid one night - or day - but who to tell? His reverie was broken by Paul.

"Hey! Whatsamatter with you, you goin' to sleep standin' up or somethin'?"

"Nah. I was just worried about last night, that's all!"

"Shit. There's no need to worry. I bet Father never even saw us, well, not clear enough to know who we were." Paul encouraged. "Come on, let's go over to the park before school and play on the swings!"

They left the park and arrived at the school just as the bell sounded to summon all to classes. Stevie and Paul felt guilty as Sister Vanessa bid them a cheery "Good morning boys". They returned the greeting and quickly looked away. Sister pursed her lips as she entered the school building, a thoughtful frown upon her brow. After morning prayers were said, Sister Vanessa cast a pleasant smile over the class then fastened her eyes upon the two mischievous lads.

"Father Trengrove tells me -" she addressed the class at large "- that there were visitors to the Presbytery last night." Her gaze still upon Stevie and Paul, she continued. "Now I wonder if anyone here knows about it."

Sister's gaze travelled completely around the class, coming to rest upon the two boys again. They shuffled uncomfortably but remained silent. Sister spoke.

"Ah well, Father thought someone in this class might know something about it, perhaps they will go and tell him later - possibly at confession?"

She began the lessons. Paul and Stevie had a rather uncomfortable day; however something that Sister had said was important to Stevie. Father Trengrove! Of course, he was the one to tell about the man of the night before. All day Stevie wrestled with his problem, not quite sure how to go about talking to Father of the incident. It was out of his hands. After school Stevie and Paul were summoned to call on Father about altar duties. When that matter was settled, Father Trengrove asked the boys if they had anything further to say, Paul shook his head; Stevie looked at his boots. All were silent for awhile.

Father "Harrumphed" then said. "I would not like to be disappointed in my Altar Boys, you must have faith, are you sure there is nothing to tell me?"

"Aw, we was just catchin' pigeons Father!" Paul whined.

"Both of you?"

Stevie and Paul nodded.

"Well, in future ask beforehand and you will not get into trouble, however, as you did not ask and ran away when I called; you must be punished. I may overlook the punishment this time if you are both prepared to serve an extra week at the Altar." He looked enquiringly at the boys.

They were trapped. Of course they would be glad to serve, thank you Father. Disheartened at the extra duties, they left the Presbytery. Stevie told Paul to go home without him, he had something to do. Paul tarried but Stevie insisted and Paul knew how stubborn his mate could be on occasions, so he left. Stevie was scared but knew he had to talk to Father about the man; he had to be forgiven for breaking the bottle and desperately needed to clear his conscience. Father Trengrove was surprised when the lad was ushered into his study. The stern features and furrowed brow gave the boy misgivings about informing.

"Well Steven, what is it. Think you may be able to talk your way out of your duties, do you?"

He glared at the boy.

"No Father, it's not that - I - !"

"Come, come - do not stammer boy - out with it, quickly!"

Stevie baulked edging to the door, wishing he could back out of it now. Maybe it was a stupid idea anyhow, to tell Father.

"Good God boy, I do not have all day, what is it?"

Stevie trembled.

"It's - it's - I'm scared, please Father -!"

Father Trengrove suddenly mellowed; he sensed the boy had a deep problem.

"Come here lad." He said, gently, as he sat down and clasped his hands on the desk.

Stevie stood awkwardly before him, tears welling in his eyes.

"Well now, let us not be soppy."

Father unclasped his hands and held one out to the boy pulling him around the desk until Stevie was beside him.

"What is your problem Son, school work?"

Father put a reassuring hand on Stevie's shoulder. The boy felt more at ease now that Father was not shouting at him.

"No Father, school's all right. Its - it's a man. He tried to take my pants off!"

Stevie looked wide eyed at his mentor. The youngster related the night's events and gave Father Trengrove a description of the man. He was told not to worry about the bottle as the breakage was accidental and only used as an excuse for the man to attack him. He was a good boy for coming to Father about the assault and he would not tell Stevie's parents of the escapade regarding the pigeons, provided the boy behaved as expected and did his duties properly as an Altar Boy. A relieved Stevie went home, clear of conscience and knowing his parents would not know he was out late at night. Meanwhile, Father Trengrove had assumed responsibility of the boy's troubles. Because the lad was visibly upset and deeply worried, he was the main concern. So it was that Father had ironed out his worries, however the law dictated that the rogue must be apprehended, after all; there was the responsibility to his diocese. Detective First Class Mason Caulding being a former pupil and now a close friend of the Father, it was he of course who answered the call when necessity arose. Having got a description of the attacker, Detective Caulding assured his friend that he knew the man in question. He was a known offender; all they needed was proof positive. To this end

Stevie's parents were called upon by the detective and his assistant - much to Stevie's chagrin.

'So much for Father Trengrove's promise' thought the lad, saddened that his trust had been abused. Detective Caulding explained to the parents that Father had called and was worried for their son's safety. Even though Father did not directly tell his parents, Stevie knew that indirectly he had. Within two weeks the man was apprehended, tried and sentenced. After serving three months he would be back on the streets again. Stevie was a different boy by this time. The police questions, the ordeal of the courtroom, the indignant way his parents had reacted. All had taken their toll. He was wary when alone, sometimes moody, sometimes restless, always worried and with a far away look in his eyes as if seeking that which would never come. He and Paul were sitting on the grass by the swings in the park one Saturday morning. Stevie, as was his habit, was morose.

"Can ya keep a secret Stevie?" Paul guardedly asked.

"S'pose." Uninterestedly came from his glum companion.

"No really Stevie, I can't tell ya 'less I know you won't blab!" He glanced at his mate. "It's a truly secret, me parents don't think I know but I overheard Dad on the 'phone!"

Stevie began to show a little interest.

"Nah! I won't blab, what is it?"

Paul moved closer and whispered in his mate's ear.

"It's me Uncle - Dad's brother. He got put in clink!"

"Whaffor?"

"I dunno, but he's in for three months!"

Paul screwed up his nose as he lay on his back watching the leaves idly waving in the slight breeze, and then continued.

"He ain't a bad guy really - just gets funny now and then."

Stevie lay on his back too beside his cobber, they were silent awhile.

"What do ya mean; he gets funny - like a clown?"

"Nah, it's somethin' else, don't think I'd better tell ya. Reckon ya'd pimp an' then I'll get inta trouble."

Paul rolled over onto his stomach and plucked at the grass. Stevie was curious now, coming out of his shell.

"I won't pimp Paul, we're mates aren't we? Tell us!"

"True, God's honour. Cross your heart and hope you may die if ya pimp!"

He rested his head on one hand the better to see his mate's avowal.

"Sure, cross my heart and hope I may die if I pimp on ya."

Stevie spat on his fingers and crossed his heart then waited expectantly.

"Aw, I dunno." Paul drawled. "I can get into lots of trouble if ya dob an' anyone finds out!"

"Huh, some friend can't even trust your own mate. I crossed my heart didn't I?" Stevie demanded.

"Well, okay but you better not dob!"

"No, I won't. C'mon."

"It's me Uncle - the one in prison - he fiddles with me!"

Stevie sat bolt upright, staring at Paul in disbelief, then subsided without a word; thinking.

"It's true, doncha b'lieve me?" Paul felt he had to prove the point. "Well, doncha?"

Stevie did not answer immediately, then absently -

"Yeah, I s'pose so!"

They lay quietly for a while, each with his own thoughts. Paul could not stand it any longer.

"Hey Stevie, ya not gonna dob are ya, you promised?"

Again Stevie did not answer immediately; he rolled over to gaze at his cobber.

"Nah!" He murmured. "I promised so I won't tell." Pause, then. "Paul."

"What?"

"Did he hurt ya. I mean, was ya frightened?"

The subject had become important for Stevie. Talking about it may be the therapy he needed. Knowing it was a rude subject, having experienced an attack recently and with the fear and the awe of the church hanging over him; the boy was confused. Here was his best pal admitting he too, had been attacked yet he did not appear to be stressed by it at all; except that he may get 'dobbed in'. Paul answered.

"At first I was, about a year ago when Uncle John first squeezed me bum an' undone me zip-per. But he never hurt me. I liked him a lot, still do I s'pose."

"Did you tell ya mum?"

"Nah! I thought about it but Uncle John promised he wouldn't ever hurt me an' would give me things an' would take me out." Paul gave a grin.

"Anyhow, I liked it - it tickled."

"What tickled?" Stevie was wide eyed.

"When he tickled me thing - you know!"

It was Stevie's turn to wrinkle up his nose.

"Argh. It's rude. I reckon you oughta tell your mum!"

"Shit Stevie, if we're still going to be friends, you gotta keep your promises."

Paul was becoming agitated.

"I like Uncle John; I don't want him in prison forever." Paul lapsed into moody silence.

"All right, I'm not going to say anythin'." Stevie assured.

He would remain silent; after all, they were pals and should stick together. Reassured, Paul jumped up.

"Want to play on the swings?"

"Okay."

They enjoyed fifteen minutes of swinging then played chasey until exhausted. They again sprawled on the grass.

"Know what Paul." Stevie began. "I reckon it was because of me your Uncle is in jail!"

"Huh! How come?"

Stevie explained the circumstances and occurrence of the past months. The ordeal of the court, his extreme fright on the night of the attack and how he went to confession after telling all to Father Trengrove.

"That's why I wanted ya to go home when we got sprung about the pigeons." He finished with.

"I went back to tell Father, I thought you'd make fun of me if ya knew!"

“What makes ya think the bloke was MY uncle?” Paul frowned.

“I dunno, seems likely don’t it? Your uncle is in jail an’ so’s the fella what got me! ‘Sides, he was in this suburb – ain’t that where your uncle lives?”

“Ugh-huh.”

Paul arose and climbed onto the fence of the playground. He sat astride it then called to Stevie.

“If it was Uncle John, you won’t tell anyone, will ya? I mean, I don’t want all the kids to know me uncle does that!”

Stevie was becoming irritable.

“Nah. Let’s drop the subject, we should not be talking about it anyway – if Dad finds out I’ll cop it an’ we won’t be able to play together, I won’t say nothin’ an’ you don’t say nothin’ – right? Now let us forget it. I’ll race ya to the bandstand.”

He was off, Paul bringing up the rear. The weeks drifted idly by, Stevie was beginning to become his old mischievous self again and his friendship with Paul strengthened as the result of them having a common pact. The events that were the basis of their worries, long forgotten. Happily strolling home from school one day, the two boys took little notice of a man approaching until he was well upon them. Paul recognised him immediately.

“Uncle John!” He cried, running towards him.

“G’day Paul, how’s me mate?”

The man glanced at Stevie who, upon recalling those beady eyes, tried to hide behind an outcropping privet hedge. Terror stricken and agitated, sure he would be bashed for ‘dobbing’ and causing the man to go to prison; he trembled.

“Who’s your little cobber, Paul?”

Uncle John came toward Stevie who would have run off had the beady-eyed man not grabbed him firmly by the arm, to detain him.

“Don’t – don’t hit me please!”

Stevie realised the futility of running and pushed further into the hedge.

"Please Uncle John, he is me best pal – he didn't mean to dob on ya!"

Paul laid a restraining hand on the arm holding Stevie.

"Yes, he's the one – he's the one all right!" The beady eyes glared, and then softened as he cooed.

"Come boy, stop shivering, I won't harm you!"

Stevie tried to pull away.

"I wanna go home, lemme go!"

"Look son, I just want to talk for a bit. I will let you go if you don't run away – please son – Paul knows I won't hurt you, don't you Paul?"

Paul stood beside Stevie.

"'Cause he won't Stevie, I tol' ya he was alright didn't I; trust me!"

Uncle John released the boy and sat on the small brick fence over which the hedge grew. Stevie was behind Paul but stayed put, visions of that terrible night returning, his heart thumping; he waited.

Uncle John smiled at Stevie as he explained.

"Y'see, I been wanting to tell you I was sorry for scarin' you – I really wouldn't of hurt you that night – I just can't help meself sometimes. I'm not supposed to be talking to either of you; I'll get into trouble if I'm caught with kids for a bit. I come on purpose to talk, hopin' I'd catch you both. B'lieve me son, I'm sorry for what I've done, givin' you a fright an' all. Try an' forgive me, will you?"

Stevie shrugged.

"I s'pose."

The man turned to Paul.

"Well little nephew, I got to go away for a little while. You may not see me for a bit, I'm goin' interstate. Will you keep our little secret? I know you don't want me to go but it's better for all our sakes."

He gave Paul a squeeze then departed, saying. "Goodbye boys, remember no tales!"

Paul turned to Stevie.

"See. He's alright, ain't he?"

Stevie shrugged.

"Still don't like him much. Glad he talked to us but, I don't think I will worry so much now, I was real scared; y'know?"

Paul put an arm around his mate's shoulder as they went home.

"Y'ain't afraid no more, ya not gunna dob are ya?"

"Nah!"

"You comin' to my place now Stevie?" Paul asked.

Somehow Stevie felt happy, as if a great weight had suddenly been taken off his shoulders; he felt good.

"Okay!" He affirmed, then. "Paul, wanta ask Father if we can catch some pigeons tonight."

"I reckon, let's ask our parents!"

They ran off, jabbering.

The End.

Howard Reede-Pelling.

5 Cory – The White Bomber. 30/12/1977

Cory was eight, a wiry little fellow with rather plain features, not ugly but not what you would call handsome either. Most noticeable was his shock of blonde, almost white hair; accentuated by the green cardigan and shorts that were a birthday present from his Grandparents. It was school holiday time and Cory came back to the school ground for something to do, hoping to find one of his mates to play with. However, the only people there were strangers to him. He stood by the fence watching, they were playing a game of cricket, it was Cory's favourite game. Two men were fielding, one acting as 'keeper' the other near the mid off boundary. Two small boys of about his own age in the 'slips' position and two older boys comprised the group. One of these last was bowling. They seemed to be having a good game. Cory climbed the fence and came in closer, hoping the ball would come his way and give him the opportunity to join in. It did not, he moved closer. The older boy who was bowling called out.

"Hey, you with the green jumper, if you want to play move there where you'll be useful."

He indicated a position near one of the men. They played for about two hours. Cory felt he did well, more than held his own in fact. He made a great one-handed catch falling on his face and took a turn at batting. He scored seven runs before being caught out and they said his bowling was pretty good too, for a little bloke. As all were leaving, one of the men called him over to look at the mark on his face. It was only a graze from the fall when he caught the ball but the man insisted taking him to the car and treating it. With his face daubed with acriflavine Cory stood and watched as the group departed. He enjoyed the game and wished it could have lasted a little longer, but as the day was drawing to a close he knew it was near home-time. Cutting through the school yard the little lad noticed a teenager at the window of one of the prep grades. Curious, he sauntered across just as the window was forced open and the youth climbed in. Cory stood on the box the youth had used. He could barely see over the sill at what was happening within. The teenager was ransacking the teacher's desk; he turned suddenly and caught the boy watching him. Putting a finger to his lips to warn the boy to silence, he crossed the room. Cory seemed glued to the spot.

"Whatcha doing, you should not be in there, should you?"

For answer the youth grabbed the boy and hauled him over the sill and into the room. Cory began to scream but the youth smothered his cries with a large hand and held the little fellow so hard it was hurting.

"Shut up damn you." The ruffian hissed. "I'll break your bloody neck if you don't quit making a racket, shut up I say!"

Cory could not scream if he wanted to, he could barely breathe. The youth took his hand away from the child's mouth and held a fist up menacingly.

Cory shivered with fright but only softly whimpered.

"I won't yell, please don't hit me!"

"Right." Said the youth. "Now sit there, don't move and no noise."

He continued rummaging through the desk, occasionally putting things into his pockets and glancing at the boy who was too scared to move. The youth went further a field looking through more drawers and cupboards. Cory heard a car pull up by the school fence near where he had been playing cricket. Cory looked towards the car, the light was fading but he recognised the man who attended his graze. Making a sudden dash the boy was through the window and running to the man, shouting.

"Hey Mister, wait!"

The man stopped and turned just as the youth made his exit and scarped around the corner. As they met the man asked.

"What is the matter, what is going on?"

Cory wrapped his arms around the man and hung on tightly.

"He grabbed me and I was frightened – he is stealing!" The boy sobbed.

Realising that the youth was well away and he was needed more by the child, the man comforted Cory and gently coaxed the story from him. It was dark by the time they arrived at Cory's home and his parents apprised of the day's happenings. They expressed their thanks that the man had to return for his son's pullover and for his timely assistance to their son, whom they promised, would be kept closer watch upon. Two days later when Cory was sent to the shop on a message for his mum, he was surprised to see the youth from the school incident, playing at one of the pin-ball machines. Cory hurried from the shop. The youth pretended not to notice the boy but quickly followed as he left. The youth caught Cory just as they came to a lane way and pushed the boy into it, a threatening fist raised aloft which he knew would hold the boy to silence. Not a sound was spoken for almost a minute, Cory because he was afraid this time the bully would use the fist and the youth because he was not sure what to do now that he had the boy.

"I ought to smash you one, nicking off like that on me and dobbing." The big fellow snarled.

Cory, with fear in his eyes and heart, stood his ground silently, not daring to speak. The youth continued.

"What did you tell your old man when he came for you the other night?"

"P-pardon?" The boy stammered.

"Your father, what did you say to him about me when we came out of the school-room? Well, tell me!"

"He – he was not my father, I just played cricket with him. Can I go now? I have to get home with the message mum sent me for."

Cory tried to wriggle away but the youth held him against the fence by the shoulder.

"How much change you got left?"

Cory put his hands behind his back.

"It is mum's money; I have to take it back!"

Placing his closed fist against the lad's nose, the bully snarled.

"Hand it over Sonny!"

Cory spilled the change into the youth's hand and was then tripped and pushed into the grass verge of the lane way. The youth fled. Cory picked up his mother's goods and crept to the corner to see if the youth had really gone. He was in time to see the ruffian enter the shop, presumably to buy a packet of smokes with his ill-gotten gains. Cory waited until the youth came out of the shop, then at a good distance, followed him; hoping to find out where his tormentor lived and perhaps have his dad belt the youth. The boy worried how he was going to keep up with the big bloke, who seemed to have legs like stilts. Cory had to virtually run to keep him in sight. To the boy's relief, the youth eventually went into a house about three streets away from where Cory lived. He waited awhile to give the bully time to get well inside before creeping up to get the house number. Then he ran like billy-oh back home. Cory was just turning the corner of his street when he came face to face with the bully again. With one hand the bully held Cory against the fence (a habit he had) and with the other slapped the face of the startled lad two or three times. The child broke into frightened crying.

"Followed me eh! Thought I went home did you? Well I didn't, that's an empty house. I saw you through the window and raced over the back fence to cut you off, you little bugger. I warned you not to get smart and dob me in again – didn't I?"

The youth shook the sobbing boy violently. Cory fell to the ground and the youth rubbed grass into his face, and then kicked the packet that the boy had gone to the shop to get for his mum. That was the last straw, the youngster's fright turned to anger. He picked up the broken packet and hurled it full into his tormentor's face, yelling as he ran helter-skelter home.

"I'm gonna dob on you now, my dad'll getcha, you'll see!"

With flour in his eyes and covered head to toe in a puffy white cloud, the youth made to go after the lad but as he saw the child enter a house, thought better of it and departed. As the boy was sobbing his story to mum and dad, a knock on the door sounded the arrival of the man from the cricket game. He had come at his son's request to invite Cory to play with them again. When all was explained and they decided to put a stop to the bully, the question arose as to where to find him. Cory had the answer.

"Just follow the flour marks; they will either lead to an empty house or the bully's home. He would have to get cleaned up!"

Now that the ruffian is in a detention centre, Cory has no trouble going messages and he has some nice new friends who love cricket and always come by to pick him up when they are playing a game. They call him by a 'nickname' now – Cory, the white bomber!

The End.

Howard Reede-Pelling.

6 Gone Fishing 28/9/1995

"G'day Troy!" I exclaimed upon meeting a mate as we queued at the check-out counter of the local supermarket. "Where are you off to this week-end?"

It appeared that Troy had been deep in thought prior to my familiar greeting, as he gave a slight start of surprise.

"Oh! Hi Jules, I er, I think we will go up to the lake camping and fishing."

Troy gave me the impression of guilt. I have no idea why I got that impression at that point; it just of a sudden crossed my mind.

"Oh, really – camping huh?"

I raised my eyebrows in disbelief. After all, Troy was not the outdoors type. I mean, really, he had always been the intellectual one of our group of teenagers. Troy was more at home tinkering with inventions or unscrambling conundrums and the like at his computer. No, camping and fishing definitely was not his forte! Evidently he sensed my disbelief.

"Yes, just a mate and myself, we thought it would be fun – a bit of a change – you know?"

Troy did not look me straight in the eyes for very long at all. He grabbed his change and the goods he had purchased, and then hurried off.

"Would you like me to come with you?" I shouted after him.

"No thanks, we'll be right!"

He was gone.

I pondered the incident at some length during my walk back to the car. Troy knew I was a very keen and experienced fisherman and I could have been of invaluable assistance to him and his friend on the camping trip. Perhaps his friend was also an experienced fisherman. But why did I think he reacted guiltily upon our meeting; why should he feel guilty? I shrugged the thought and the feeling away and went about my business. That Friday evening as was my wont, I called upon my young lady friend. Amber and I had been going steady for some months. It was our usual habit to attend the local 'night spot' for a little dancing, drinks and a convivial chatter with our friends. To my great surprise when I called for Amber, her flatmate informed me that she had already left.

"Oh! Really, did she happen to mention where she would meet me?" I asked.

Lana seemed quite vague in her reply.

"Er – no – no, she just went out. I did not speak with her – I was in the shower when she left – I think!"

Puzzled, I returned to my car. Perhaps Amber had some business she had to attend before our evening out. It was quite possible she was unable to contact me as I had been shopping. No doubt she would meet me at the nightclub. I went alone. For the better part of an hour I awaited Amber at our usual Friday evening venue. With the milling crowd it was a very lonely place for me without her, I began to have vague apprehensions that I was missing something. I sought out Lana. Perhaps I could glean a clue of Amber's whereabouts, should I speak a little more with her flatmate. Lana saw me coming and I was sure she was attempting to avoid me. In that packed room, she had difficulty moving away. Her eyes warned me that she was hiding something.

"Come clean Lana." I demanded. "What is going on – where is Amber? I am sure you know, please tell me!"

"Oh Jules, I really can't tell. I promised Amber that I would not tell you where she went for the week-end. You do understand I can't say anything, don't you?"

Lana's plea hit me like a bombshell. Gone for the week-end and she said nothing to me of it. I was devastated! Troy had also gone away for the week-end – uncharacteristically. He always did have eyes for my Amber!

I know my face showed anger as I swung about and charged out.

"Jules!" Lana called. "Don't do anything rash. Where are you going?"

I called out angrily.
"Me – where am I going, I'm going fishing!"

End

© Howard Reede-Pelling.

7 Through the half open Door 12/10/1995

Gerry struggled with his bonds, hell they were tight! The circulation was being restricted and his sweating so profuse that the salty streaks down his neck were beginning to sting. With face pressed against the cold metal floor of the large van in which he had been unceremoniously dumped, Gerry searched frantically about for a sharp object. Even a screwdriver may be of some use to free him from the pain of that damnable rope. A protruding screw caught his attention. If only he could get his body into the right position so that the bonds which held him, could be chafed against that screw; perhaps he could escape. In desperation Gerry scuffed and scrubbed frantically and with urgency, mindless of the fact that skin was also being torn away with his desperate efforts. The rope was fairly thick and strong. It appeared that more skin was being chafed away than rope. Gerry persisted with his attempt at gaining his freedom. Of a sudden, footsteps were heard hurrying towards him. The van door was flung open and two of his captors began loading goods into the vehicle. Gerry lay still, pretending to be submissive. The men finished loading then slammed the door shut and began driving the vehicle away, ignoring Gerry completely. He re-recommenced his escape bid. It seemed that the van was on a free-way, for the desperate man on the floor could feel the speed at which the stolen van was travelling. Gerry hoped and prayed that these rogues did not damage his van, it was his livelihood and he still had instalments to pay on it. At last, the rope was being chewed to threads; the tension eased and another few Herculean yanks caused the rope to come asunder. Gerry was free at last! He wiped the bloodied wrists upon his overalls and rubbed circulation back into his numb arms. Now, what to do? The door of his van had an outer latch with a padlock for security. No way to open that from the inside. Gerry mentally noted he must do something about that! Boxes were stacked up covering the window of the cabin, so those in the front of the van could not see what was happening in the hold of the van. Gerry was loathe to attempt to kick his way out through the van walls; he doubted if it was possible anyway! Without warning the van left the free-way quite sharply. This was made painfully obvious to Gerry as he was rolled across the floor to crash heavily against some boxes.

"Careful, you'll wreck the goods!" He heard one of those in the cabin yell.

Two minutes later, another turn, a little slower and then a very rough and bumpy ride left the passenger in no doubt that they were traversing a corrugated country lane. Five minutes of travel along this track and the van came to a stop. Those in the cabin alighted. Gerry steeled himself to spring a surprise attack so soon as they opened the rear door of his prison. For sure they would expect he was still bound and helpless. As the door was unlatched, Gerry threw his weight against it. This action knocked two of the thieves over, then Gerry swung to the ground and raced for his life to the cabin, luckily the keys were still in the ignition switch. As Gerry started the engine and set the van in motion, the third of the trio who was fumbling with a lock on the door of the barn at the rear of a farmhouse, where the stolen goods were to be stored; hurried to a tractor over by the fence. By the time Gerry had turned his van in that fenced in yard and was on his way to the gate, the third man had the tractor moving. He rammed the side of the van, causing it to tilt awkwardly against the farmhouse. Gerry, jolted from the driver's seat, had his legs jammed as the cabin door came ajar. Whilst attempting to free his trapped legs as he lay on the cabin floor, Gerry saw one of the men charging towards him wielding a tomahawk. The man swung a deadly blow full at Gerry's face. Gerry saw death coming through the half-open door!

Howard Reede-Pelling.

8 Beloved Child! 9/11/1995

Simone tearfully brushed aside the bouncing honey-brown curls which fell across her line of vision, as she soothingly stroked the small cheek of her sleeping child. Belinda looked so beautiful and appeared to be one of the healthiest children one could ever have imagined. Ah! Looks can be so deceiving. Although the pretty little girl slept a peaceful sleep of calm serenity and those gorgeous large blue eyes were no longer visible, Simone knew the depths of despair to which she had sunk were as nothing to the very real possibility looming in the future; that those heavenly eyes would glaze over in the peace of death! Fresh tears glistened upon her own cheeks as Simone recalled the fateful words of the specialist.

"Belinda's condition is terminal! Perhaps six or seven months – I am sorry – nothing can be done!"

Oh, the thud of her heart thumping in erratic beats seemed to echo about the room as of a doomsday chorus. The shock as realisation that her daughter, that wonderful little being, was doomed to die, nevermore to be there to brighten their lives. It was too much for the distraught mother. She fainted. Simone remembered awakening to the trembling caress of her equally devastated husband, Jeremy, who doted over his pride and joy with the unbridled passion and tenderness of a loving father. With this same tenderness, he attended her mother. That horrid episode did not seem to have occurred half a year ago, yet time had raced away ever too soon. Now with the forecast so close to its inevitability, Simone wept for the beloved child of their bodies. One of her tears splattered upon the back of her hand as she gently, tenderly, softly brushed the tiny cheek of her dying baby. Simone hastily dabbed at her own pretty face lest the little girl be awakened by a wayward tear. She could feel the closeness of Jeremy as he lightly squeezed her shoulder while he sat beside his grieving wife, a grief they shared. His touch gave her the strength to hold herself together as she must, at least until it was over. Over! Over! Oh, dread the thought. That their beloved child would be gone and gone forever – no – no, perish the thought! A miracle that is what they needed, a miracle. Simone turned to Jeremy, he read her thoughts.

"Darling, we have prayed, we are still praying. We cannot expect miracles but" he smiled wistfully at her "we will always have our memories and those captivating photographs. Belinda will always be with us and while she still lives, let us enjoy her to the full. Look at her wonderful curls – just like yours – and that cute little button of a nose. Oh, our little Belinda is so precious I just want to kiss and cuddle her to pieces, I – I - !!"

His faltering voice choked to a whisper and he shook with silent sobs. Simone placed a hand over his as it rested upon her shoulder. She squeezed the hand, sharing his sorrow; then whispered.

"Our child, our only precious little girl, our dearly beloved child!"

Her voice trailed away into nothingness. They watched the quietly sleeping little girl. The beautiful little love of their lives, faintly fading – fading - .

Howard Reede-Pelling.

9 Sam by © Howard Reede-Pelling 15/9/2003

Butterflies have a habit of just flitting away when one is interested enough in them to try and pick them up, so it was when Sam approached a particularly finely coloured one. That he took an interest in the butterfly but a moment since had no bearing upon the fact that it alighted just at that moment and could at least have had the decency to wait until Sam had some sort of a chance to acquire the wonderful little creature. But away it flew and new worlds had to be conquered, with a 'pfft' and a shake of the head, Sam aimlessly sought some other interest. A grassy slope dipping away at his right lent itself to new wonders. He would investigate and see what was below. As this fearless five-year-old came to the rounded knoll before the grassy slope, he looked all around him; not another being of any sort was about. The slope was not at all steep and if it had been just a little more so, Sam would have enjoyed rolling down. He tried but barely moved. 'Pfft' and a slow getting to his feet so he could look about again had him just stand and stare. There was nothing exciting to do that was the trouble. Slowly he made his way to the bottom of this rather dismal slope, not the fun he imagined he would have had when first he became aware that the slope existed. What a let-down. He looked for more butterflies – no – that was the only one and he missed it, ah well, nothing down here so he may just as well go back to the top of the gradient again. Sam turned to return from whence he came. The trouble of being on one's own was that there was no one else to play with. He heard a kid next door playing and hoped he would be going outside his back yard. Alas, when he got out there was no kid there that is when he spied the butterfly. They could have had such fun running and romping about. Ah well, Sam decided it was better to go back home, the trouble was, there was nothing to do at home either. That was why he ran out of the back gate in the first place. Then he remembered, wasn't that a ball that he saw in the woodpile near the back veranda? Yes, a beach ball. That was better than nothing; Sam would go back and play with that! Just as he got to the back gate Sam heard the childish voice from next-door again. He waited, hoping the boy would come out and they could play together. He listened intently. A car door slammed, the motor burst into life and Sam heard the vehicle gradually disappear in the distance. Once again all was quiet. 'Pfft', he snorted. Then the back door of his house opened and a voice called.

"Here you rotten little twerp, where have you got too?" As Sam was still outside the gate he could not be seen. Then the voice yelled.

"Goodness gracious, the gate is open, Sam is missing. Hey you lot, get out here, Sam is running loose out in the meadows!"

"Oh dear me, my sweet little boy is missing, come on, help me to find him!" The middle-aged lady urgently called back at her friends as she rushed towards the rear gate of the property. Sam nonchalantly walked through that gate as if nothing were amiss.

"Oh there you are!"

The lady said as she reached out for Sam.

"Who went and left the gate open so Sam could get out?"

She reached down and clipped the lead on.

"Naughty dog" she said as Sam wagged his tail.

End.

10 Koomar the Mighty. © Howard Reede-Pelling 15/9/2003

Koomar was a fierce warrior. At two and a half metres tall he towered above his adversaries and they were many. Huge muscles seemed to be bulging out of his tough attire, the heavy pelt of a grizzly bear was draped about the top half of his wide shouldered torso and there were criss-crossed leggings clinging tightly to the powerful legs, legs that were tucked into strong footwear. The fact that the footwear stood out because it was adorned with the hide of a rhinoceros gave aggressors cause to linger. A fearsome looking blade of immense proportions was held in a hostile position overhead as if it were ready to smite down any adversary who ventured too close. Although the be leagued warrior stood his ground and looked so ferocious that whoever dared to approach too closely should be doomed to be cut asunder, still the angry horde ever slowly advanced. Perhaps a dozen fierce tribesmen from the village into which Koomar had stumbled, confronted him. They were clad in pelts too, however their pelts were from the lesser beasts such as was common to the area in which they lived. Deer and Okapi with an occasional monkey pelt was the main attire of these primitive tribesmen. This strange giant stood out from them very distinctly. His steady fierce gaze that was unblinking bored into the tribesmen until each felt that he was selected alone as a victim of the powerful man they had surrounded. The tribesman who appeared to have seniority muttered gibberish which was addressed to Koomar, he could not understand a word of the man's meaning. The tribesman appeared a little in awe of the ferocious warrior. As the giant stood immobile during this discourse, the leader began to get annoyed and moved threateningly closer. Koomar swirled his large blade around his head. The tribesmen fell back in fright believing that the single warrior was about to attack. Koomar just gazed at them disdainfully as if they were not worth fighting. At last the spokesman realised that this giant of a man was ignorant of his tongue, so he lay down his spear and faced the giant timidly. A raised hand put to his head, heart and then reaching out to the lone warrior, was a signal that he hoped the interloper would respond to. Koomar sensed that the gesture was one of peace. He slowly lowered his weapon and stood waiting for the next move. Upon seeing the big man less aggressive looking, the leader turned to his followers and spoke. To a man they too, likewise put their spears upon the ground beside them. A smile changed the stern features of Koomar, he mimicked the actions of the leader but did not relinquish his sword. Smiles all around beamed from the once angry horde, the spokesman selected a stick from the ground and commenced to draw a picture in the soil. The picture depicted a group of people – Koomar interpreted them to be the tribesmen. Assaulting them the picture of a wild animal was drawn, it was an animal the like of which Koomar had never before seen. It was essentially a dragon but its tail was thick and had a horn protruding from it which appeared to be a deadly weapon. The animal had four stout legs similar to a rhinoceros but its head was as no head ever before seen by Koomar. Instead of being dragon-like or even bovine, the beast resembled that of an alligator, with four great big sabre-like teeth jutting from its lower jaw. Truly a fearsome creature. Koomar shook his head and opened his arms expressively, denoting that never before had he seen such an animal. The spokesman for the tribe pointed to his mouth, then a wave of his arm encompassing the men behind him and pointing to the picture and again at his mouth, gave Koomar to believe that this fabulous animal was eating the tribesmen. A grin let the horde know that Koomar believed these men were making the story up, but for what purpose he could only guess. The mob began to have a heated discussion; more than one look was directed at Koomar with outward disgust. They were not behaving as if their leader was joking. At that moment a heavy hissing sound was heard coming from behind the men. The sound was not very far off. The action of the horde was instant. With many yells they rushed past Koomar as if he were not there, to disappear without trace into the jungle. The giant was left alone, a stalwart figure contemplating just what was happening. He had not long to wait to find out.

Into the small clearing where the confrontation with the tribesmen took place, a most ferocious and fearsome creature appeared. Upon seeing what it took to be a meal, this monstrosity reared up on its hind legs and an awesome hissing of thunderous sound emanated from its gaping, drooling mouth. The fore legs waved in an inspiring manner as if the large animal had at last found a morsel to satisfy the cravings of its stomach. It lunged at Koomar coming down atop of the lone warrior, straddling him and at the same time the gaping jaws reached beneath to snap the strong body as a piece of twig. Koomar had instinctively raised his sword to ward off the dinosaur-sized reptilian creature that was endeavouring to devour him. His blade was thrust home heavily into the huge chest which was now above Koomar. With a continued hissing, something of a scream of anger burst from the wounded colossus. It fell just to the side of the stalwart warrior and began writhing in its death throes. Careful so as not to be trapped within the threshing legs and that awesome tail, Koomar withdrew his sword with a great strain and again thrust it home into the heaving gyrating body. The threshing tail caught him a massive blow to the head as Koomar tried valiantly to avoid such a happening, he staggered away from the dying creature to the comparative safety afforded by the nearby forest. Koomar fell to the ground, slowly sinking into oblivion. To the soothing feel of a damp bunch of cocoa nut fibre, he awoke to find an ugly female of similar appearance to that of the tribesmen who accosted him before. Her face broke into an awful grin upon noting that Koomar had regained consciousness. She gibbered to an outside body. It was then that the warrior noticed he was lying upon a bed of monkey pelts in what appeared to be a native lean-to. Almost immediately the same spokesman, whom Koomar took to be the leader of the tribe, entered and without a word, bowed low in defence to this stranger in their domain. A very large smile was upon the savage face and he fawned upon Koomar. Clapping his hands, a procession of savages entered with gifts which were piled upon the floor at his feet. Bundles of food such as bananas, berries and nuts, a great piece of meat – half cooked – which he later learned was from the monster that he slew, and the great spiky horn which once adorned the tail of that monster; was left for him. Then he heard the sounds of laughter and joyous dancing emanating from without. It sounded as if the tribe were having a joyful get-together. Of a sudden the noise stilled only to become excited. It appeared as if all were converging to one side of the compound. A villager who appeared to have some seniority quickly entered the lean-to and addressed his leader. Their gibberish annoyed Koomar but he awaited the outcome. The noise of the throng without came nearer. An imposing man of Nubian features barged in, a few words of gibberish were exchanged then the newcomer addressed Koomar. He spoke a few words that were more in keeping with a worthwhile language but it was not legible to Koomar. Then the newcomer spoke words that Koomar understood, it was his own language.

"Do you speak this tongue?"

His frown deepened then changed to an enlightened grin as the giant responded.

"Yes, this is my language – who are you who understands?"

"Ah, it is good. I am Banuta the Head Man of the Ukabunga tribe; I have travelled for three days to this village for our quarterly barter. I bring two loads of pelts from monkeys and okapi to exchange for food. Our two tribes barter each change of seasons. I will take back nuts and fruit for them. There are not many animals for the Tubunga's to make warmth with now that the fierce Thrombilla roams these mountains. I am told that you are he who has slain one of these enormous beings and you did it alone – we salute you O Mighty one – but others will take its place. Each Thrombilla roams a mountain range and makes it home. Another will come to take its place but for perhaps two moons there will be peace here. Might I ask what brings you to this area, perhaps I may be of assistance?"

"I am the mighty Koomar – I need no assistance – however I shall tell of my mission. Somewhere in these ranges is the old city of Moorko, legend has it that the jewel of Moorko is still buried beneath the ruins. My mission is to return the jewel to my King and so win the hand of the Princess. That is why I am passing through this place."

Koomar stood beside the bed of pelts on which he was laid to rest and looked to this interpreter who would undoubtedly relate his words to the Tubunga tribe.

"Ah, I can help you. My tribe – the Ukabunga's – is only one march from the ancient city. It is taboo for anyone to enter the ancient village, for none who have entered have ever returned."

"Moorko has the jewel and it is my mission to take the jewel to my King. That is what Koomar will do."

"As you wish O Mighty Koomar, might I accompany you as far as my village? Two are better than one for the dangerous journey and I also have a following of twelve of our best fighting men accompanying me here. We will be the more powerful together!"

After much bartering and heated discussion, the villagers of both sides were happy with their deals.

"If you are ready Mighty Koomar, we are returning to our village. Will you accompany us?"

Koomar nodded and strode forth, the dozen fighting men struggling to keep up with his long strides. Their beasts of burden, now laden with foodstuffs, were easily able to keep pace with the mighty warrior. Something similar to oxen but more in line with the fleet deer with large, broad backs. Koomar learned they were common animals of the Ukabunga region; they were so fleet that they could easily outdistance the terrible Thrombilla. Progress was rapidly made through the mountains of the Tubunga's.

"Care must now be taken O Mighty Koomar, ahead lies a new mountain range, this one will undoubtedly house another Thrombilla. If we go cautiously it may not notice us and we can pass unscathed. If we are sighted we must make haste and quit the mountains forthwith, else we stand to be demolished. Great stealth is our one defence."

"I have slain one – I can slay another!" Koomar stated with authority.

"Your courage is without question but it were better for all if we can avoid a confrontation, O Mighty Koomar!" The Nubian cautioned.

"So be it, we shall travel cautiously." Koomar replied simply.

The party of warriors crossed the mountain range and were hastening towards the lower slopes, when in the distance could be heard an angry hissing. A Thrombilla which was on the far side of the range from where the intruders were passing became aware that trespassers of the range were about. The crashing of its body as it charged sounded like a veritable earthquake was approaching. It was too far away when it became aware of the party and because the Thrombilla is not built for speed, the warriors were able, with haste, to quickly depart from its territory. The warriors of Ukabunga breathed a sigh of relief when they began scaling the rocky heights of the next range of mountains. This was a very rocky mountain. Long chasms and high outcroppings made haste very slow work but they doggedly pushed forwards, the beasts of burden cautiously picking their ways along deep ravines and over treacherous rocky hills. The last of the party had but barely climbed an awkward slope when Koomar, who was leading, cautioned all to stand still. Just visible beyond the range they were climbing, a Thrombilla could be seen. Koomar held his trusty great sword at the ready. Banuta, the head man of his tribe, motioned for them all to creep into a fissure not far away. It would afford the party great protection from the Thrombilla should it become aware of them.

Koomar boomed.

"Let the Thrombilla come, I am not afraid!"

Banuta wisely stated.

"Of course not O Mighty one, but should we have a confrontation, one or more of my warriors may inadvertently come asunder beneath the monster or mayhap its awesome tail may not be averted. It were prudent for us to avoid the beast if at all possible O Mighty Koomar. Let us try the fissure and maybe the Thrombilla will move away!"

Reluctantly, Koomar submitted and all were safely filed into the fissure. The beasts of burden could barely squeeze themselves and their laden packs in, still, as there was a long continuous passage; they strung themselves out comfortably. Banuta led the file, then six of his warriors followed by the two beasts of burden and the other six warriors. Koomar, ever on the offensive, was the last man to enter. All without was silence. The men waited, listening. There appeared to be no threat. Koomar, chafing at the thought that he had submitted to the humiliation of running and hiding as a scared deer, cautiously back-tracked to have a last glance about. Although they were safe from the Thrombilla in the fissure, he did not wish to be cooped up like some timid animal. Barely had he got to the entrance of the fissure, when the fearsome ugly long snout of a Thrombilla blocked the opening. Amid a terrifying hissing roar of displeasure came the powerful stench of the carnivore's rotten breath. Barely able to breathe Koomar retreated to get away from the dreadful stench. The panic-stricken beasts of burden hurried deeper into the fissure forcing those ahead to make haste. It was useless trying to get out the way they came in, so the group continued along the fissure to see where it led. A large cavern with a high roof was entered; the party breathed a sigh of relief for none were comfortable in the restrictions of the narrow passageway. They had negotiated perhaps three quarters of the journey across this huge chamber, when without warning and with great speed, an animal as large as a lion sprung at them from its concealment among a cluster of fallen rocks. Had it been smaller one would have thought it was a rat, for the whiskery snout and the long tapering tail was quite reminiscent of such a despicable vermin. This creature came at them with express speed and a silence which in itself was alarming. Banuta who led the dozen warriors, shouted out a warning as he managed to duck beneath the vicious claws and snarling, gaping mouth. His spear futilely struck the wild beast a glancing blow on its shoulder. Two of his men were not so fortunate however and that their demise was swift, although a blessing for them was not a great barrier to the animal's onslaught. Koomar saw the danger so soon as did Banuta and was very quick to rally into the fray. His mighty sword flashed in the twilight of the caverns dimness and with a swiftness almost too blurring to comprehend, he had inflicted mortal wounds before the creature was aware that it had an adversary worthy of attack. Bloodied, the large member of the rat family writhed in its final death throes to eventually subside upon the bodies of the dead and a few who were wounded.

"That was mighty quick and I feared that we all may well have died had you not gone into the midst of danger, O Mighty Koomar. It was indeed good fortune that you chose to accompany us this day. Let us not take these caverns lightly, there may well be more dangers ahead, we must take more care in our progress and not become complacent!"

Banuta cautioned, as he stood in awe of the reaction afforded by the big man. Hero worship was apparent in his demeanour.

"Just a hiccup in our travels." Koomar responded.

"Let us get along; mayhap these caverns have an opening on the other side of this range. It is quite possible that we may travel right through the mountain range and emerge upon the other side. The Thrombilla may be aware of the other exit but that is a chance we must take. Follow me with caution for there may be other dangers ahead!"

Koomar led the way in his apparently off-hand manner, but there was nothing off-hand in reality. The mighty warrior knew full well that in this labyrinth of caverns would be more than just the one danger. His apparent care-free attitude belied the wariness of the man, for his every sense was attuned to the slightest hint of anything untoward. Although he moved with apparent ease and somewhat of grace and heartening aplomb, his natural instinct of survival surged to the fore; this was no careless adventurer. Having left the large chamber where the reptilian monster was slain, the entourage' continued its wary way through another winding water-worn passage, ever so slightly downwards towards the other side of the range through which their journey took them.

Perhaps a kilometre of dark, damp travel brought them to another large cavern. Not quite so big as that in which the rat-like monster was encountered, yet a relief from the restrictions of the seemingly unending windings of the dark passageway. All breathed a sigh of relief at this respite. Koomar cautioned Banuta to warn the tribesmen that there could well be another predator within this chamber, all looked about cautiously. As the crossing of the chamber was accomplished without further threat, aside from some minor small rodents which scuttled away at their approach; another similar passageway was entered. This one had a faint illumination emanating from the walls, and the going was much easier. A slight draught could be detected giving rise to the thought that mayhap an exit into the outside world was approaching. Two more turns of the passage verified this belief, for there only a matter of one hundred metres, was an opening into the outside world. The majority of those following gave grunts of pleasure at the sight. Koomar had Banuta warn his men to silence; they must proceed carefully and silently. One never knows what dangers could be lurking without. At the exit, Koomar looked about with much care. There was no danger that could be detected, just a clear sunny day that looked as if it were waiting to be picnicked upon. Koomar took no chances; he knew that a predator could be about just waiting for some misfortune to blunder into a trap. There was no need to worry, after having ascertained that the way was comparatively clear; Koomar advanced fearlessly. The tribesmen were a little apprehensive but followed in the footsteps of their leader, Banuta, who hastened to keep pace with the mammoth strides of the great warrior. The way was downhill as they were almost at the bottom of the range through which they had only just emerged, and a few more boulders and bushes had to be negotiated before the next mountain was to be tackled. At the bottom a quite wide river flowed but it was very shallow, the group stopped as Koomar held up a hand for silence. All listened attentively. The silence was only disturbed by the slowly flowing water. “There seems to be no immediate danger, we will stop and drink.” It was almost an order. All were weary and thirsty so there was no demur. Having sated his thirst, Koomar sat very alert for danger while the men rested a little.

"Just over the next range and we come to my village of Ukabunga tribe. Ukabunga, the king, will be most happy to welcome you O Mighty Koomar. It is rare that one can greet a man who has bested a Thrombilla. You will be made very welcome. Perhaps you will stay with us awhile and we can show you some hospitality, that way you may be rested for your next march up to the old city of Moorko."

Banuta looked to Koomar for some sign of acquiescence. The warrior shook his head.

"No, I will forge ahead for my own king waits impatiently for my return. I have no need for rest as I have done little but travel and that is no good to one who is impatient to return to his lover. Once the jewel of Moorko is in my king's keeping, the fruits of my efforts may be rewarded and enjoyed. No, Koomar will push on; there is still a task to be done!"

With a sad shake of his head, Banuta followed the warrior as he set off to cross this last range of hills.

"There is little or nothing to fear between here and my village O Mighty Koomar. My tribe is a fearsome fighting force and they excel in clearing this range of unwanted predators. There have been many great battles on these hills as the Thrombillas attempt to take over the territory. There is little food left for them as my fighting men keep the range clear of game. The Thrombilla can only find my tribesmen for food and we make a great noise and our numbers annoy the monsters. It is rare that one finds a Thrombilla here." The party of fighting men soon crossed the range and were welcomed home with their precious cargoes of foodstuffs. Koomar bid farewell to his associates at the edge of the village and continued his journey over the next range. Banuta and the ten warriors that were with him waved as the giant diminished amongst the trees of the forest. There was little food available so close to the village for many were the scavengers in the vicinity who pillaged these home hills.

But, as the warriors did on their journey back from the village of the Tubunga's, feeding on the fruits and tubers they passed and what occasional small animals which came within range of their spears; so did Koomar feed with them. He was not hungry as yet but knew he must obtain nourishment soon. As there was little or nothing to be had on this first range after the village of Ukabunga, Koomar looked forwards to feasting well on the following range. He was at the summit of that range and had only to negotiate two more, before the old city of Moorko was to be reached. It was atop this range that the frantic hissings of two or more ferocious Thrombillas could be heard in the forest on the range through which Koomar must pass to reach the old city. By the sounds of them, they were fighting; no doubt it was a territorial matter for them. Koomar hurried across this range knowing that he may not be accosted by the Thrombillas as their energies were more taken with their own interests. He passed the loudly hissing and threshing beasts unnoticed and went his way unscathed. Towards the lower slopes of this range an Aranchid fell to his great sword. This small animal of the deer family just happened to be feeding on the other side of a large boulder that Koomar was stepping over and with almost instant reaction, it lay bleeding under the mighty sword. The warrior fed well as he made his escape from that noisy range and headed for the last of the hills that hid his destination. A slight hiccup stemmed his rapid progress at the halfway mark up the following range. It was in the form of an interested new player in the territorial fight on the range behind Koomar. This new player was a Thrombilla and its interest was the outcome of the fight. It was very hard to distinguish between a male and a female of the Thrombillas as they are almost identical in looks and size. Koomar guessed it was a female over which the two were fighting. As this one was keenly trying to see what the outcome of the battle was, Koomar deemed it possible that he could also pass be this one unnoticed too; this was not to be the case. The Thrombilla, either sensing his presence or sighting a slight movement, hissed and turned towards him. Koomar stood still, his mighty sword at the ready. A fresh outburst from the fighting pair had the Thrombilla hurry back to its vantage point, looking towards the sounds of combat. Koomar took his opportunity and fled up and over the range; he was long gone ere the Thrombilla again looked for the interloper. Koomar charged down the hill to lose himself amongst the shrubbery of the valley floor. He drank and rested for a few minutes, checking that all was clear; no sign of pursuit. One more range to go and Koomar was at the lost city. He strode forth with confidence; he would locate the jewel of Moorko, even though he had no idea in just what form the jewel took. It could be a precious stone, a golden mask, even a totem of some kind; it would stand out Koomar was sure. His journey to the summit of the last range was hard going. The scenery changed, gone the grazing lands to be replaced by very large well-girthed trees and clinging vines. The denseness of foliage was more in keeping with a jungle. Monkeys that were unknown to Koomar ranged and chattered incessantly and there were large denizens of the jungle about that remained unseen by the alert man. A man who must stay with very keen senses if he were to survive in this place. No doubt the jungle was too overgrown and intense for there to be enough room for Thrombillas to roam here. But the warrior knew instinctively, that lion sized predators were slinking about. The odd noises of their movements were borne to Koomar even though he never sighted a threat to his passing. Once the mighty warrior crested the range, he had to climb into an enormous tree to sight ahead. The climb was taxing as there were creepers and small animals that scampered away at this intruder into their domain. A very large group of small monkey-like beasts hurriedly quit the tree that Koomar was climbing, only to stop and chatter as they looked with interest at this strange being that had invaded their privacy. Koomar paid them scant notice for he had more important things on his mind. As he had climbed as high as his weight could safely be accommodated, the man scanned the downside of the range, looking for some remnants of the old city of Moorko. At last he espied a turret protruding from the deep jungle. Just about half-way down the other side of the range and he would be there. There was a low moaning that could be heard coming from the old city. Koomar fancied it was an animal of some kind. It sounded eerie and dismal. Koomar took a deep breath and began the descent of the tree. As the great warrior left the tree he became aware that a gathering of large beasts of some kind had encircled him. Occasionally he could just catch a glimpse of baleful eyes watching his forwards march. They were wide spaced eyes, only about a metre from the ground, evidently carnivores of some type. He made sure his grip upon the trusty sword, which was his only defence, was firm and the mighty blade was ever at the ready. Silently, without warning he was beset by what appeared to be a pride of lion-like beasts. Two sprang at him while another four charged with lithe springs of their short stubby legs. That his blade struck true was the only thing that stemmed the initial charge. The four that were not slain with that first rally, quickly departed when their two companions were laid low; the bodies writhing in their death throes. Koomar looked about for a renewed charge. It did not come immediately. The animals which attacked had melted into the jungle. Koomar waited, but no further charge was made until he had traversed a couple of hundred steps. This time it was not a silent advance; there were roars and screams coming from all sides. The mighty warrior stood his ground and that fearsome blade appeared to be a propeller so quickly did it flash and scintillate in the flickering rays of sunshine that filtered through the canopy of vines and leaves. Once again after three of the beasts were slain, the rest had disappeared back into the jungle. It was a pattern that was repeated time and again as Koomar slowly made his way to the old city. He stood at last only a stone's throw from the crumbled outer walls of the ruins. Covered in blood from his adversaries and by now almost breathless from his exertions, the warrior stood motionless. That low moaning could be heard more distinctly now. There was something eerie in its mournful tone. Again another charge was made at him by those slinking beasts. Koomar turned to face them and his demeanour left them in no doubt about his intentions should the beasts come at him too closely. Their charge was halted by him facing them. He made to lunge in their direction, the animals had charged him before and were bested, they were fearful of attacking whilst their quarry was aware of them. The bodies of their pride were testament to the fierceness of this engine of destruction. The animals prudently kept their distance; they preferred to attack when the quarry was unaware of their presence. Koomar cautiously advanced to the city's outer wall, such as it was. Carefully negotiating the wall and entering the old city of Moorko, Koomar looked about for a likely starting point for his search. As the confines of this overgrown habitat of a long-gone race, appeared to be deserted Koomar pushed forwards, just jungle and vines neatly marking the place where the people once had their dwellings. There was no life what-so-ever. Neither animal nor bird life existed within the city walls. Even those lion-like creatures which attacked him would not enter beyond the walls. No doubt the continual moaning scared the jungle life away. It was indeed a scary place. Scary that is, to all but the intrepid Koomar who did not easily frighten. A small domed edifice appeared to be the centre of the city; it was from here that the awful moaning was emanating. Naturally that is where the giant headed. When the domed structure was reached, Koomar doubted his ability to enter for the thing was little more than a circular room with a door. It was certainly not built for one of his large stature. Gingerly tapping the inside with his sword in case there were any animals hiding there, the man waited for a moment. The constant weird moaning emanating from within was beginning to irk him, he would soon put a stop to it; no animals were inside at that point so Koomar doubled himself up and forced his way in. Trying to tap the floor his sword waved in the air, there was no floor. As his eyes became accustomed to the dim interior Koomar realised that this was just an entrance. There was a flight of steps going downwards at a very steep angle, had he just barged in no doubt he would have come asunder, falling to goodness knows where in the darkness. The steady moaning continued. Koomar carefully placed his feet as he squeezed through the doorway. Once within he could stand reasonably erect, just a slight bowing of his head was necessary for him to negotiate the steep descent. That terrible mournful moaning continued incessantly, putting this irritating scourge aside Koomar continued his slow and careful climb down these treacherous steps. One slip and he could have plummeted to goodness knows where in the dimness of the interior of this abandoned abyss down which he had ventured. It was so eerie within the confines of the well and other than fresh air that was constantly whistling past, he felt as though he was alone; a sole being in this abandoned old village. He had descended some one hundred and fifty metres when finally his feet were on a solid floor of some kind. Now the light had brightened just a little and the warrior stood quite still as he assessed his surroundings. The mournful moaning continued. Looking around intently and cautiously, Koomar sought out any abnormality that may appear as a possible threat to him; there was none. He was quite alone and unhindered so far as an interruption to his advance was concerned. That abysmal moaning persevered monotonously, Koomar was determined to find the cause of it and eliminate the bothersome noise. It seemed to be getting louder as he advanced and the great warrior grasped his mighty sword more firmly with the blood-spattered blade leading the way. The light of day was getting brilliant now as if he were out in the open air, yet Koomar knew he was many metres underground; possibly one or two hundred. How could there be such light within these catacombs? Determined to find the source of the light and also to put a stop to that continual moaning, the great warrior forged ahead across this large open area to where the light appeared to emanate from. Rounding a turn in the far extremes of the open cavern, the source of the light became obvious. In a niche of the wall the brilliance shone through. It was coming from behind a carved image of what appeared to be a god of the once populous village. The image was made of a green stone, fluorite. It stood about one third of a metre high, was very stout and had a mysterious magical look about it with the strong light coming from behind. It was the most beautiful object that Koomar had ever before witnessed. This, he believed, was the jewel of the lost city of Moorko. When he grasped the green image and lifted it from the niche, the source of the light and the moaning became obvious. Behind the image was a polished crystal, and daylight, evidently beaming down through a hundred metres shaft, was reflected into the green image giving off the myriad colours that gave the image an appearance of iridescence. This no doubt would have intrigued the lost inhabitants of the isolated village. The light, Koomar later discovered, was picked up by another crystal at the entrance to the shaft high above and diffused downwards, thus allowing the hidden chambers to be illuminated. The moaning was caused by the downdraught passing across cunningly placed hide strips of a very thin nature that were strategically placed across the shaft and hidden behind the green god-like image. No doubt the high priests used this medium to instil fear and awe into the villagers and so keep the powers of order and obedience in the priesthood. Once the image was taken from its resting place the light no longer illuminated the way. Darkness suddenly was thrust upon the lonely warrior. He steadfastly returned the way he entered the catacombs carefully feeling his way now that he could no longer see through the deep darkness that engulfed him. It was a slow and sometimes painful experience. Because of his mighty bulk the warrior constantly bumped his head on the low ceiling of the stairwell. The open chamber held no dangers as it was fairly large and would have housed quite a throng of the villagers as they came to worship their god, but having successfully negotiated that and having located the stairs; Koomar found that he was constantly coming into contact with the roof of the tight enclosure. Keeping well bent and holding the statue very tightly, the warrior made his way slowly up the long stairway being very aware that he could miss a step and go plunging to the bottom. Far above the opening into the warm sunshine beckoned. Koomar steadfastly pressed on. Happy that he had found that for which his endeavours had been exerted successfully to accomplish, and in urgent desire now to fulfil his obligation to his king and peoples. Happy also, that at last he may reach out for the lady of his desires; his love!

When Koomar finally reached the top of the steps, he cautiously poked his head out to make sure that he was not ambushed. Anything might have happened while he was down in the depths, perhaps an animal may have stalked him and it could be waiting without, or perchance he was followed; although this last was very unlikely. The way was clear, not a sign of a predator or an enemy were in sight. Hoisting the quite heavy stone image under his left arm, to leave his right arm free in the event that he might have to fight off an animal or some such as he quit the old city; Koomar boldly strode forth. At the outer wall of the overgrown village, he was beset by the lion-like horde that slinked after him on entry. They must have patiently waited knowing he would return. Seeking a safe place to stow the prize he had won, Koomar put his full attention on the job at hand. He knew he must slay the entire pride of some twelve angry looking beasts, if he was to have any sort of a safe trip back. The sheer numbers of the pride left Koomar in no doubt but that he would have a gruesome fight on his hands. Somehow he must get them separated. If they all attacked at once then he would have little hope of survival, two or three at a time the warrior knew he could handle. But how to separate them, that was the question uppermost in his mind. Keeping the wall of the old village at his back Koomar tried to coax one or two of the beast's forwards. They were cunning. He warily stepped a few paces forwards, daring the animals to come and get him. They licked their drooling mouths and crouched ready to spring but held their ground. Koomar remembered his slaying of the Thrombilla, he fell to the ground warily holding his trusty sword upright. The ruse worked and the lion-like beasts charged, almost as he fell Koomar was up again and facing the fierce animals. When they became aware that they had been tricked, they about faced and began a panic-stricken retreat. Koomar took advantage of their retreat and attacked. He had laid low two of them and was attacking a third when the retreating animals noticed that he no longer had his back to the wall. A fresh onslaught was made towards him, Koomar fought valiantly as he endeavoured to regain his safety barrier. He was heavily beset by the other nine of the pride. The flashing of his whirring blade dealt a destruction that he was sure the fierce animals had never before seen. With the ferocity of his desperation there lay dead and dying another four of the beasts when finally Koomar regained the comparative safety of the wall. Now he could no longer be attacked from behind. He stood facing the remaining five animals, their defeated brethren lying at his feet. Slowly the rest of the pride slunk into the jungle to disappear from sight. Koomar knew they would not go far but would lay in wait, patiently biding their time until the ferocious man tired of waiting and ventured forth; then they would attack when the odds were in their favour. Koomar did not wait. Retrieving his green stone idol the warrior strode forth as if there was nothing to fear. His trusty blade at the ready in one hand while the other arm cradled his prize, ready to drop it and fight immediately should he be attacked again. He managed to travel over the first range without interference although he could hear the other five lion-like beasts travelling abreast of him, waiting patiently for an opportunity to sneak up unnoticed. Although he appeared to be taking little notice, the mighty warrior was as alert as ever he could be. The animals must have sensed this; else they would have begun their attack sooner. As Koomar descended the ridge, the next range loomed ahead. There would be no respite for the man as he was aware that Thrombillas would be ranging on that range. The lion-like animals knew this too so they made a last ditch affront on their escaping quarry. The five of them charged simultaneously at the wary man, he was ready for some such onslaught and struck out even as he lowered the idol to the ground. Two more of the beasts lay at his feet dead ere the remaining three disappeared back from whence they had come. Bested by the ferocity of this man-beast, a most powerful adversary. They left him to his own devices and he started up the range alert for any sign of a threatening

Thrombilla. Surprisingly, no attack of any sort was made against him and he approached the following range. Another two ranges and he would be near the village of the Ukabunga tribe. At the summit of the next range he came to a standstill for ahead were two huge Thrombillas. They were tearing at a carcase of what seemed to be one of those lion-like creatures that Koomar had only just fought. Although he could not be certain for he knew that the ones he had slain were far behind now, and as the Thrombilla was quite a slow animal, there was no was they could have passed the mighty warrior so quickly. This must be a kill of some other sort. Koomar hoped that the feeding giants would be too engrossed with what they were doing to notice him. He hurried onwards trying to keep out of sight of the monstrous beings. It was a forlorn hope for the Thrombillas turned and made as if to threaten him. Koomar steadfastly hurried on. Surprisingly, the huge beasts returned to their feeding seeing as this latest intruder in their domain was but a passing entity and not vying for their meal. They ignored him and the great warrior was allowed to go his way. Last but one range before the village of Ukabunga and the monkey life was active. They appeared to be running away from something, it soon became apparent just what that something was; a party of warriors were on the hunt and monkey pelts were the prime target. When the fighting men became aware that there was another man in the region, they became quite warlike. However the very large size of the man assured them that he was no threat to them. Banuta, the head man, howled with pleasure at the sight of Koomar.

"Ah my friend, that we should see you again, we thought that you would have succumbed to the Thrombillas. It is indeed a great thrill that you would honour our village with another visit. How come you to escape the large monoliths and also the Sitars for I see you have reached the old city of Moorko. Is that the jewel of Moorko?"

His welcome was genuine as was his surprise for no one before had ever returned who dared to travel to that city. The giant warrior stated matter-of-factly.

"I am Koomar!"

As if that explained everything, to most of the fighting men it certainly did, for he had fought his way to the city, acquired the jewel, and returned safely. They stood in awe of the mighty man.

"Your monkeys went that way." Koomar jerked his thumb after the monkeys.

"We shall forgo the chase O Mighty Koomar and escort you to our village. The Kandoes can wait another time for us to skin them. King Ukabunga would chastise us if we allowed you to travel alone any further when we are here to assist if needed. We shall all go back and celebrate your safe return, O Mighty Koomar."

"As you will." Koomar replied without stopping.

They marched triumphantly back to their village where there would be great rejoicing. And there was great rejoicing. King Ukabunga paid homage to this fierce warrior from another place. It was a privilege for the king to finally see the treasure of the lost city of Moorko, for rumour had it that the jewel was there for the taking. Although many a warrior had sought the jewel, none had ever returned and it was given up as an impossible task for any man to ever come back alive with the jewel. Indeed, even to get so far as the city itself was deemed to be impossible. For someone to have survived the rigours of the jungle, fought his way through the colossal of the ranges (the thrombillas), acquire the jewel (no man knew where it was) and then to return through the dreaded ranges of the Thrombillas again; was a feat unheard of before in the memory of man. Koomar was feted as a true warrior, bold and fearless; the envy of all who witnessed his triumphant return. And still his journey was not yet over, for he had to return to his own village with the coveted jewel. Many thought that he was fortunate indeed to have succeeded so far, few thought he would ever get to his own village alive. There were those who hatched plans to somehow acquire the jewel for themselves, now that the most dangerous part was accomplished; poor fools. There was this fearsome giant who had sought, found and won the jewel, to give as a token to his king as a gift in exchange for the hand of the king's daughter.

How could a mere tribal warrior dare to take it from him? The foolish racked their brains for ways and means non-the-less. King Ukabunga deemed it a worthy trophy for his own village.

His unspoken thoughts were of ways and means to acquire the trophy himself, for if any village deserved it; it was the village of Ukabunga. Koomar was unaware of these thoughts and blissfully accepted the adulations put forwards for his benefit. It was while he was asleep after his ordeals and having eaten that the unthinkable happened. Koomar awoke to find his trophy was missing. He immediately demanded to see king Ukabunga himself.

"Ukabunga!" He stated. "The jewel of Moorko has been taken while I slept. If it is not returned forthwith, I shall unleash carnage upon your village. Koomar has spoken!"

He drew his sword and stood defiantly. There was a hushed and stunned silence. Ukabunga the king trembled as he knew that this was no idle threat. When he ordered his aides to stealthily creep in and confiscate the magnificent artefact, he gave no thought to the anger of the warrior when he awoke. Ukabunga the king haughtily drew himself up making as he thought an imposing figure.

"The jewel is the rightful property of the Ukabunga tribe and has been set aside as our new totem. Warriors, take the stranger, he has no right to our totem, bind him to a tree on the range of the Thrombilla – that is your king's wish!"

He motioned for his warriors to advance. Not a man moved, they knew the fighting strength of Koomar and a man who had bested a Thrombilla, was not to be taken easily. None wished to be the first to die. The king was beside himself with wrath.

"Fools, he is but one man, you are many and my fighting warriors who are fearless, how dare you disobey your king. Take the meddling interloper and do as you are ordered or there will be others to feed the Thrombillas!"

Many were the mutterings of the fighting men, still none moved. Banuta, the head man spoke. "My King, Ukabunga, this man has come in friendship to our village. He has proven himself worthy of our respect and admiration, did he not single-handedly slay a fearful Thrombilla. It is against our customs to so belittle and betray such a mighty friend and ally. Give the warrior back the image that he so strenuously fought for and earned. We do not need such a totem for we have our own glorious King Ukabunga. Let not one fighting man die needlessly especially when all admire this great warrior so!" The king was taken aback by this show of authority by his second-in-command. He faltered, and then shaking his head demanded that his orders were to be obeyed. Amid many mutterings and fearful wide-eyed looks of distaste, a few fighting men advanced. As Koomar was about to step forwards with the intent of slaying as many as he could in the first onslaught, Banuta defied his king and held up a hand to stop them. Backing up to Koomar, he stood beside him menacing his own people.

"I fight beside a fellow warrior against you all; it is not the way I wish to live in a village where there is little respect for one so glorious to strangers. I will go with the Mighty Koomar and together we will regain his relic and I shall accompany him to his journeys end. You are no longer worthy of my support. We fight to the death!"

His words were spoken in the language of Ukabunga, which Koomar did not understand; however his mien and actions spoke louder than mere words. Koomar understood that he had an ally in the bold Banuta. He awaited the outcome.

"Death to both of these who would stand against Ukabunga your king. They are no longer welcome in the village of Ukabunga; Banuta has defied his king and therefore must perish. Rise O warriors and defend your king and village!"

Ukabunga had a mad lust for blood in his eyes, waving his arms dramatically for the support of his fighting men. The more ignorant and savage of his warriors massed together and slowly advanced and their intentions were clear. Koomar did not wait but savagely surged forwards wielding his mighty sword with devastating effect as a whirring propeller, Banuta was immediately by his side. Together they caused much mayhem and the blood of their adversaries flowed freely.

Six corpses were at their feet and another three had great gashes upon their bodies as the two stalwart warriors fought side by side. It was the greatest battle that Banuta could remember fighting and he was giving his all for his hero. Koomar relentlessly forged ahead through the mass of fighting men who threw themselves with reckless abandon at these two whom their king decreed must perish. It was a losing battle. Never had mere fighting men of the village seen such ferocity in a foe as this giant man from another place. The fighting men of Ukabunga withdrew under that fierce onslaught, and looking about, saw their dead and dying comrades.

"All right, enough, I will surrender the jewel. Cease this carnage or my village will have no one to defend us!"

King Ukabunga held up his hands for the fighting to cease. Koomar, not understanding a word that was spoken in the dialect of the Ukabubgans, fought on. Banuta placed a hand upon Koomar's shoulder and bid him to desist.

"Stop fighting my friend, King Ukabunga has declared an end to it all, the fighting men are retreating."

Banuta cautioned Koomar to bide awhile, which the big man did. Presently the king returned with the prized jewel and laid it at Koomar's feet. Koomar picked it up and quickly quit the village, Banuta at his heels hurrying to keep pace. After the two men had traversed some three or four ranges, Koomar announced.

"This cave we are approaching is where I made camp when I first journeyed to your village. It is a good and safe place where we may rest and find food before we begin the last part of our journey. Come friend, let us rest up and get ourselves presentable for my triumphant return home. You will take a position of high import for your assistance and friendship to a perfect stranger. Great will be our welcome at my home and village. You will stand beside me as a great fighting man and friend. Come; let us rest for our triumphant homecoming! We have but a few more ranges to travel to our journeys end and I look forwards to greeting my new wife; the king's daughter."

The End.

Howard Reede-Pelling. Finished 28/10/3003.

11 Hobbies, Pastimes, Recreation.

Numismatics February 2002

Number one of a series.

Coin collecting is known as numismatics. This covers the collection of tokens, medals and anything of bartering capabilities, such as Bone Money, Wampum Beads and the like. It can be a nightmare for the uninitiated.

I first became a numismatist in the late forties, when I was a teenager. My expertise at that time was just with pennies – all that I could afford. I never ever managed to collect the whole 'set' as it were, because that is an impossibility. Some years just did not have the coins minted. As I grew, so did my collection. In 1960 as a mature adult I had over two hundredweight of specially selected coins of all denominations, from all countries. One will soon realise that it is almost impossible to complete one country's coinage, so I began to specialise. I collected only from Australia and then only varieties. Even so, my collection was still unwieldy but I persisted. I fast became the Guru of Australian Coinage.

At thirty years of age I joined the Numismatic Society of Victoria and it was not long before my writings and papers on the subject became 'must read material'. I became such an expert on the subject, that I could look at the obverse and accurately tell what the date of the coin was on the reverse. This was accomplished because of various factors in regard to the manufacture of the piece and the wear and tear of usage. I was thirty years a numismatist.

In regard to numismatics, one should first learn the basics. Obverse means – heads, reverse means – tails. Pellets are the dotted edging, legend is the wording around the peripheral – usually Latin and patina is the surface finish of the coin. A numismatist always holds any piece between finger and thumb by the outside edge; NEVER place a digit upon the surface of a coin as that causes dis-figuration and disintegration of the piece in time. Even when one is not hot, there is often dampness on one's fingers and deterioration of the collectable is begun. Ten years hence the piece is often damaged, the patina is gone, the value of the coin diminished.

Too numerous are the varieties, but here are a few of the rarer specimens: - Penny 1918 Heaton mint, 1930, penny (uniface) 1937, Penny 1946, Penny 1948 Perth mint. Halfpenny 1923, Halfpenny 1939 Roo, Threepence 1916 Three-legged emu, Threepence 1921-2 over date, Threepence 1933-4 over date, Threepence 1942 Melbourne mint. All silver coins of 1910. Sixpence 1916 Heaton mint (Eng.) Shillings 1913,14,15,20,21star,29. Two shillings 12,13,14,14h,15,15h,20,23,32. All coins of the abdication in 1937 are extremely rare and collectable. These are just a few of the rarer pieces.

Howard Reede-Pelling.

Hobbies, Pastimes, Recreation.

Lapidary

Number Two of a Series.

Lapidary is the art of gemstones. I first joined the Lapidary Club of Victoria in 1962. It was inaugurated by Dame Elizabeth Fry at the I.O.O.F. hall in Valetta Street, Malvern. This is the club where I got most of my experience on committees. Before long after having joined, I was enticed to do committee work to keep the club viable. I was initially under secretary, then after a year I became showcase manager, a position I maintained for most of my thirty years at the club. During this time I held positions as social secretary, field officer, secretary and then I did a seven year stint as editor of the local magazine, The Lapidarian. For most of my time there I submitted three or four articles a month to the magazine.

Lapidary is an art form whereby one collects the raw material from the earth and with the aid of experienced club-mates, turns them into things of beauty and value. I began by embarking upon a field trip seeking jasper, clear quartz and also tourmaline. In this I was successful to the extent that I was able to fashion some beautiful cabochons. Many field trips followed. Sapphires, gold, peridot, topaz, garnets, citrine, serpentine etcetera. I became well-versed in the art form. As many of these field trips took us to rivers and streams, we were constantly delving into the riffles seeking that elusive El Dorado – Gold. My many forays into the waters gave me the expertise I needed to pass on my considerable knowledge to others – the 'new chums' as it were. I have samples of gold from numerous areas – all different.

With many of these clubs there were exhibitions put on for the public to gape and drool over, hence my expertise into the 'show world', many shows were set up in all sorts of places, mostly local town halls. We often had to hire school halls and gymnasiums as the town halls were inadequate for our growing wealth of specimens. I can recall hiring the Lower Melbourne Town Hall for one exhibition

There is no greater satisfaction than taking some raw material from the earth, a stone if you will, and cutting, shaping and polishing it into a glamorous art-form. All one's own work. The satisfaction of having done so is far and beyond the bonds of imagination; it is factual! Have yourself a ball – join a Lapidary Club and experience the out doors. One memorial trip was to Flinders for zeolites. We gathered gmelignite, clear quartz crystals, aragonite and sharks teeth. I've experienced the outdoors life – have you?

Howard Reede-Pelling.

Hobbies, Pastimes, Recreation.

Gold Panning.

Number Three of a Series.

During my times as a Lapidarian, I learned and practised the art of panning for gold. It is a very basic and fundamental thing to do, Gold Panning; however there are some pitfalls for the un-initiated. The first of which is 'keep an eye out for snakes', the second is to be aware of the dangers of getting in over your depth and to look out for snags. Safety considered, and one should already have checked equipment, the next step is 'where to find the best spot to do your fossicking.'

Usually a gravel bed of a creek will afford a good source of 'specimens', if that satisfies one. Me, I look for natural 'riffles' along the side of the creek or river. Usually these are found by studying the lay of the land around about the area. A rock formation that extends into the water often has water-worn gullies or riffles. These are caused by many decades of water running over the rock, leaving the hardest surfaces to jut out above the softer surfaces, thus causing these 'riffles'. Gold being one of the heaviest of the minerals usually settles into these riffles amidst the heavier stones and mud.

Method of extricating the gold from the mud and stones is by panning. A small spade or scoop, even a spoon can be used to get the residue out of the riffles and into one's gold pan. Now the trick is to separate them. Having put three or four shovels full of gravel, mud and hopefully gold, into your gold pan; give the whole lot a vigorous stir with your hand, making sure that you do give final rinse of that hand to remove any specks that may adhere. The heavier gold will almost immediately find its way to the bottom of the pan; therefore one may remove forcibly, the majority of sticks larger pebbles and muddy water.

The residue left, usually about an inch of muddy water, will have what gold is there, in it. Now by gently stirring and letting a little of the muddy water at a time escape from the pan, one may notice many specks and perhaps a small nugget, to appear. With care, one is able to drain the entire lot of muddy water out of the pan, leaving only the gold, which is heavier, in the pan. With a small phial of water at hand, one may be able to press a finger onto each speck and transfer them into the phial. Upon contact with the water in the phial, the specks of gold will again sink to the bottom. Very soon, a continuity of this practice will see the phial fill appreciably. Good fossicking!

Howard Reede-Pelling.

Hobbies, Pastimes, Recreation.

Beach Combing.

Number Four of a Series.

The pastime of beach combing sounds a little like seeking pieces of flotsam, far from it! This can be a very lucrative activity, more in the line of gold seeking; in fact it is very much the same. I must admit to having spent much of my time in the latter years of my life, wading the shallows in an effort to keep fit, as arthritis has permeated my body. It was purely by accident that I discovered how lucrative beach combing could be!

Early one morning I was wading the shallows. The tide was out and the sea was calm. Looking where I was stepping because of the rocks and reefs in the area, I was amazed to see the glitter of a coin. I picked up the coin, a twenty cents piece, and glanced about in case there were others. There were. In all, over an area of ten square feet, I retrieved eight of these pieces and a couple of six cent pieces. Greedily I looked further a field. Not only did I find coins but there was a gold ring and a bangle, also a chain with a crucifix attached. Due to the changing tides a large area of sand had been washed from the sea floor, leaving the heavier objects such as I had found, well exposed. Bolts from boats, sinkers, bullets (the area was a rifle range during the war) and an old rusted gun, just a few of the items found.

I fashioned for myself a rectangular plastic basin, two thirds of a metre long and half a metre wide and deep. This I fashioned into a window with a plate glass bottom similar to a van window. Now I could see the sea-bed clearly even on a day when wind rippled the water. Over the next ten years I managed to recover from the sea, five thousand dollars worth of old coins, damaged gold and dozens of toys of the leaden type of years gone by. At times it was back-breaking work, especially when the sea became rough; I persevered.

Beach combing is related to gold fossicking in that one has a need to use a flat bat as a paddle, something the size of a table tennis bat, to wash away the sand from deep crevices and ridges on the sea bed. Many a gold ring and even the odd gold coin can be covered by the sand in these pockets. On a sunny day I detected a glitter in a shell hole about six inches deep. Upon paddling with my bat I made a gold sovereign of English origin, emerge from the hole. It was dated 1850 and was in E.F. (Extremely Fine) condition due to having been protected by the elements down the hole; possibly for a whole century. The piece sold for two hundred dollars. I also found a two ecru gold piece (about the size of a threepence). I've had fun beach combing, have you!

Howard Reede-Pelling.

Hobbies, Pastimes, Recreation.

Boomerang Throwing and Making.

Number Five in a Series.

Mine tinkit you long way from somewhere – ay? Aborigines have come a long way since the days of such sayings. Nowadays the Aboriginal people are vying for an equal place in society along with many so-called, foreigners. They have become politicians, judges and in fact pillars of society. We ourselves are actually just newcomers to this wonderful land. We have much to learn, especially in the art of fashioning and throwing that ancient of weapons – the boomerang.

Now I am no expert but I do have a little expertise in this direction. I was instructed by Bill Onus, whom I first met at Koranderrk just before Healesville on the Yarra flats. He was the caretaker at the time of the aboriginal burial ground there. I was just eighteen and driving a motorcycle, I camped upon the property. He taught me to shoot properly and how to hunt and track animals. One thing that I dearly wanted to learn was the correct way to throw a boomerang; this he taught me. Bill Onus was a fine aboriginal and a gentleman. Later, he set up and produced for export many varieties of boomerangs and other native artefacts at his factory at Belgrave, on the way to Kallista.

To make a boomerang, the best material is seven-ply. Cut the shape of a boomerang at about 160 degrees, slice flights on the leading and trailing edges of the bottom flat surface. The top flat surface has to be rounded on the circumference. A pattern may be etched if one so desires. This rounded edge in conjunction with flat bottom of the boomerang, gives the article 'lift'. The flights also assist in this area. Once you are satisfied with the finished product, it is time to seal it with a coat of lacquer. This is necessary to protect the wood if it gets onto damp grass.

The art of casting your boomerang is laid down in most manuals. First it must be held correctly. Firmly hold the short end in your hand with the index finger facing the ground and set to give the boomerang a flick. The boomerang should be held at shoulder height and firmly cast in a straight line parallel to the ground at shoulder height and in an upright position. At fifty metres it will lie over and travel in an upwards direction from which it will begin to circle around and return. If the wind is blowing straight at one, the boomerang (for a right hander) should be aimed at ten degrees to the right whereupon it will return at ten degrees to the left. There are two ways to recover your boomerang. If it returns above you and hovers, a hand can be placed through the centre hole as it spins; if it returns at a lower and faster velocity, then it is wise to close the open hands one above and one under, the weapon. Have fun and enjoyment with your boomerang.

Howard Reede-Pelling.

Hobbies, Pastimes, Recreation.

Bottle Collecting.

Number Six in a Series.

I was a member of The Western Antique Bottle Club for eighteen years. In that time I sat on the committee in various portfolios. Social Secretary, Secretary, Treasurer, Editor and President. We had many memorable shows including one at the Show grounds in 1983. At that time I was Secretary and had the pleasure of firstly inviting and then presenting with a gift, the Miss Australia winner, Sharon McKenzie, whom I then escorted on a tour of inspection; of our Bottle Show. Many shows at town halls and exhibition centres were made. Including one at the Williamstown Town Hall where I had the pleasure of escorting The Right Honourable Joan Kirner, just before she became Premier.

Antique Bottle Collecting is a lucrative and very interesting hobby. The value of these pieces is remarkable. Two thousand dollars for a single bottle is commonplace. One must specialise in particular areas as the house would tilt otherwise. Bottles are quite heavy when one gathers huge amounts of them. My first experience with bottle collecting came during my days at a Gem Club. A mate and I were a little tired of delving fruitlessly for agates and haematites in a gold mining area at Castlemaine, when my mate suggested that we dug out one of the mullock heaps of an abandoned gold digging. We toiled for a half of an hour before we found our first bottle. It was only a Kruses Oil bottle, but it was an 1880's piece and it was found by myself; my very own link with the past. I became quite interested in Bottle Collecting.

With Bottle Collecting it is most important to specialise. My first area was with the then quite common milk bottle. There are 625 different dairies in the Melbourne district and I had one or two bottles from each of them by the time I sold the lot to the Clunes Historic Society and concentrated upon the stoneware Ginger Beer Collection. I still have the best collection of Victorian Stone Ginger Beers in existence.

Some of my bottles are valued at over two thousand dollars each. On an average the Victorian Collection of Ginger Beer Bottles are worth one hundred dollars a bottle. I have a total collection of five hundred and ten Ginger Beer Bottles. My complete collection including the Codd Bottles, Pointy enders (Hamilton Patents) and various others including Wines, Scents and Stone Flagons; would exceed $80,000. As well as antique furniture, I might add.

To properly relate the exciting possibilities with Bottle Collecting one would need an entire newspaper. This I don't have access to, so I hope that I may have inspired some of you a little. Advice is free, so if you so desire feel free to be enlightened by myself in regard to Bottle Collecting.

Howard Reede-Pelling.

Hobbies, Pastimes, Recreation.

Bird Observing.

Number Seven in a Series.

This is a most relaxing and serene of recreational activities, the observation of our natural bird-life. The feathered creatures that abound in our habitat are indeed a natural treasure, but on the whole, we, the so-called ruling majority; take little if any notice of one of nature's wonderful gifts to mankind. Bird life is an amazing and diverse feature of our universe, yet we take most of it for granted without looking deeper into this vast and informative area of living beauty and diversity. Take just a little time out to think and ponder of the possibilities in this field. Think well of the various sizes, shapes, types and colour variations of these our feathered friends, set there for our enjoyment to wonder at and witness, yes and even to learn from and gain much in living together in harmony, even as we of multiple races have not yet learned to do.

Bird life has its own set of rules for the harmonious co-existence of the species. This is a rule, not of kill or be killed, but more of a 'look before you leap' existence. True, birds do prey upon each other in many cases, however, this is not the rule; there are many species of birds that are not cannibalistic or indeed, meat-eaters. Although the vast majority of our native birds are insect or honey-eaters, there is a large field where the bird-life are grain-eaters. Even the carnivorous of our feathered neighbours are not so aggressive as to be war-like; no indeed, their aggressiveness comes merely as a need to eat to survive. Birds such as the eagles and kestrels. Many birds need sea-life upon which to live; Gulls, Pelicans and the like. But this paper is not just a guide to the eating habits of birds but a prelude into the wonderful spectacle of witnessing the colour and beauty, and indeed, the idiosyncrasies of the more common types of birds to be found in our neighbourhoods.

It is a fact that more and more clubs and gatherings of bird observers are now becoming quite the norm, it is a relaxing, peaceful pastime and is gathering much momentum because the interest and beauty are there, to witness free of charge and to get one out in the open air. When first one takes the time to sit quietly in a natural country-like setting in one of the areas set aside for the purpose, close to the city; say for instance Yarra Bend Park, when all about is still. That is when one can see the native birds in their natural habitats doing what birds do, chirping, flirting, eating and even playing. To witness a couple of tiny tits seeking insects, although they may be just a drab grey colour, their lively antics keep one enthralled. Then there are the more colourful varieties, parrots etc. Swallows and the fleet swift. I am a Bird Observer, are you?

Howard Reede-Pelling.

Hobbies, Pastimes, Recreation.

Upholstery – Restoration.

Number Eight in a Series.

That shabby old chair or divan one has in the attic or garden shed, either Grandma's old couch or Dad's favourite chair, just laying there gathering dust; now is the time to restore it! Upholstery is not a mystery any more; even you can do something about making an effort to at least give it a new outlook. One does not have to be an expert to restore it to something of its former glory; just a little common sense will suffice. A couple of metres of new material just draped over it and tucked in at the seat will give it a new, clean look. But, if one needs something a little more substantial – read on!

Now if the need is for diamond or spade buttoning, perhaps then one should have the piece expertly done; however, for just the odd easy chair or divan, they may be restored with a minimum cost and be made to look good. The secret is to first remove the outside arm and back covers. Now one can see how the inside arm and back materials are fastened. When covering your furniture it is basic to stretch the material evenly and firmly into place. Replace springs that are broken or have slipped, and be sure to tie them properly to prevent them slipping again. Sometimes the supporting Hessian has to be replaced as it may have worn. Carefully note how it is attached before removing it, so that you can replace it as it was.

If your furniture has stab buttoning, then that is easily restored. Just get the button which has come undone or a replacement, and a trip to an upholsterer will supply you with the necessary needle so that the button may be re-attached. Look how the others were done and simulate them. If extra padding is needed, that is where the upholsterer will come in handy again. If you wish to have the tacks covered, be sure to take note of how the outside back and arms were attached. Back tacking is the simple means of cutting strips of cardboard and putting the tacks in a straight line along it; the cover is then folded down and tacked to the underside of the furniture. The sides are then slip-stitched and your furniture is as good as new.

If it needs a polish, do not despair; a quick wipe over the woodwork with a touch of shellac and Metho will take most surface scratches off and give your piece a warm sheen. Make sure if you are recovering, that you do not make the mistake of putting on a too gaudy cover as it may not suit the polish. Pastel colours are the evergreen trend and a safe guide for a comfortable unit. Remember, you may have to live with it a long time.

Howard Reede-Pelling.

Hobbies, Pastimes, Recreation.

Skating.

Number Nine in a Series.

Have you ever experienced the pleasure of gliding along with the freedom of flight, the very smooth rhythmic flow of good balance and the wind in your hair as you glide majestically through the suburbs, up hill and down dale, in and out amongst mere pedestrians and trees, along smooth bitumen paths or around a car park? Then you don't know the glory of skating. Skating is fun, be it upon the ice, on cornered wheel boots or in-line-skates, it is freedom of flight and ease of movement flowing along with grace and poise. It is an exhilarating form of sport, exercise and relaxation.

A few precautionary tips. Make sure you are well protected in case of a fall, and you will fall occasionally, due to the very nature of the sport. Matches, sticks and stones, even other pedestrians can cause a downfall for the unwary. Proper protective padding is a must for the skater. Headgear, elbow pads, knee pads, wrist guards and even shin pads are a necessity for your safety to enjoy this most pleasurable of pastimes. Care and respect for others is also a must. All have the right to co-exist in safety, so be aware of the needs of others. Just because you have a pair of skates does not give you an automatic right of way!

To fully appreciate and enjoy the thrill of skating, take care and go slowly at first. It is much better to properly master the use of your blades, be they ice or roller, before you can go hurtling along at breakneck speeds. Instead of lifting your feet one after the other, try letting your weight pull you along. With a little practice this is easily done by first of all putting the weight evenly upon both blades, and then ease the skates away from your body by leaning to the fore with the weight upon the heels. After one has moved about one metre, the weight should be transferred to the toes and pull the feet together. This will bring one to the upright position again and you will have moved about two metres. This movement is called 'wows' and should be repeated for as long as it is practical.

Wows keeps one evenly balanced, remembering to always lean slightly to the fore, and as one practices, skating by lifting each foot in turn will automatically follow. Let the body flow forwards and movements is made possible by stepping forwards rather than pushing forwards. Skating can be very hard on the ankles at first as one is using muscles that are seldom exercised so vigorously. Take care not to overdo it for the first few weeks. Later, the muscles will have hardened and skating will become second nature. Have fun!

Howard Reede-Pelling.

Hobbies, Pastimes, Recreation.

Story Writing & Poetry.

Number Ten in a Series.

There is nothing more satisfying than to be able to put thoughts in your head down on paper, be it in book form, prose or poetry. Writing can be described as an art form, indeed I think that in some cases it is so; but a rank amateur can and is, able to put pen to paper and make some sort of a fist at it, given a little leeway. After the first book or fifty or so poems, one does acquire a 'knack' of imparting their thoughts with somewhat of a bit of respectability. I know, I have been there – done that – so I have experience at it. After having written fifteen books, including 450 pages of poetry and countless articles for magazines of clubs to which I have been associated, I do have some expertise in this area.

When one writes, there is a need to have a format. One must have a beginning, a middle or body of the article, and an ending. It is also advisable not to deviate from one's goal, put the thoughts in their proper perspective, and make the story viable. One must keep the reader interested and keen or the plot will be lost and the reader will cast away the article and pick up the comics. In writing a story, there must be interest at all times. That is one of the reasons for making chapters. A chapter is in itself a story. A whole book encompasses maybe twenty five chapters and even though they are related, there must be an interest at the ending of each one to keep the reader enthralled. To make the reader look at the next chapter just to see how the story is going, what the next exciting episode is all about. Do not go out at a tangent unless you are going to return to the gist of the story at a later time, for one may forget what the plot is about and end up on a different tram.

Prose and poetry are the same. Although prose has a story to tell, it does not rhyme as poetry does; it is merely a statement of an idea. Poetry on the other hand, not only tells a story but it does so with rhythm and sound alike words.

Poetry has a ring to it which is easy to listen to and is easily understood. But, as in story writing, one must stick to the story-line and not deviate. A good piece of poetry or prose must have a meaningful beginning, the two or three middle verses should have the body of the story and the ending must be just that – an ending. Keep the reader enthralled!

Good poetry can easily be made into songs; just work on the syllable system when composing your piece. Each first, second or third line, in fact right throughout the piece, have your syllables symmetric and all will fall into place.

Howard Reede-Pelling.

Hobbies, Pastimes, Recreation.

Camping -- Bush Lore.

Number Eleven in a Series.

Ah, the call of the wild! Nothing is as good as camping, communing with nature if you will. But beware the pitfalls, and there are many of which the city dweller may not fully comprehend. Just a few reminders for city folk. Be sure to pack the can opener, a box of matches and a torch. There are many things of creature comfort which we take for granted, but may not remember in the bush. A toilet roll, extra blankets, a container for water, a spade, the medical kit and most importantly – let someone know what you are planning and where you are going.

Setting up camp is like planning a house. One must look to safety first! Don't just plonk down in the first shady spot you come to, look for the dangers. It may be there are bushes or logs about that could harbour spiders or snakes, which could come out and creep into bed with you for warmth at night. The river bank upon which you have erected your tent may be unstable and give way, casting you into the water at night. Perhaps the shade tree you have decided to camp under is a blue gum, which are notorious for dropping healthy looking limbs of great weight upon you unexpectedly. Then again, the gravely bank a little away from camp may be just one massive bull-ants nest!

Given that one has not neglected safety, all has been remembered that is necessary and the camp has been set up respectably; if one is fishing, the next step is to locate bait and a good fishing spot. Most people will rely upon the spade for the recovery of worms for bait. Not good enough! Fish do not rely on worms alone for feed; they eat the natural things which fall into the rivers and streams. The little white moths that abound near wattle trees, witchetty grubs that fall into the water from the same trees, spiders that can be found under the loose bark of gums and acacias, grasshoppers and locusts from the grasses and yabbies from nearby dams. A good angler will have the outer cable-case of a push bike handy. They can be stored in one's creel quite easily. A lone ghost gum in a paddock is a good place to scrape the ground-cover leaves away and expose the bardy grub's web. A flick upon each hole will tell you whether a grub is home or not. A dull thud means he's at home, a ting means he has already been taken. A twist of the cable down the hole and you are able to extricate the grub as bait. Scrub worms are also good bait.

Have fun safely and catch plenty of fish. Above all, take heavy boots to guard against snakes and scorpions.

Howard Reede-Pelling.

Hobbies, Pastimes, Recreation.

Swimming -- Teaching.

Number Twelve in a Series.

I first began teaching swimming at the age of seventeen. I had two pupils. It was not until the 1956 Olympic Games that I began in earnest, and then I was so taken by the likes of the Konrads and John Marshal, that I adopted their 'new' style of swimming – the third stroke breathing method. This is an evergreen style that is as near to breathing at a walking pace, that one can get. I shall endeavour to pass on to my readers, this little gem of information; read and put it into practice for the betterment of your stroking.

The Third Stroke breathing Method is not unlike that old favourite 'The Australian Crawl'. With the Australian crawl one takes a deep breath and holds it until one has swum an entire lap, pulling up at the end of the lap through sheer lack of breath. With the Third Stroke Breathing Method, one does just that – breathe on every third stroke! Not only can one breathe normally when swimming, there is also stability to your stroking inasmuch that the body does not rock sideways at each stroke. A steady even pull such as a sculler is also evident.

For Third Stroke swimming, one does the crawl but on the third stroke, turns the head to one side sufficiently enough to take a breath. The breath is taken BELOW the water level for with the forward propulsion of the body, a hollow is left after the head has moved forwards. It is in this hollow that one takes their breather, blowing out gently with the head straight down for two strokes. On the third stroke (which is now upon the other side of the body), the swimmer should take the next breath. With a minimum of movement the head moves from side to side with the third stroke, only the chin moves from side to side. During two strokes, the head should be held in a straight forwards position. The feet should be kicked two, four or six times during the entailing three strokes. Depending upon the distance to be swum, marathon, two to six laps or sprint.

This method enables the swimmer to gain maximum speed with very little exertion. An easy stroke for practice laps and a purposeful stroke for an average distance. More frenzied can be left for the last half a lap in a sprint race. As a rule, an easy purposeful stroke will eat up the laps and get the swimmer from A to B with little exertion. The Third Stroke Breathing Method of swimming is a proven practise drill and a world-class winner in marathons. Enjoy your swimming.

Howard Reede-Pelling.

Hobbies, Pastimes, Recreation.

Philately.

Number Thirteen in a Series.

Philately is the hobby of Stamp Collecting. We all did at one time or another; delve into the fascinating world of the most ancient of pastimes; well, for the last century or so at any rate. Because of its diversity there is an interest for all, young and old alike. The young because it is really fascinating; the old because of the fiscal benefits. Stamp collecting has a very large following and it has an extremely large diversity. For instance, there are collectors for charity, those that have no real interest in philately but they know others do have, and get together all the stamps that would otherwise have been wasted and send them to institutions, mainly as money earners. Then there are the beginners, children mostly, who have the curiosity to learn of the different cultures and variety of stamps. Those fledglings that begin a collection and then lose interest. But far and away are the serious collectors who steadfastly adhere to the rigid guidelines of philately and properly store, tend, and preserve these icons of yesteryear and of the future purely for, not only their monetary value but because they have a genuine love of stamps.

A true philatelist is one who takes a genuine interest in the hobby and acquires all the necessary utensils to adequately consummate their ideals of The Collecting and Storage of Stamps. A couple of pairs of tweezers, fine and heavy, the correct drying material for used stamps, good pocket albums for the correct storage of their treasures, most importantly, two pairs of eyeglasses for the finer inspection of the stamps to take note of imperfections and variations. A nice airy office and an uncluttered desk for the laying out and sorting of these sometimes very scarce and valuable items.

As the years roll by, stamp collecting is becoming more and more of a mind-boggler. The new varieties keep coming as the governments realise that huge incomes can be gained for the public coffers, due to the enormous interest that is encouraged by new variations and 'sets' of stamps. It would seem that everyone is trying to cash in on the enormity of stamp collecting. Personalised stamps, stamps of the different flora and fauna of countries, even motor racing and yachting events are catered for, anything from which governments are able to raise monetary gain is being exploited. While the interest is there, and it looks like the interest always will be there, people and governments are out to make a profit. And why not? When there is a genuine need and people are happy with it, make it viable; there is no harm in promoting that which does some good for all involved. I like philately, do you?

Howard Reede-Pelling.

Hobbies, Pastimes, Recreation.

Ephemera.

Number Fourteen in a Series.

Ephemera! What is it you may well ask? Fair enough! Ephemera is paperwork and the art of collecting it. Such as old tickets, newspapers, photographs, cuttings, programmes, posters, postcards, in fact anything of historic value of our past in paper form. There are clubs and associations dedicated entirely to it and indeed, they hold exhibitions, displays, buy and swap stalls etcetera. Take for instance the 1956 Olympic edition of the newspapers. A copy of that newspaper in mint condition is worth $100 - $1000. A boarding ticket for the titanic, if one still exists, would possibly be in excess of thousands. A ballroom ladies card for the Trocadero (now well demolished) would set one back hundreds of dollars. This is just a small sample of what ephemera collecting is all about!

A search through any drawer could well reward one with many items forgotten about in every home. People do not put much stock in such things and are very liable to pass them by as unworthy, not worth the effort; I must clear that drawer out someday! Be very careful; what you may regard as just a mundane scrap of paper, could be worth many dollars to a collector of trivia. It may pay you well, if when you do clean out that drawer, if you look up the appropriate clubs in the yellow pages and have an expert determine what is rubbish and what is to be thrown out. Look before you leap is a well-known saying, never has it been truer than when clearing out rubbish.

Everyone knows how valuable those old tobacco cards are; they are ephemera! Look in any antique shop or a second hand shop and you will see dozens of items of ephemera. They would not be there if there was not a quid to be gained by having them. It does seem to be a pity that not a great deal of interest has been engendered in the very real and profitable art of collecting ephemera. It is one of those easily overlooked hobbies that so many people just ignore; until they realise the money-making potential!

In the wonderful world of collecting ephemera, the collecting of cards is just one of a plethora of diversities. There are people who collect only newspapers for example, or magazines (I had a valuable collection of T.V.weeks, from Vol. 1 No. 1 up to ten years without missing an issue), which when disposed of, it brought more that the face value. I can recall a friend who has a similar story to tell of his collection of playing cards. Some of them dated back to the seventeenth century. Have you the makings of a collection?

Howard Reede-Pelling.

Hobbies, Pastimes, Recreation

Number Fifteen in a Series

The Art of Billiards

Instruction by Howard Reede-Pelling

As a thirty year old I took advantage of an offer of instruction in the manly game of Billiards. My tutor was one Mister Bourke who just happened to be the husband of Dolly Bourke (nee Lindrum) who took over and ran the famous Lindrum Billiards Rooms in Flinders Lane and then in Flinders Street, just past the offices of The Herald-Sun.

Dolly Lindrum lived in the same house as Walter Lindrum, in Kerferd Road, South Melbourne, where Mister Bourke gave instruction on the very table which was made famous by Walter; it was situated at the rear of the premises and was self-contained. Walter Lindrum spent much of his early lifetime at that particular table.

These were the main points that I was taught:-

Stand square on to the table. Bridge at a half arm's length and use the rest, do not stretch. Use the nine points of the cue ball and strike gently according to the position required. Play the ball; don't just shut your eyes and bash; that is for pub players. Leave the cue ball to your advantage, NOT your opponent's. Control the ball, do not let it control you and above all, have respect for the table.

Take the fifteen RED balls off the table leaving only the six coloured balls and the cue ball. Imagine that the pack has been broken and you are left with only the coloured balls to pocket. From a position left or right of where the triangle of red balls were, now pot all six colours in order one at a time making sure to leave the cue ball in a position to pot the next colour. This is an exercise to control the cue ball to its best position to pot each ball in turn, from the most advantageous position.

Enjoy your potting.

Howard Reede-Pelling.

Interested persons take note:-

Howard Reede-Pelling has written
fifteen papers in regard to:-

Hobbies, Pastimes, Recreation

These papers are also in a booklet available separately.
The first of these papers is on the subject
of NUMISMATICS. (Coin collecting)

Below is a list of the papers as written.

Numismatics (coin collecting)
Lapidary (gem collection)
Gold panning
Beach combing
Boomerang making and throwing
Bottle collecting
Bird observing
Upholstery – restoration
Skating
Story writing & poetry
Camping – bush lore
Swimming – teaching
Philately
Ephemera.
The Art of Billiards

Persons who have more than a casual interest in any of the above subjects, and wish it to have them elaborated upon; Howard is at your disposal.

12 Monstrous Escape © Howard Reede Pelling

The screams of unseen wild predators permeated the steamy jungle. I could feel the vibrations of their passing beneath my hide-bound feet and the terrible gape of the cavernous jaws permitted that horrific stench to foul the air. Although out of sight, I knew a Brontosaurus was stalking me, it's tiny vision seeking me out amongst the bramble of foliage. I hastened to the protection afforded by my cave, knowing that once within it's comforting walls, I would be safe; the huge animals unable to penetrate it's formidable covering.

I was but a bare twenty metres from its safety, when my way was impeded by an angry Tyrannosaurus Rex; a huge lizard-like creature that walked upon its hind legs. It towered above me, emitting the most frightful screams imaginable. I was trapped. With a cool head I looked about for a means of escape. The Brontosaurus stalking me suddenly broke into the clearing and charged, giving voice to a murderous roar as it did so. The Tyrannosaurus Rex charged past me, screaming. The two prehistoric monsters engaged in mortal combat metres away, allowing me to hasten off lest I be swept from my feet by a giant gyrating tail, or worse still, crushed under the weight of a falling monster.

"Come on Byron, we'll be late for school!"

"Huh? Coming!" I gently placed the ladybugs in my hand upon a leaf and continued to school.

Howard Reede-Pelling.

13 Jenny © Howard Reede-Pelling.

The biting wind cut through the crocheted shawl which Jenny grimly clawed tightly to her shivering body, as she huddled ever more deeply into the cramped niche towards the end of the cobble-stoned lane in which refuge had been sought; from the elements. The evening darkness seemed to have appeared suddenly as though the sun were inadvertently switched off. So Jenny made her way with haste down that dreary cul-de-sac in a forlorn attempt to attain a place of comfort, to while away what would surely be an uncomfortable, cold and frightening night. That shawl was the last of her worldly possessions which at all could be classed as valuable. Not in monetary terms was it of value but heavily steeped in intrinsic value, as this was her only heirloom and connection with her forebears that Jenny had to cherish. Great grandma had been the one to fashion this lovely garment and family history handed down to later generations, reported that the old lady wore her masterpiece with elegance and grace. So too, did Jenny's grandmother. Oh yes! Grandmother was the talk of the Social Set in her day and did prance about her Tea-Parties with style, proud of her mother's great handiwork. Jenny recalled that her own mother was not at all taken with the shawl, when family tradition deemed it be passed on and kept in the family. The shawl spent most of Jenny's life-time in her mother's linen-closet; bespangled with naphthalene flakes. Upon the few occasions when mother displayed the family heirloom, Jenny could only stare in awe at the beautiful wrap and the skills of her great grandmother. Then came the unexpected bombshell! Jenny had asked her mother if she could wear that wonderful shawl to her friend's house, as she had been invited to a slumber party. The theme of the evening was to be that each person had to wear an article of old-time clothing. Jenny's item was the treasured shawl! Early morning had the Police waking the household to alert Jenny that her house had burned to the ground overnight, taking her parents with it! Six months had since elapsed. Jenny was comforted by her many friends and they attended her immediate needs, but only one family would take her until she became self-sufficient. Her lot was made worse and most intolerable by the son of the family, who made Jenny feel indebted to them. When he began to force himself upon her and insinuate that it was time for her to be nice with him, as he and his family were nice to her; Jenny then grabbed her few possessions and left. A week of trundling along both familiar and unfamiliar streets took their toll. Jenny became most disillusioned with her lot and life in general. Safe havens were as scarce as the meals for which she was forced to beg. Poverty and helplessness drove her to take comfort in that one link with her past which was tangible – great grandma's shawl! Jenny huddled tighter into her niche and tucked the precious shawl in about her frozen legs as the dark, cold and friendless night drew its cloak of loneliness and despair about her. Tears of hopelessness trickled down her pale cheeks but no cry escaped her lips. Jenny had already cried herself out – many times – her fears for the future grew to gigantic imaginings of an awesome fate. Jenny had visions of herself prone in the gutter with the pitiless rain beating fervently at her shrivelled remains as mangy frightened and starved, once domestic pets, fought over her lonely body. Not a soul to care what had become of her, not a tear shed over her unhappy demise – and her beloved shawl – oh the pity of it being torn to shreds by scavenging animals to be left rotting in the dirty, damp gutter; perhaps finally to enshroud Jenny at her last resting place. Numb of body and mind, Jenny became aware of strangers bearing along the cul-de-sac towards her; she raised her weary head a fraction to see what threat invaded her privacy now. To the heavy beating of her heart, which pounded as of a thousand drums, the silhouettes of a man and woman reached towards her. Jenny could feel the comforting shawl being taken from about her face and piteously prayed aloud.

"Oh God, please don't take my shawl – please!"

Kindly voices and tender hands assisted Jenny to her feet as a sweet modulated voice offered comfort.

"Oh you poor Dear. Please let us help you, we will get you nice and warm soon and you will have a good solid feed into you, then a more comfortable place to rest up. Come dear, you are safe with us – we are Soldiers of the Salvation Army – you and your precious shawl seem as if they could certainly do with some tender loving care!"

Jenny once again pulled her shawl about her and as the tears came more profusely, she was comforted in those caring arms.

Howard Reede-Pelling

END.

14 Wayne by © Howard Reede-Pelling 1996

The pier at first appeared deserted as I gazed along its length on a mild still Sunday morning in mid-September; Kerferd Road pier always appeared deserted early any morning for that matter. Today the sea was calm; perhaps the fish would take the bait and reward my patience. I was more than half-way along the rough loose boards that moved and thumped beneath my weight, when I realised I was not alone out here – there, in the far extreme of my splintery path – a movement; ever so slight. I studied it as I approached and beheld a scruffy little urchin of some ten years, a reasonably clean face glared at me with a forlorn expression from under a fringe of unruly collar-length black hair. I gave a quick wink and a cheery

"G'day Tiger'" as I set about the business of fishing.

A quiet half-hour elapsed. Two more people were now at the end of the pier trying their luck, the lad had not stirred other than to watch my fruitless efforts. I reeled in and tried a change of bait, perhaps a couple of sand-worms to replace the octopus fillet. I cast out casually. Two seconds and Bingo! The float fluttered then dived beneath the surface and away, I let it run a little, and then struck. The excitement of the chase had my full attention. The fish was of a fair size by the feel – at least two pounds – a good fish to catch off a pier. I played it as best I knew how, it was well hooked. Elated, I flipped the fish onto the pier, right at the feet of the lad. The 'Couta had plenty of fight in it and my line was becoming tangled with its threshing about. The boy came to life and planted a foot on the fish, I passed my spike and he deftly cracked the 'Couta on the head then impaled it. As I removed the barb from the vicious mouth and glanced at the boy, his face was transformed – gone the glum expression – replaced by a keen interest; the deep brown eyes alight with excitement.

"She's a beauty Mister! Ya don't see many big 'uns come in here no more. Can I put her in ya bag?"

He was already doing it.

"Sure." I answered with a chuckle.

"You have done a bit of fishing yourself, haven't you, Son?"

"Yair, 'til Dad died."

He turned away as he answered and lapsed into silence. I resumed my fishing, the boy again glum, stared out to sea.

"There is a spare rod here if you want to try your luck". I offered.

"Nah!" He shook his head.

With a shrug, I looked at my float, it began to dance again. Hoping for another big 'Couta, I studied it; one more jiggle then it remained calm. The boy was suddenly sitting beside me.

"Yair, I think I will Mister!"

I passed the rod, some bait and left him to it. By lunch time we had caught between us, nine fish. The first was the only big one but never-the-less, we had a couple of meals there. During the course of the morning, the boy had divulged that his name was Wayne Sonning, he was an only child and his mother worked at the Supermarket. His father was killed in a level crossing accident ten months ago. Wayne spoke quite a lot of his dad, he must have been a fine father for the boy respected and loved him; they were mates.

"What's ya name Mister?"

"You can call me Fred". I said as I began to gather my gear.

"Are ya goin' then?" Came from the boy, rather wistfully.

"Lunch-time." I answered. "The old tummy is rumbling and I am dying for a cuppa!"

"My Mum'll give ya a cuppa, I only live over the road, Fred – if ya wanna!"

I smiled down at the eager face, recalling the glum expression so often upon it.

"Thanks Wayne, but no, your mum would not take kindly to a stranger popping in on her."

As I drove away I could see the boy was again looking all forlorn, sitting on the beach wall watching my departure, the fish he caught dangling from his side. Unmoving, he watched me out of sight.

I had no intention of returning to the pier that afternoon, Golfing was my wont as a rule – but here I was, striding along those creaking boards as if it were my duty. Perhaps it was that wistful look in those sad brown eyes – I do not know. As I reached the terminus – there he was.

"I knew ya'd come." Wayne drawled. "I wanted ya to!"

I offered a rod and we fished again. An hour or more passed and we chatted idly, the boy seemed brighter. After a pause in the conversation he said, rather shyly.

"Me Mum said if I liked I could ask ya to pop in for a cuppa." Another pause then. "Would ya Fred, please?"

It was more of a plea than a request. I had the feeling that his little world would shatter again if I refused him. I studied the eager face, then impulsively.

"Sure, why not? I think I'd admire to meet your mum!"

We gathered the fishing tackle, which might just as well have been left at home and I followed this ragged little lad, who somehow got the better of me, to a rather weary-looking small flat on the beach road. Wayne eagerly rushed inside, shouting.

"Hey Ma! He came – Fred came – he's here!"

I felt like a great foolish oaf and wondered what the hell am I doing, when of a sudden it all became well worth while.

"Oh shush Wayne, what's come over you?"

A curiously soothing mellow voice said, and then she appeared and apologetically asked me in. Wayne had the most beautiful mother. Trim, very capable looking with sparkling brown eyes and a halo of auburn hair caressing a slightly pink-cheeked face that smiled a welcome as I was ushered to a chair. The well moulded figure would be more in place at a beauty parade than at a chain store counter; I thought. Missus Sonning was speaking.

"I must thank you for the fish, we'll have them for tea; I hope Wayne was not a bother to you?"

"Er, no-no." I stammered, aware that I had been staring.

"He was no trouble at all, he is a keen fisherman."

A frown accompanied her reply.

"Well, he used to be" - pause - "when his father was here; he has not fished since; until today. Misses his father you know, they were very close."

"Yes, Wayne told me, I'm sorry, didn't mean to pry, he just all of a sudden let it all out; you know?" Missus Sonning nodded.

"Just as well I suppose, it has been bottled up since – since -; anyway you seem to have given him a new interest in life. He has been so listless lately, I have been worried!"

Wayne appeared. "I got the kettle on Ma, ain't we got no cakes?"

Her exasperation began to show.

"Must you speak like that, Wayne? You know better. No, we haven't any cakes; there's biscuits!"

The boy disappeared into the kitchen. His mother was addressing me again.

"He just seems to have lapsed since his dad went; his pet dream is to have a pony. John – that was my husband – promised him one if ever we moved to the country, but we didn't have any hope from the start. We were stuck here with a poorly paid eight to four-thirty, mundane job and since John died I have had to make ends meet at the Supermarket. It doesn't pay much but we get by and the pony is just a dream, still, Wayne has hopes – poor kid!"

The rattle of cups and saucers announced the arrival of Wayne with a tray and we sipped tea silently. I was quite entranced by Missus Sonning, she had charm, poise, dignity and a curious affect on me, I felt I wished to see her again; to get to know her. I broke the silence and blurted hopefully.

"The Royal Show is on at the moment, there are lots of ponies there in the arena events. If you like, I will take you and Wayne one evening!"

The boy was on his feet beside his mother, almost upsetting the tray.

"Oh Ma! Could we please Ma, perlease – I'd love to see the show?"

"Wayne, hold on now, we don't even know the man, we just met him. I mean – we can't - ?"

"Aw gee Ma!" Wayne grizzled. "His name's Fred!"

I butted in.

"I'm sorry, fancy not even introducing myself – Fred Pelling – I'm an Antique Dealer. So sorry, I should not have presumed - !"

"Oh, it's all right Mister Pelling –"

"Fred" I interposed.

"Well, Fred." She smiled. "I am Yvonne and thank you so much anyway; it was nice of you to offer."

"Aw gee Ma!" Came from Wayne. "We don't go nowhere anymore."

"Anywhere!" She frowned.

"Well, we don't – c'mon Ma – please, pretty please?"

The look and attitude was intended to melt his mother's heart, it may have worked with dad, but mum was a resolute person and Wayne's cause seemed lost.

"Tell you what." I suggested. "I will be going myself in any case, so how about me popping in on my way – say seven-thirty on Thursday evening. If you decide to go we will have a fun evening – if not – well, no harm done. Can we let it ride until then – give you a chance to mull it over?"

Wayne glanced expectantly at his mother. She smiled.

"We will leave it at that then."

I took my leave with a thumping heart.

"Hope to see you Thursday!" And left an excited little boy clamouring about his mother. Thoughtfully, I drove home, visions of a winning smile cupped in a halo of auburn hair lingered pleasantly. Each day dragged by like a week until at last, there I was approaching her door. Odd thoughts were racing through my mind. 'The lights are on, at least they are home, and thank goodness they did not go visit an Aunt or something. I know she is expecting me, please be ready and willing to go. Now, the big moment – where is the bell button? Ah, there!' Faintly, in the rear of the flat, was an answering tinkle, then voices and hurried footsteps, the door flung open. Wayne stood, bright-eyed resplendent and glowing, a huge grin relieved my tension – they were to accompany me. I tried not to let my relief show.

"We're goin' Fred!"

Excitedly came from Wayne as his mother emerged from a doorway down the dim length of the hallway. 'Truly a gift from the Gods', I thought, as she neared with extended hand. I took it gently as if the dainty thing were fragile and eyed her person approvingly. Her plain white dress in all its simplicity topped by a fur half-coat, white accessories and scarf from which that beautiful hair peeped coyly, had me spellbound.

"My prayers are answered that I should escort an angel." I offered. "And thanks for accepting my invitation."

Her smiling reply was that she and Wayne were becoming stick-in-the-muds and should get out more, was very gratifying indeed. Soon we were purring along the highway. Long before we reached the Show grounds, brightness in the sky above attested that all was in full swing. Wayne, excited, pointed out the huge Ferris wheel towering over the myriads of life beneath. It was like a great heart pulsating life and energy throughout the milling throng. As we passed through the gates from the car parking area, the presence of the sheep, goats, pigs and cattle became quite obvious and remained so for some time, as the boy led us willy-nilly hither and yon, flitting from one of nature's wonders to the next. Eventually we put a stop to it and Yvonne suggested we look for the Arts and Crafts Pavilion.

After an hour or so jostling through crowds and standing staring in awe and wonder at the various exhibits, the old legs demanded a reprieve; so the next port of call was obviously the arena events where one could sit and watch. Three weary people that we were, had merely begun the climb up the steps of the Grandstand, when the building beneath us fairly shuddered as a resounding – thoomp – whistle – then pop, followed by the brilliant glare of coloured stars glittering gently earthwards, was herald to the opening of the fireworks display. Fifteen minutes of spellbound beauty had the vast audience agog with oohs and ahhs as each succeeding burst of glory outdid the last. Then the arena lights came on and we were entertained by the Victorian Police Motor cycle Squad, who amazed the young and old alike with their intricate manoeuvres and feats of balance, while riding at speeds of up to eighty kilometres an hour. They had such perfect control of their vehicles and were so resplendent in their smart uniforms; they were indeed a sight to behold. Wayne laughed uncontrollably at the two clowns representing 'Keystone Kops' on a pair of Mini-Motorbikes, Yvonne and I could not repress a chuckle or two as they were quite amusing and clever. Tent Pegging was the next item on the agenda but we were not quite so enthralled with it.

"Crikey!" Wayne suddenly shouted. "We haven't seen the horses. When do they come out, Fred?"

"Oh, just a sec', I have the programme here somewhere!"

A hurried search revealed the clipping in a rear pocket.

"The Grand Parade preceded the fireworks, so we missed that. No! No more horses tonight 'Tiger', we may be able to see them in the stalls as we are leaving though; we have to pass the pony stalls on the way out!" I said, with a pout.

That glum expression was again evident.

"But you promised, Fred."

Yvonne came to the rescue.

"You must not be selfish Wayne, Fred gave us a lovely evening out, be thankful for that. He can't help it if the ponies were not on!"

I tried to square myself.

"Perhaps they were on during the daytime. Tell you what Wayne – maybe – just maybe, your mother might let me take you both up to my farm at Digger's Rest. There is three hundred acres of land and old Jim, my caretaker, keeps a couple of hacks in trim. You will not only see horses, you can ride them!"

I glanced enquiringly at Yvonne; with wide eyes she was looking at me.

"I must say Fred, you are full of surprises!"

"Well?" I queried.

She pondered a minute, then with Wayne nodding vigorously beside her, said.

"We'll see, I will have to think it over."

A sparkle was in her eyes, Wayne was bubbling over and I smiled contentedly. I was picturing many such outings ahead, with that winning smile cupped in a halo of auburn hair beside me and that odd Saturday or Sunday at the pier fishing, with a quiet but happy little urchin with unruly black hair, for company.

THE END.

15 The Fairy

I had never before seen one, well, not that I could remember anyhow. I mean – they were just in one's imagination – or so I thought, that was until the day that I just happened to be wandering alone by the merrily rippling brook on a bright sunny day; unless I dreamed it of course. But no – it was too real - I could never have dreamed that beautiful little being and the gorgeous face and deportment so brilliantly depicted upon my vision. No, it was not a dream for I can remember well the scintillating flair of her beautiful movements and the wonderful conversation we had, so interesting and inspiring with her most melodious voice and cheerful laughter. But then, the dainty little thing stood but a mere one half of a metre in height and the gossamer wings were silent, almost invisible so swiftly did they flutter. She just had to be a fairy, there was the wand upon which a glistening star twinkled as she pranced merrily about. A real true-to-goodness fairy and I was there to see her. My heart stood still.

As I stood in stunned admiration of the lovely sight upon which I had inadvertently stumbled across, she smiled and the sweet dulcet tone in her melodious voice held me enthralled as I listened.

"Oh, you are the caring one who freed the butterfly from the web of the tree-spider in your garden. I have been sent to make a like service for you in appreciation, from the land of beauty. My homeland would be honoured if we could make your happiness a thing of joy. There is one overbearing trouble you have and we are about to clear it from your mind. Think of that trouble and the trouble will abate." The fairy waved her wand and was about to leave, when I whispered almost to myself as I was not absolutely sure that I was not having a vision.

"Who told you that I have an overbearing trouble – er – miss?"

Her scintillating smile and the cocking of her head as she replied let me know what a foolish question I asked.

"Just like a grown up. The children would not question because they believe as they should, that we know all. We do not have to be told of your troubles for we know about them already. Just do as I have outlined and your trouble will be past. This is your reward for caring about the little things – look to the future."

With that she raised her starry wand and disappeared. I stood perplexed, what trouble?

The one trouble that I had was that of infertility – a fairy would not know of that – still, she did say to think of it and it would abate. Now that got me to thinking and worrying again. There was nothing that could be done about it. The doctors had taken tests and it was a permanent thing. May belle would just have to adopt if we were to be parents. I went home a little bit downhearted. I had tried to let that side of things just fade – but a fairy – a bosh. May belle was bubbling over with excitement when I got to the house. Her happy smile greeted me.

"Darling, good news, I have just returned from the doctor, we are going to have a baby!"

I was stunned, fairies, whoever believes in fairies – well – maybe I do!

16 POTTERY

As a prelude to my Pottery Collection I deemed it appropriate that a few words of explanation were in order. Old World pottery in Victoria, Australia is not very well known at least the sort of pottery listed here. I have been collecting this type of our heritage since 1965 and have amassed a very nice gathering of pieces. There were three very serious collectors in my time; Max Longford who only collected very mint pieces, Graeme Fyfe who took any piece he could add to his lot and me Howard Reede-Pelling. I collected even broken articles that were relevant to my interests and became an expert in restoring them, to replace them when I could as a mint copy became available. I collected most of the Australian Ginger Beer bottles at first, then as my collection was getting too large and costly I decided to collect ONLY VICTORIAN bottles which of course had to include border towns such as Albury-Wodonga. Max Longford has disposed of his collection, they were dispersed amongst other collectors including Graeme and I but to my knowledge, I have the only near enough to complete collection of Victorian Ginger Beer bottles in the world. Graeme had a quadruple heart bypass in 1999 but was still collecting then, however the bush fires of 2009 swept through the small settlement 8 kilometres from Horsham where he lived at the time and I do not know if the bottles survived or not. Graeme did have an underground store room for them but their fate is uncertain. My collection of Pottery comprises of 510 Ginger Beer Bottles and almost 100 other Pottery pieces relevant to them; such as Demi-Johns, foot warmers and bread and grain containers. I have about sixty bottles that Graeme needs and he has a similar amount that I need; if we had joined our collections we would have the complete collection of Victorian Ginger Beer Bottles covered except for unknown bottles that may exist.

Now there are very few bottles in my collection that are repaired only very hard to replace bottles, most of mine are now mint. As this collection may be the last of its kind I need to have it preserved for posterity, to this end I have chronicled the following pages and am currently attempting to find a permanent home for them so that they can be put on display for the public to view and be well kept for the future generations. Bendigo Pottery was the first concern that I tried but they preferred to keep ONLY Bendigo pieces, as I wished to retain the collection as a whole I tried elsewhere. The National Gallery will be a last resort as they will most likely only get an airing once and then be stored away. The same fate is expected of the Victorian Museum, at the moment I am negotiating with The City of Greater Bendigo in Victoria, Australia, to have my collection displayed at the Deborah Gold Mine at Bendigo. As the majority of the collection is from Bendigo, it appears to be only fitting that this historic collection should be housed for the peoples of Bendigo to appreciate as a priority. I am still trying to house them where they will be available for public viewing permanently.

My bottles are displayed according to their areas, one shelf of Horsham, two shelves of Bendigo etcetera. One entire book case is devoted to Melbourne and suburbs but almost eighty-five per cent are bottles produced at the Bendigo Pottery or its subsidiaries. The earliest Ginger Beer Bottle in my collection is about 1854 and the most recent are a couple from the 1935 year. All of the different closures are explained along with relevant sizes, colourings and types. The collection is colour coded. Also part of the collection is a comprehensive account of most of the potteries at the time. Howard Reede-Pelling.

Pottery

Victorian Ginger Beer Bottles and Country Border Towns

Name	Dates	Place	Variation	Pottery	Type	Value '96	Value '04Kn
Addicott F.F	1915-26	Frankston		7 Ben	Ch	400	4
Albury Brew Co-op		Albury	Diamond	(Ben) 7 No	D	70	
"		"	Mtn	7 Ben	D	85	
"		"	Mtn	Pin	D	85	
Alpha	1910-22	Mildura	Ord	7 Ben	Ch	45	
"	"	"	G.B	7 Ben	Ch	65	
"	"	"	Square Sh.	7 Ben	Ch	200	4
"	"	"	wide G.B.	7 Ben	Ch	60	
Barrett Bros.		N. Fitzroy	Sm. Mono	Tay Int	Ch	50	
"		"	L.Oval Brewed	(Ben) 7 No	Ch	40	
"		"	Circ. Sm. Circ.	(Ben) 7 No	Ch	40	
"		"	Sm. T/M	7 Ben	Ch	40	
"		"	Lge T/M	(Ben) 7 No Int.	Ch	40	
"		"	Und. G.B.	(Tay) No Int.	Ch	70	
Bartlett J & Co.		Tatura		19 Gov	C/s	110	6
"	"	"		13 Gov	C/s	85	
"	"	"		(Ben) 7 No	C/s	90	6
"	"	"		4 Ben	Ch	85	
"	"	Rushworth	'Royal' Open	19 Gov	C/s	450	600 10
"	"	"	No Reverse	7 Ben	Ch	75	
Bennett G.H.		Richmond	No G.B. Wavy Flag	(C.A.P.)	Ch	70	
"		"	G.B. Sm Oval	7 Ben	Ch	70	
"		"	G.B. Apple Grn	7 Ben	Ch	400	
"		"	G.B. Dk Grn	7 Ben	Ch	400	
"		"	G.B. Lt Grn	7 Ben	Ch	400	600

"		"	No GB. Rippled Flag	(Ben) 7 No	Ch	80	
"		"	Open Stamp T/M	(Ben)7 Ben	Ch	500	2
"		"	Trade Mark	(Ben)7 Ben	Ch	80	
"		"	"	(Ben) Hoff	Ch	80	
"		"	" Lge GB.	(Ben)7 No	Ch	80	
Billson A.A.	1888-1904	Beech/ Tallan'a		2 Ben	Ch	200	2
Billson A.A.	1893-1904	Bee/Tall/ Ruthg	a/o/w	(Ben)2 No	D	50	
Billson Bros B.B.	1888-92	St. Kilda		2 Ben	Ch	90	4
Billson G.H.	G.H.B.	"	d Smaller St K. etc.	2 Ben	Ch	60	
"	"	"	Lge Shield	3 Ben	Ch	30	
"	"	"	S Smaller Shield	3 Ben	Ch	35	
"	"	"	d Lge Shield	3 Ben	Ch	45	
"	and Co.	"	"	(Ken) No	Ch	80	
"	"	"	Smaller 'T/M'	(Ben) 7 No	Ch	?	
"	"	"	"	Ken	Ch	60	
"	& Co.	"	"	7 Ben	Ch	85	
Boon Spa	1920-37	Footscray		Ben) 7 No	Ch	250	5
Border United C0-0p		Albury	Mtn	t/t 3 Ben	D	50	
"		"	a/o/w	(Ben) 7 No	D	80	
Brown D.O.		Castlemaine		7 Ben	Ch	100	6
Bray Les.		St. Arnaud		7 Ben	Ch	250	3
"	"	"		(Ben) 7 No	C/s	100	5
"	"	"		% (Ben) 7 No	Ch	200	8
Bray W.	1902-1909	St. Arnaud		not complete 7 Ben	Ch	(300)	3
Bryant & Shiel	1917	Wangaratta		Pin	Ch	100	
""	"	"		7 Ben	Ch	100	
Butchart G.		Mildura		(Fowler) No	C/s	90	
"	G. Jnr.	"	With G.B.	7 Ben	Ch	70	

Name	Dates	Place	Variation	Pottery	Type	Value '96	Value '04Kn
Bollington	1894-1908	Collingwood	Hop Beer 26ozs.	2 Ben	Int Bl	400	6
Bollington (Blyth G.)		Geelong	Long Mono (R) ck/st	7 Ben	Ch	300	1
"	"	"	"	7 Ben	Int Ch	250	6
"	"	"	"	7 Ben	Ltg Ch	275	3
"	"	Short Mono		(Price) No	Ltg Ch	350	9
" "	"	"	"	20 Tay	Ltg Ch	250	8
Botanic The Dandenong	1923	Melbourne		5 Ben	D	120	
Bruce & Sons	1891-1900	Bendigo	impressed a/o/w	Ben	Ch	200	2
Bruce W. & Sons	1909-1912	Bendigo	NoG.B.	2 Ben	Ch	100	
" "	" "	"	G.B.	2 Ben	Ch	100	
Burns P.	1911	Maffra		7 Ben	D	400	7
Butler V.E.	1912	Maffra		7 Ben	D	125	12
Chapman Bros p/l	1927-1930	Nth. Fitzroy	Blue/t	5 Ben C/s	D	450	
Cohn Bros.	1917-1925	Bendigo	Straight GB	5 Ben	C/s	60	
" "	" "	"	4 Lines on back	5 Ben	C/s	60	
" "	" "	"	3 " " "	5 Ben	C/s	60	
Colac Aerated Waters	1917	Colac	Blue/t (Ben)	7 No	D	225	6
" " "	1921	"	Lge/t	7 Ben	Ch	40	
Cole Chas. & Co.		Geelong	*	7 Ben	Ch	150	
" " "		"	*	7 Ben	Ch Bl	150	
" " "		"		7 Ben	Ch	150	
" " "		"	Trade Mark (Sm)	22 Ken	Ch	170	
" " "		"	Trade Mark c (imp) Poss (Ken)	22 No	Ch	170	
" " "		"	poss int. th. (new top)	?	Ch	?	?
Crystal Spa Co. Ltd.	1908	Hamilton	Tri	7 Ben	Ch	120	

Darby A.	1897-1900	Warrnambool		2 Ben	Int Bl	200	6
Darby Bros.		Shepparton	a/o/w	5 Ben	C/s D	80	(200 3
" "			Blue/t	5 Ben	C/s	300	3
" "			t/t (Ben)	7 No	C/s	70	
" "			t/t	9 Fow	C/s	120	
" "			a/o/w	9 Fow	C/s	70	
" " Pty. Ltd.		"	a/o/w	9 Fow	C/s	80	
" " " "		"	a/o/w	15 Fow	C/s	80	
" " " "		"	a/o/w	13 Gov	C/s	70	
" " " "		"	(Diff) a/o/w	13 Gov	C/s	70	
Deans & Co.		Ararat	(8 imp.) Poss (Tay)	No	Ch	40	
" "		"	Blob	3 Ben	Ch	200	4
" "		"		7 Ben	Ch	40	
" "		"	(21 imp.) (Ben)	7 No	Ch	40	
" "		"	Dk/t Poss (Tay)	No	Ch	40	
" "		"	Smaller Poss (Tay)	No	Ch	40	
Davis & Grant	1903-1915	Gisborne		7 Ben	Ch	400	3
Dixon & Co		Prahran & Melbourne		7 Ben	Ch	150	
Dixon's J.	1904-1906	Prahran		7 Ben	Ch	200	
Dixon P. G. & Co.		Melbourne	Sm. Lion Poss (CAP)	No	Ch	150	
""	"		Lge Lion	7 Ben	Ch	150	
""	"		Sm Oval	2 Ben	Ch	150	
""	"		Lge Oval	7 Ben	Ch	150	
""	"		Sm Oval	Hoff	Ch	150	
Dolphin O.		Nagambie	Tonic Ale imp. Int.	2 Ben	Ch Bl	700	2
Dunham & Hill	1930	Echuca	'Royal'	21 Gov	C/s	750	15
Durham George	1909-1920	Terang & Nhill		7 Ben	Ch	300	4

Name	Dates	Place	Variation	Pottery	Type	Value'96	Value '04Kn
Eberhard & Co.		Clunes		(Ben) 7 No	Ch	30	
" "		"	Brewed	7 Ben	Ch	50	
Edhouse H.		Stawell		7 Ben	Ch	80	
Egan D.	1905-1919	Bendigo	Union Cordial Works	7 Ben	D	150	
Egypta	1920-1924	Melbourne	Egypta slanted	(Ben) 7 No	Ch	175	
" "		"	Products P/I	(Ben) 7 No	Ch	175	
" "	"		slanted circ stamp a/o/w	9 Fowl	Ch	300	
Elliott G. H. P/I		Melbourne	'E' brewed	(Ben) 7 No	Ch	100	
" "		"	filled 'E' "* b/t	7 Ben	Ch	200	
" "		"	" "*	7 Ben	Ch	80	
" "		"	" "* (C.A.P.)	7 No	Ch	80	
" "		"	thin 'E' "	14 Tay	Ch	100	
" "		"	imp 'E'"(Ben)	7 No	Ch	80	
" "		"	Circ label"	9 Fow	Ch	500	2
" "		" * *	Elliotts (Ben)	7 No	Ch	80	
" "		" * *	(Ben)	7 No	Ch	80	
" "		Carlton		a/t Ben	Ch Bl	250	
" "	"			a/t Ben	Ch	250	
" "	"			a/l/t 2 Ben	Ch	200	
" "	"	O.E est.1845	lt/br (Ben)	2 No	Ch	500	2
" "		"	O.E. a/t (Bou)	16 N.D.	Ch ring	300	1
" "		"	open 'E' brewed at base (Ben)	7 No	Ch	100	
" "		" " "	sm badge	(Hoff) No	Ch	100	

" "		" " "	thin badge	(Hoff) No	Ch	100	
" "	"	" " "	" "	Hoff	Ch Bl	120	
Franklin & Co.	1904-1909	Balaclava		7 Ben	Ch	75	5
Frankston Springs A.W.Co.	1895-1910	Melbourne 'Open	Stamp' fish	2 Ben	Ch	300	
" " "	1893-1910	" "	"	2 Ben	Ch	350	
" " "	1893-1910	Collingwood	(Ben) " t/t	7 No	Ch	125	
" " & Co.		Melbourne	" b/t	7 Ben	Ch	300	
" " "		"	Registered	" t/t 2 Ben	Ch	200	
" " "		"	FSCo lge inits. b/t	7 Ben	Ch	250	
" " "		" " "	sml inits. (Ben) b/t	7 No	Ch	200	
" " "		" " "	(Ben) t/t	7 No	Ch	200	
" " "		"	Hop Beer 26ozs. fish	2 Ben	Ch	1000	
Fraser Jason	1902-1915	Stawell		Hoff	Ch	250	12
Gamble H. J.	1920-1921	Melbourne	(Ben) dk/br	7 No	Ch	400	3
G.A.W		Geelong	with G.B.	(Hoff) No	Ch Bl	250	
"		"		(Hoff) No	Ch Bl	250	
Gibson J.	1886-1909	Yarrawonga		7 Ben	D	75	8
Goodfellows		Ballarat	(Ben)	7 No	Ch	250	
Goodfellow & Co. P/L		"	"	'Royal' red	21 Gov	C/s	500
Goodfellow & Co.		"	"	brown	19 Gov	C/s	500
Goulding C. R.	1901-1903	Prahran	C.R.G.	7 Ben	Ch	200	7
" "		"		Hoff	Ch	450	4
Gow J.		Footscray		Tay	Ch	275	10
Grant Davis and	1903-1916	Gisborne		7 Ben	Ch	400	
Gray's Castlemaine			int.	2 Ben	Ch Bl	80	
""				2 Ben	Ch	75	
Gray A.		"		7 Ben	Ch	150	

Name	Place	Dates	Variation	Pottery	Type	Value '96	Value '04Kn
Harrison	Nth Fitzroy		int.	7 Ben	Ch Bl	600	1
"	"		(poss)	Hoff	Ch	120	
"	"		Thick Btl. 26 ozs	7 Ben	Ch	80	
"	"		Diff Symbol 'a'	2 Ben	Ch	35	
"	"		" " 'b'	2 Ben	Ch	35	
"	"		" " 'c'	CAP	Ch	100	5
"	"		(Ben) " " 'd' dk/br	7 No	Ch	100	
"	"		sharp stamp 26 ozs " " 'e'	6 Ben	Ch	150	
"	"		26 ozs " " 'f' (Ben)	2 No	Ch	120	
"	"		" " 'g'	7 Ben	Ch	45	
"	"		" " 'h'(Ben)	2 No	Ch	45	
"	"		Burned Label	7 Ben	Ch	100	
Harrison Pty. Ltd.	(Ben)	1927	Real (harr on back) dk/t	2 No	Ch	120	
" "	"	"	" " lt/t	2 Ben	Ch	90	
" "	"	"	" " (harr on back) lt/t	5 Ben	C/s	500	2
Harrison's Hoppetta	"		(Ben) 26ozs a/o/w	2 No	Ch	120	
" "	"		Diff 26ozs a/o/w	2 Ben	Ch	120	
" "	"		Smaller (Ben) 26ozs a/o/w	2 No	Ch	150	
Hatchett Jos.	Murtoa	1923		5 Ben	Ch	150	
Herron H. W.	Sale	1913-1920		7 Ben	Ch	400	8
Heywood F. C.	Stawell	1923-1930	a/o/w	9 Fow	C/s	90	
Hunter Bros.	Bendigo			7 Ben	Ch	200	4
Hunter Stewards &	"	1914-1917		7 Ben	Ch	300	
Hunter T. O.	"		Circ label	13 Gov	C/s	70	
" "	"		" Diff	17 Gov	C/s	55	
" "	"		lge botl (Ben)	7 No	Ch	120	

" "	"			5 Ben	Ch	180	
" "	"		epsom	5 Ben	C/s	80	
" "	"			7 Ben	C/s	80	
" "	"		26ozs (Ben)	7 No	Ch ring	200	
Hunter Jos.	Horsham		Tri	7 Ben	Ch	400	
" "	"		(Ben)	7 No	Ch	150	
" "	"			5 Ben	Ch	100	
Ice Volcanic	Prahran		(Dixon)	2 Ben	Ch	600	2
Jackson A. E.	Corowa	1925		9 Fow	C/s	80	
Jackson C. S.	"	1914		Pin	Ch	150	
Jackson Bros.	"	1918		(Ben) 3 No	D ltg	150	
""	"	1920		7 Ben	Ch	70	
Jacobson's	Footscray			7 Ben	Ch	200	
Jacobsen's	"		(rare) (yet to acquire)	7 Ben	Ch	?	
Johnson F.	Riddell	1911		7 Ben	Ch	500	3
Jones & McEwan	Castlemaine	1924-1932	(Ben)	5 No	C/s D	400	10
Kinpton's	Abbotsford	1895-1903	26 ozs a/o/w	2 Ben	Ch	700	5
Larcombe R.	Echuca	1926-1929	dk/t	15 Fow	C/s	90	
" "	"	"	" "	9 Fow	crC/s	90	
Leak Bros.	Benalla		G. B. (Ben)	7 No	Ch	200	
" "	"		(Ben)	7 No	Ch	200	
Leak & Sons W.	"		Bird	7 Ben	Ch	80	
" "	"		(Ben) " Aerated dk/t	7 No	Ch	80	
" "	"		(Ben) " G. B. lt/t	7 No	Ch	80	
" "	"		(nbw) 'Open'	2 Ben	Ch	400	
Lindner Dolph	Dimboola	1911-1924	t	7 Ben	D	50	
" "	"	" "	dk/ br	5 No	D	50	
" "	"	" "	lt/t	5 Pin	D	50	
Manallack St.	Arnaud	1909-1924	(Ben) G. B. bo) rev	7 No	Ch	100	
" "	"	" "		7 Ben	Ch	50	
" "	"	" "	rev	7 Ben	Ch	75	
" "	"	" "		7 Ben	Ch	90	

Name	Place	Dates	Variation	Pottery	Type	Value '96	Value '04Kn
Manallack & Co.	"	1925-1933	G. B. rev gr/t ?	No	C/s	400	
Manallac & Co.	"	" "	rev gr/t ?	No	C/s	400	
Manger & O'Niel	Echuca		blk label a/o/w	9 Fow	C/s D	55	
" "	"		brn label a/o/w	9 Fow	C/s D	55	
" "	"		(sm/bo) (Hoff) bl/t	No	Ch	100	
" "	"		bl/t	5 Ben	Ch	150	
" "	"		lge bottle bl/t	7 Ben	Ch	175	
Mason S.		Wodonga	G. B.	4 Ben	Ch	90	
" "	"		G. B.	Pin	D	85	
" "	"			Pin	D	85	
" "	"			7 Ben	D	85	
" "	"	1880-1923	a/o/w	2 Ben	D	50	
Mc Donald & Co.	Melbourne		G. B. lge stamp	7 Ben	Ch	150	
" "	"	"	sm stamp	2 Ben	Ch	250	
Mc Gavin J.	Corowa	1912	lt/ bl lip	7 Ben	D	450	
" "	"	" "	dk/ bl lip	Pin	D	400	
Mc Gaw L.	Maffra	1922	tan	5 Ben	D	50	
" "	" "	1923	bl neck	6 Ben	C/s	180	
" "	"	" "	bl shoul	5 Ben	C/s	180	
Mc Gee	Rochester			7 Ben	Ch	100	
Mc Martins	Nhill	1911		Pin	Ch	85	5
Medwin H. A.	Tongala	1930	(Ben)	4 No	Ch	70	
Merbein Cordial Works Pty.	Ouyen	1921-1930	red	18 Gov	C/s	120	
" "	" "	" "	l imp on neck t	19 Fow	C/s	120	
" "	" "	" "	(Fow) t	19 No	C/s	90	
" "	" "	1923	t	5 Ben	Ch	160	
" "	" "	"	br	Pin	Ch	160	
Mitting H.	Irymple		dk/ t	Pin	Ch	400	4
Murray & Meade	Albury		lge bottle	Pin	D	50	
" "	"		a/o/w	2 Ben	D	90	

" "	"			Pin	D	50	
" "	"		-- on stamp	Pin	D	45	
Morrow G. A.	Wangaratta	1918 - 1947	bl/ neck	5 Ben	Ch	400	
" "	" "	"	(Ben) dk/ tan	7 No	Ch	200	
Neilson & Co. Nth.	Fitzroy	1921-1926	bl/l ?	No	D	400	
Nugent James	Wahgunya	1907-1916		Pin	Ch	175	8
Orb (George Bollington)	Richmond			7 Ben	Ch	400	3
" "	"	"	int.	7 Ben	Ch	500	1
" "	"	"		7 Ben	Ch Bl	500	2
Oswald D.	Eaglehawk	1922-1925	Epsom	4 Ben	Ch	170	
Oswald & Metcalf	Eaglehawk	1902-1909		7 Ben	Ch	160	
Oswald J. H.	Corowa	1908 - ?	Int.	2 Ben	Ch	65	
" "	"		Blue label	23 Pri	D ltg	200	
" "	"		Circ label	9 Fow	Ch	65	
" "	"		" "	9 Fow	C/s	70	
" "	"		Oval label	5 Ben	C/s	70	
" "	"		" "	7 Ben	Ch	65	
O. T. Ltd.	Melb. & Sydney		?	No	C/s	300	4
" "	" " London			7 Ben	Ch	300	
Ouyen Cordials Pty. Ltd.	Ouyen		(Fow) t/t	15 No	C/s	350	
" "	" " " & Mildura		a/o/w	15 Fow	C/s	350	
Palling J.	Heathcote	1905-1914	G. B.	7 Ben	Ch	200	5
Phibb Bros.	Corowa		G. B.	7 Ben	D	50	
" "	"			7 Ben	D	85	
" "	"		straight writing	7 Ben	D	50	
" "	"		lge bottle " "	7 Ben	D	55	
Phibbs L. C.	"		a/o/w	7 Ben	D	120	
" "	"	(Ben)	t	7 No	D	80	
Phibbs P. J.	"		dk/bl/lip	7 Ben	D	150	

Name	Place	Dates	Variation	Pottery	Type	Value '96	Value '04 Kn
" "	"		G. B. lt/ bl/lip	7 Ben	D	150	
" "	"		G. B. dk/ bl/lip	7 No	D	150	
Priddle Bros.	Queenscliff	1914-1918		7 Ben	Ch	400	
Pritchard G.	Bendigo	1895-1922		7 Ben	Ch	200	
Purcell O'Sullivan	Melbourne	1891-1914	G. B.	7 Ben	Ch	Bl	300
" "	"	"	"	7 Ben	Ch Bl	300	
" "	"	"	"	7 Ben	Ch	100	
Reed Bros.	Bendigo			13 Gov	C/s	35	
" "	"		(Gov)	13 No	C/s	35	
" "	"		'a'	13 Gov	C/s	35	
" "	"		'b'	13 Gov	C/s	35	
" "	"		'c'	13 Gov	C/s	40	
" "			lge B.R. & G. B. 'eyebrow'	4 Ben	C/s	400	
" "	"	"	"	4 Ben	C/s	250	
Reeves R. V.	Hamilton	1921-1929	(Ben) no reverse	7 No	Ch	65	
" "	"	" "		7 Ben	Ch	65	
" "	"	" "	old style writing	7 Ben	Ch	75	
" "	Warrnambool		bl/t	9 Fow	Ch	270	2
Rochester Aerated	Waters	1914-1924	(Ben) bl/lip	7 No	Ch	350	
Ride E.	Benalla		small sheep	Pin	Ch	60	
" "	"	- 1937	(Ben)	7 No	Ch	65	
" "	"			Pin	Ch	70	
" "	"			7 Ben	Ch	70	
" "	"		circ. stamp	10 Syd	Ch Bl	100	
" "	"	"	"	9 Fow	C/s	100	
Ride J.	Benalla		int.	7 Ben	Ch	250	3
" "	"		a/o/w	2 Ben	D	300	7
" "	"			7 Ben	Ch	250	3
" "	"	1908-1915		(7 Ben	Ch	70	
" "	"			7 No	Ch	70	4
Ride William	"	1860 - (1937)	(Ben) a/o/w	7 No	D	60	
" "	"		a/o/w	7 Ben	D	70	

" "	"		(Ben)	7 No	Ch	80	
" "	"		(Ben) brewed	7 No	Ch	80	
Rogers Bros.	Malmsbury st.	1923	oval stamp bl/n	5 Ben	C/s	600	8
" "	" "	1918-1923	" " (Ben) bl/t	5 No	Ch	160	
" "	Church st.	" "	circ stamp bl/t	7 Ben	Ch	100	
" "	Burwood Rd.	" "	" " bl/t	7 Ben	Ch	100	
Rosel A.	Echuca	1914-1920	dk/t	Pin	Ch	200	
" "	"	" "	(Pin) br/neck	No	Ch	175	
" "	"	" "	(Pin) brown	No	Ch	210	
Rowlands E.	Ball, Syd, Mel		'a' (Ben)	7 No	Ch	35	
" "	"		'b' (Tay?)	No	Ch	35	
" "	"		(diff rev) 'c' (Ben)	7 No	Ch	35	
" "	"		'd'	Tay	Ch	40	
" "	"		'e' lge stamp	7 Ben	Ch	50	
" "	"		diff 'f' lge stamp	7 Ben	Ch	50	
" "	"		imp 'r' C.a.p.)	No	Ch	70	(175)
" "	"		5 lines rowlands up rev	Fow	Ch	60	
" "	Syd, Melb, Kat, Ball.		4 lines down rev	Fow	Ch	60	
" "	Ball, Melb. Syd.		F & M ?	No	Ch	300	
" "	"		F & M a/t ?	No	D	175	
" "	"		(Ben) diff G. B. l/t	2 No	Ch	70	
" "	"			2 Ben	Ch	20	
" "	"		diff stamp	2 Ben	Ch	35	
Rowlands E.			imp. F & M ?	No	D	250	
Rowland & Lewis		1854-1876	imp. a/t ?	No	D	200	10
Russell & Powell Pt.	Fairy	1881-1904	int.	2 Ben	Ch	300	8
" "	"		crazed int. 26ozs.	2 Ben	Ch	100	5

Name	Place	Dates	Variation	Pottery	Type	Value '96	Value '04 Kn
Rowley J. S.	Warrnambool	1908-1910	G. B.	7 Ben	Ch	70	
""	"	"	"	7 Ben	Ch	65	
Savage & Co.	Wahgunyah	1897	(Ben) hop ale int.	2 No	Ch Bl	200	
Schweppes	Abbotsford		4 lines the king dk/t ?	No	D	70	
"	"		3 " sm rare " " dk/t ?	No	D	70	300 3
"	"		" " " "lt/t ?	No	D	70	
"	"		" "H.M. " " lt/t ?	No	D	70	
Schweppes	Abbotsford (faint)		3 lines by appt. dk/t ?	no	D	350	2
Sharpe Bros	Australia		int. a/o/w	Fow	D	200	
Skeyhill J. P.	Hamilton		b/t	7 Ben	Ch	130	
" "	"		"	Pin	D	80	
Sloan S.	Hamilton		lt/t	7 Ben	Ch	45	
" "	"		(Ben) "	7 No	Ch	45	
" "	"		dk/t	7 Ben	Ch	45	
" "	"		(Ben) "	7 No	Ch	45	
Stacy T. G.	Melbourne		non-alcoholic bl/lip	7 Ben	Ch	300	3
" "	"		olde english bl/lip	7 Ben	Ch	350	
Stevens E. C.	Warracknabeal	1905-1915	(Ben) a/o/w	7 No	D	70	
" "	" "	"		7 Ben	D	70	
Thornley & Howlett	Sale	1920	(Ben)	7 No	Ch	400	
Thornley W. J.	"		(Ben)	7 No	Ch	35	
" "	"			21 Gov	C/s	500	
Thornley W. T.	"	1911-1915		Pin	Ch	110	
" "	"	" "	(Pin)	No	Ch	120	
Trait J. J.	Geelong	1891-1919	ltg	Cap	Ch	250	
" "	"	" "	(Ben)	7 No	Ch	150	
" "	"	" "	lt clean stamp	Pin	Ch	150	
Walker J. A.	Dalyston & Wonthaggi	1920	(Ben)	7 No	D	200	6
Wangaratta Brewery	Wangaratta		a/o/w	9 Fow	C/s	90	

" "	"			6 Gov	C/s	80	
Ward W. R.	Yarrawonga	1911-1915	(Ben)	7 No	D	75	
" "	"	1915-1921	(Diff) (Ben)	7 No	D	75	
Warrnambool Cordials Pty. Ltd.	Warrnambool		(Ben) dk/t	7 No	Ch	250	
Waterfield A. T.	Horsham		(andrew street)	7 Ben	Ch Bl	50	
" "	"		(" ")	7 Ben	Ch	40	
Watson D. S.	Albury		a/o/w	7 Ben	D	100	
Watson E. C.	Rutherglen		a/o/w	2 Ben	D	70	10
Watson & Young	Albury	1893-1908	(Bou)	12 No	Ch Bl	250	
" "	"	" "	int.	2 Ben	Ch	200	
Wilding Henry	Queenscliff		'open stamp'	2 Ben	Ch	600	6
Wilcox Bros.	Dandenong, Lilydale & Frankston	1901-1915	t/t	7 Ben	Ch	300	3
" "	"	" "	(Upper mark missing)	7 Ben	Ch	400	2
" "	"	" "	bl/t	7 Ben	Ch	300	
Wilmot G.	Colac		bl/l	7 Ben	D	200	
" "	"		(Hoff) sp bl/ sh	No	D	275	5
" "	"		bl/sh	Hoff	D	300	2
Wilmot George	"		int.	2 Ben	Ch	220	4
Wilson's	Albury		(Ben) (rev U. F. Wilson)	2 No	Ch	50	
Whittaker W. & Sons	Dunolly		smaller stamp	7 Ben	Ch	90	
" "	" "	1922-1923		7 Ben	Ch	80	
Young D. C.	Corowa	1908		7 Ben	Ch	200	8
Young R. H.	Rutherglen	1914-1918	'Y' imp. at sh	9 Fow	C/s	275	
Yoxall Bros.	Melbourne		(Brewed G. B.) (Ben)	7 No	Ch	200	5
Yoxall J. P.	Wangaratta	1888-1925	int. small arm	2 Ben	Ch	250	
" "	"	" "		7 Ben	Ch	130	10
" "	"	" "	G. B.	7 Ben	Ch	200	8

In total there are 265 definite Bendigo Pottery pieces including 20 from the Pinnacle agency. There are 390 different bottles in the Victorian Collection and a total of 470 Ginger Beer bottles in all. Of the 72 incidental and unnamed ones, there are eight early stamped Bendigo bottles. This listing does not include the two Bendigo Whiskey bottles or my other pottery pieces. What has not been included in this summary, are the dozen or so 'other' Victorian bottles in my collection. These are the plain or unmarked ones. Perhaps in their day they had paper labels which have deteriorated or been washed off. There are two all/white dumps of the early Bendigo Pottery stamp - No.1 stamp - and the others have the No. two or seven stamps. Notable of these is the 26 ozs. All/white internal thread (with ceramic stopper), bottle in perfect mint condition, this has been conservatively valued at $1000 plus. This has the No.2 stamp. In my opinion it is a more desirable piece than the Aitken of Victoria Parade Brewery bottle, which has a sale valuation of $3000, although I have mentioned its value as of 1996 at $2000.

Impressed Ginger Beer Bottles

Name	Place	Dates	Variation	Pottery	Type	Value	'96 Value	'04 Kn
Dahlkes	Melbourne	1872-1888	a/grey	Dal	D	60		
Footscray	Footscray	1871-1872	a/t	Foo	D	500 1		
G.H.M	Melbourne	1857-1861	a/br (Geo. Hughs?)	No	D	80		
Jensen & Houston	Ballarat	a/br	Bal	D	100			
Mason S.	Wodonga	1880	a/br	Wod	D	120		
"	"	"	a/ dk/cr	Wod	D	50		
"	"	"	a/br	Wod	D	100		
Paulson & Stanton	?	1850's late.	a/br	?	D	100-300		

Prev^ost E. J.	Melbourne	1854-1883	a/br	Mel	D	55
Prev^ot & Co. E. J.	"	" "	a/br	Mel	D	100
Prev^ot E J.	"	" "	a/br	Mel	D	100
Rowlands & Lewis	Ballarat	1854-1876. 1917	a/br	Bal	D	200
Williams J.	?	1855-1867	a/br	?	D	300(3)
Wolton & Wigg	Rushworth	1853-1894	a/br	?	D	400(6)

Note :- There are known to be at least seven different types of Prev^ost G.B.'s.
Seven different S. Mason's.
Three different W. Frane of Pleasant Creek.
Various Rowlands, Rowland & Lewis, Lewis & Rowland Etcetera.

N.B. Many known and seen G. B.'s, are not listed as I do not own them such as W. Frane of the Pleasant Creek area; near Stawell.

Additions to Collection since 1996 audit

G. Blyth		Geelong	Vic.	Thin mono	7 Ben	Ch ltg.	200
Mc Gee J.		Rochester	Vic.		7 Ben	Ch	100
O'Sullivan & Purcell		Melbourne		no G.B.	7 Ben	Ch	100
Alpha	1910-1922	Mildura	Vic.	Large G.B.	No	Ch	40
G. Butchart Jnr.		Mildura		with G.B.	7 Ben	Ch	60

Demi-Johns

Name	Place	Pottery	Value '96 Value '04 Kn
2 Pint (one quart)			
From William Muir	North Melbourne	poss Ben	250
S.P. Co-operative Coy.	Wine & Spirit Merchants View Street	Sandhurst	150
J. Trait & Son	Wine & Spirit Merchants Creswick	transfer Ben	200
E. Manning Spirit Merchants	Clifton Hill	poss Ben	200
W. E. Mann Spirit Merchant	Camberwell	poss Ben	250
D. Whyte & Co. Spirit Merchants Pall Mall	Bendigo	Ben	150
Lewis & Northway Merchants	Koroit	poss Hoff	200
J. E. Meyers	Clunes	a/t poss Hoff	300 (1)
Plain Demi-John		Hoff	45
2 quart (half Gallon)			
H. T. Edwards Pty. Ltd. Merchants	St. Arnaud	transfer Ben	120
S. Stooke Casterton		transfer Ben	130
Ginger Ale Extract R. O' Donnell & Co.	Melbourne	poss Ben	70
L. Lloyd & Co. Botanical Brewer South	Melbourne	poss Ben	150
J. H. Wilkinson Merchant	Sturt Street Ballarat	Ben	150
John Barrow Storekeeper	Trentham	poss Ben	200(1)
Terang & District Co-operative Society	Terang	poss Ben	100

Andrew Taylor	Warracknabeal	poss Ben	120
A. Stewart & Co. Merchants	Mortlake	poss Ben	130
1/- D. Whyte & Co. Spirit Merchants	Bendigo	transfer Ben	90
Plain		transfer Ben	45
Owen's Lamb Drench Poison		poss Ben	45
The fish & Ring Brand is the best		a/o/w transfer Bou	150
Loy Bros. (NSW) Pty. Ltd.	Sydney	(wire handle) a/o/w bl transfer No	175
Plain		(open neck) transfer Ben	45

1 Gallon

Sharpe Bros.	Australia & New Zealand	transfer Fow	100
Cuming Smith & Co.	Melbourne	(sickle brand) Ben	120
Wimble Ltd.	Melbourne	poss Ben	100
Dixon & Co.	Brim	Ben	150-200

Miscellaneous

Foot Warmer	(3 Pint)	Fow	50
Crock	with lid (1 Gallon)	Cor	55
Crock G. D. Guthrie & Co.	(back and front) 1898-1912 (3 Pint)	Ben	300 (Swapped)
Crock	(mis-matched lid pot type)	(1 Gallon) transfer Ben	55

Potteries

	No.		
Ben	1 1882-1898	=	Old Bendigo Pottery Stamp
Ben	2-7	=	Bendigo pottery Epsom Bendigo.
Pin	8	=	Pinnacle Brand (Agency of Bendigo Pottery)
Fow	9 + 15	=	E. Fowler Pottery Sydney
Mau	10	=	Mauri Brothers & Thompson Sydney
Hoff	11	=	Hoffmann Pottery Brunswick
Bou	12 + 16	=	Bourne Potteries Dendy England
Gov	13,17,18,19,21	=	Govancroft Pottery Glasgow Scotland
Tay	14 + 20	=	P. W. Taylor & Co. Limited Hop Exchange London
Ken	22	=	Kennedy Glascow
Pri	23	=	Price Bristol
C.A.P.	24	=	Possibly Cornwall's Australian Pottery, Brunswick.

Also unlisted here, there are numerous impressed bottles from overseas and interstate which I have chronicled in another paper. These are mostly 'Dumps' but there are a smattering of 10 ozs bottles and some 26 oz types of the 'rare' variety.

Notably the T. Aitken Victoria Parade Brewery salt glazed all tan ring-top Champagne bottle.

This one is in near to Mint and its value as of 1996 was $ 2000 plus. I saw a couple sold at $3000 then. There are less than five mint about. These date in the late 1800's.

Other abbreviations

No	=	No Pottery Stamp visible () = possibly whatever pottery within
t.	=	Tan
bl	=	Blue
Bl	=	Blob Top
a/o/w	=	All Off White
t/t	=	Tan Top (or not mentioned - common)
g/t	=	Green Top
bl/lip	=	Blue Lip
A/w	=	All White
circ	=	Circular
D	=	Dump shape and size
Ch	=	Champagne shape and size
bl/sh	=	Blue Shoulder
sp	=	Sprayed
c r	=	Crazed or Cracked
ltg	=	Lightning Stopper
sm	=	Small
sh	=	Shoulder
mtn	=	Mountain
mono	=	Monogram
sh.	=	Shield
L.	=	Long
ord	=	Ordinary
G.B.	=	Ginger Beer
und	=	Underlined
T/M	=	Trade Mark
d	=	Doubled
nbw	=	Neck Below Wing
?	=	Unsure of Pottery, mintage or date
sm/bo	=	Small Bottle
Kat	=	Katoomba.
ring	=	Ring Seal type closure
C/s	=	Crown Seal

Mint Known Ginger Beers I do not own

Name	Place	Dates	Variations	Pottery	Type	Value '96 Value '04 Kn
Alpha	Merbein	?	(Diff) Wider G.B.	t/t ?	Ch	
Bennett G. H.	Richmond	?	(Diff) Open Stamp t/t	Ben	Ch	1
" "	"		(Bou) " "	t/t No	Ch ring	1
Billson G. H.	St. Kilda	?		t/t Bou	Ch	
Bollington G.	Geelong	?	aqu'd now) Thin Momo	t/t Ben	ltg Ch	5
Bray Les	St Arnaud		Blob Top	t/t ?	Ch	1
Brook A.	Horsham	1911-1912		tri 7 Ben	Ch	1
Brown R. J.	Rochester	Dec. 1906	(5 gross made)	t/t Ben	Ch	0
Bryant & Shiel	Wangaratta		(a butcher's)	t/t **Ben**	Ch	1
Bushby James	Daylesford	1884-1894	also without (Ben)	t/t Ben	Ch	(3) 1
Butchart G.	Mildura	?	t/t Fow		Ch	
" "	"			b/t ?	Ch	4
" "	"			b/t ?	C/s	2
" "	"		(T/M variation)	b/t ?	C/s	?
Butchart Jnr.	"		t/t Ben	Ch		
" "	"		t/t Pin	Ch		
Chapman Bros.	Fitzroy	Khaki (3) 1	lt/b - grey/t	(Ben) Ben	C/s D (also pale blue)	1
Cohn Bros.	Bendigo		(Also noT/M) Large mono	t/t Ben	C/s	1
" "	"	1909	" "	t/t Ben	Ch	8
Cole Chas.	Geelong	?		t/t Ben int.	Ch	1
Curtis S. H.	Maryborough	1923-1930		t/t Ben	Ch	3
" "	"	" "	26 ozs.	t/t Ben	Ch	8
Daniel's	Yan Yean			t/t Ben	Ch	0
Darby Bros	Shepparton	?		b/lip Fow	C/s	4
Dixon & co. P. G.	Melbourne			t/t Ben Bl	Ch	
" " "	"			t/t Hoff Bl	Ch	

Dolphin O.	Nagambi		'ginger beer'	t/t 2 Ben int.	Ch (3)	
Dyason Collis Pty. Ltd.	Mildura	1925-1930		t/t No	Ch	3
Edhouse H.	Stawell			t/t Ben	Ch	
Elliot's G. H.	Melbourne		(broken piece)	G/t ?	Ch	0
G. B.	Mildura			t/t Ben	Ch	2
Goodfellow	Richmond		Vic.	t/t Ben	Ch	0
Glover C. J.	Bendigo		'Open' stamp	t/t Ben	C/s	8
Goulding C. R.	Prahran	1912-1913	as page 3 but with 'Ernest Spry	't/t Ben	Ch	1
Green T. J.	Morang			t/t Ben	Ch	(4) 3
Haustorfer H. E. H.	Horsham	1913		t/t Ben	C/s	3
Higgins & Parer	Melbourne		(piece only) Swanston st. (Ben)	t/t ?	Ch	(1)
Heywood F. C.	Stawell	1927		t/t Ben	C/s	6
Hoskin T. G.	Violet Town	1907		t/t Ben	Ch	(5) 1
" "	" "	"		b/t Ben	Ch	1
" "	" "	"		b/t Ben	D	1
Hosies Hotel	Melbourne		J.B. Mc Arthur	t/t Ben	Ch	(2) 2
Hunter Jos.	Bendigo		'tonic beer'	26 ozs b/t Ben	Ch	0
Manger & O'Neill	Echuca			t/t Ben	C/s	2
"	"			b/t Ben	C/s	(3)
Mc Donald & Co	Melbourne		'sm stamp-diff'	t/t Ben	Ch	
" "	"		no G.B.	a/t Ben	Ch	2
Merbein Cordial Works	Merbein			t/t ?	Ch Bl	1
M.G. B. W.	Yarraville	Feb. 1907 (1 gross)		t/t Ben	Ch	0
Moonee Valley Co.	Nth. Fitzroy			t/t ?	Ch	(1) 1
Morrow G. A.	Wangaratta			g/t ?	Ch	0
Neville G.	Prahran		210 high street	t/t ?	Ch	(l) 2
O'Sullivan Purcell & Co.	Melb.		with G.B.	t/t ?	Ch	3

Mint Known Ginger Beers I do not own

Name	Place	Date	Variations	Pottery	Type	Value '96 Value '04 Kn
O. T. Limited			written parallel	t/t ?	Ch	(3)
Ouyen Cordials Pty. Ltd.	Ouyen		single line in centre 'celebrated'	a/o/w ?	C/s	(3) 1
Palling J.	Heathcote		No G.B.	t/t Ben	Ch	
Phillips A.	Bendigo	1891-1907		t/t Ben	Ch	3
Plummer & Murphy	South Melbourne	?		t/t ?	Ch	0
Reeves R. V.	Warrnambool			bl/t Fow	C/s	1
Ride J.	Benalla		short G.B. no dot	t/t Ben	Ch	?
"	"		blue print label	gr/t Ben	Ch	1
Rowlands E.	Ball, Melb,Syd.			t/t Ben	Ch int ?	1
" "	"		(Ye Olde English) Missing	t/t ?	Ch	1
Schweppes	Abbotsford		(diff) 'sm crown'	t/l No	D	3
Thornley W. J.	Horsham		sm bottle	t/t Ben	Ch Bl	3
Walker J. A.	Wonthaggi	1911		t/t ?	Ch	1
Wilcox Bros.	Dand, Fran, Lily.		(aqu'd now)	bl/t Ben	Ch	6
" "	" " "			g/t ?	Ch	0
Wilding J. W.	Queenscliff		open stamp	t/t Pin	Ch	4
Yoxall Bros.	Wang, Ruth, Melb.			t/t Ben	Ch	3

Known but damaged ()

Impressed Ginger Beers

Beard F. G.	Bendigo	1852-1854	at base	a/t	D	0		
Frayne W.	Pleasant Creek	(Spell Var)	near base	a/t	D	(3) 1		
Urquhart F. G.	Richmond	1868-1872	lge stamp	o/w Ben	D	1		
Impressed Ale								
Aitken T.	Melb		27 ozs.	a/lt/t ?	Ch	2000	3000	5

This last column with the title Kn = Known, lists the only known bottles to date - 1996 - that we the dedicated collectors know to exist; that are known to us as MINT collectables.

There are other bottles that exist of the categories, few admittedly, but these are not MINT bottles. Some are only pieces that have been found and many are damaged one way or another, but they are not good examples of the early pottery pieces. I have put these down only as a guide. It is quite possible that other mint copies of the listed bottles do exist in some unknown collections. I and other knowledgeable bottle enthusiasts have scoured the state and seen nearly every collection of old bottles, including that small collection of the origin of the Ginger Beers (Bendigo Pottery) and to the best of our abilities have come to the finding; that this listing is by far the most complete of its type.

Therefore, please be very careful NOT to let this comprehensive listing go astray. Bottle Dealers are in the buying and selling business to MAKE money out of you and me, so it is desirable not to let this information become commercially available. I trust that you will honour this commitment and maybe in the future I will be able to give you an accurate and complete account of all bottles put out by your Pottery.

Respectfully, Howard Reede-Pelling.

Histories/Potteries/Manufacturers

Fowler's Pottery

The oldest pottery to have survived in Australia was established by Enoch Fowler at Glebe in Sydney in 1837. Only local raw materials were used to first make domestic pottery and later building materials such as tiles and chimney pots. The pottery was moved to Parramatta Road, Camperdown in the 1850's by Enoch's son, Robert.

The Pottery flourished during the nineteenth century and more than 100 men were employed. In the early twentieth century most of the wares produced were 'heavy' clay products such as pipes and sanity ware. The factory now operates at Marrickville.

In the late 1920's, a Melbourne works was opened at Thomastown by R. Fowler Ltd and was still operating as late as 1940. Many of our Australian Ginger Beers were made by Fowler's Pottery.

Brunswick Pottery and Brickworks (1859-1950's)

The Brunswick Pottery and Brickworks was established in 1859 near the Brunswick clay-fields by Alfred Cornwell. Situated at Phoenix Street Brunswick, the Pottery produced mainly flower pots, chimney pots, roof tiles, water filters, stoneware pipes and general pottery ware. Alfred Cornwell expanded to Launceston in the 1870's and the Victorian and Tasmanian Potteries began which was later bought by John Campbell. The Brunswick Pottery remained in the family and closed down in the early 1950's.

Melbourne potteries in the early days used white clay from Toorak and Footscray as well as from Brunswick. Kaolin from Buller was used by the Richmond Pottery to make porcelain although this was very expensive (four pounds per ton) and so Australian production of porcelain was never commercially achieved.

Hoffman Brick and Potteries Ltd.

This Pottery was located next door to Alfred Cornwell's pottery in Phoenix Street, Brunswick. It was the largest Pottery operating in Melbourne in the 1930's. Its previous name was The Hoffman Patent Steam Company, after the famous German-made Hoffman kilns. The Hoffman Pottery closed down in the 1960's and Hoffman Brick were taken over by Clifton Brick.

A number of local Ginger Beers carry the Hoffman Pottery mark. More on the Hoffman Brick & Pottery Company can be read about in the W. A. B. C. Newsletter of March 1992, Vol 13 No 8.

Histories/Potteries/Manufacturers

Lithgow Pottery (1876-1896)

Lithgow Pottery is very collectable and very expensive as they operated for a relatively short period and many of the pieces are marked and very appealing. A skilled potter named James Silcock joined the pottery in the late 1870's. Some of the many articles made by Lithgow include :- Tea Pots, Toby Jugs, Cheese Covers, Bread Trays, Spittoons, Jars, Jelly Shapes, Spirit Barrels, Milk Churns, Bedpans, Pudding Bowls, Foot warmers, etc. The Brickworks made plain and shaped bricks, chimney pots and pipes. Due to imported overseas ware of poorer quality being passed off as Colonial Ware and the 1890's depression, the pottery closed in 1896. Edward Brownfield un-successfully re-opened the pottery in 1905 but it closed eighteen months later. (Rough of the pottery mark supplied)

N.B. This information is from the ABC Newsletter of February 1985.

oooooooooooooooooooooooooooooooooooooo

The article below is from a 1936 Melbourne Newspaper.

Pottery, an industry for craftsmen

Pottery, one of Australia's oldest industries, is also one of those in which the craftsman's skills still plays a large part. By the use of the potter's wheel, which is still used in making jars and bottles, the Australian industry is linked with the work of craftsmen of many years before the Christian era.

Although machinery is used greatly in modern potteries, individual deftness is necessary in such delicate jobs as fixing handles to pots and cups. Today, 65 factories (excluding 250 which manufacture bricks, fire bricks and roof tiles) more than 1700 people are employed and the wages bill exceeds 250,000 pounds annually. The output is more than 500,000 pounds. The raw materials used are almost entirely Australian and the range of pottery includes various classes of porcelain, earthenware, enamelled fire clay, floor tiles, wall tiles, terracotta and stoneware.

Throughout the Commonwealth there are extensive deposits for almost every type or class of pottery. Large quantities of earthenware are produced in Australia and stoneware is also produced in vast quantities. This non absorbent body is first 'fired' at a high temperature and frequently salt glazed. It is used for drainage and sewerage purposes, being strong and highly resistant to acids. The pottery trade is one of National significance in its drainage and sewerage aspect, as it has much to do with National health. Without the products of the clay worker, many electrical services could not be maintained and the activities in factories producing iron, steel and copper depend greatly on the clay products. It is an industry that enters greatly in our lives and one that plays a large part in the industrial building of Australia.

Histories/Potteries/Manufacturers

Extract from the Sun news-pictorial about April 1983

Pottery offered for sale

The recently appointed receivers and managers of The Bendigo Pottery (Epsom) Pty. Ltd. have recommended that the company be sold.

Mr. Murray Horsburgh and Mr. John Walsh yesterday invited tenders for the historic business. They said realisable assets were $1.54 million and after deducting amounts owed to creditors, $792,000 was available for unsecured creditors and shareholders. Unsecured claims are expected to total $338,000. Paid up capital is $298,000. The receivers have continued operating the business since their appointment on January 25 but said they believed there was 'a need for a change in management and funding' of the company. Directors asked Westpac Banking Corporation to appoint receivers after a boardroom dispute erupted over the company's ability to pay its debts 'as and when they fall due'.

Charles Robert Goulding (ABC Newsletter of June 1981).

C. R. Goulding ran the factory of Weaver & Co. in Hobart, Tasmania from 1876-1881, after which time he left Hobart and moved to Launceston where he entered into partnership with Robert Mc Kenzie. These two took over a cordial factory formerly operated by Peter Barrett on a lease basis, but did not purchase the plant and fittings. For some reason Goulding ceased to be a partner after 1883, although he stayed on as an employee of Mc Kenzie but left after a short time.

It seems he moved to Melbourne around 1885 and his activities there are better known to Melbourne collectors, than to me. It is of interest that a Ginger Beer bottle used by him, shows him as being an aerated water manufacturer in High Street, Prahran; although a Mister Hynes is the proprietor of the factory. His ex-partner in Launceston, Robert Mc Kenzie, continued the business for several years but lost the cordial factory to William Ignatius Thrower who purchased it outright. Mc Kenzie was very bitter about this episode and was so hostile towards Peter Barrett, that he inserted an advertisement in the Launceston Examiner of 4th. February, 1889 expressing his feelings.

Leaks and Morrow (ABC Newsletter August 1981).

Leaks first started in Oxley, probably in the 1870's. No bottles have been seen with Oxley on them. They operated breweries in Wangaratta, Tungamah and Benalla. They bought out P. R. Cornish of Tungamah in approximately 1910. It was necessary for Mr. Cornish to sell out when the well which supplied the water for his product ran dry. Leaks continued trading until 1918 when they were bought out by G. A. Morrow. Morrow bought out Leaks in Riley Street, Wangaratta in 1918. This must have been the start of Morrow in the aerated water business as there is no reference to him before 1918. He continued until 1947, when he was bought out by the Donnelly Bros. They continued until 1950 and moved to Albury after buying out Wilson's. The old Morrow factory was then taken over by Alpine Cordial Works until 1954 when it once again changed hands the buyers being Bynon's, Wangaratta.

Histories/Potteries/Manufacturers

G. P. Milsom, Launceston (ABC Newsletter August 1981).

George Milsom commenced business in 1865 in the Kaiapoi borough of New Zealand and had achieved nearly thirty years practical experience as a cordial maker when he arrived in Tasmania. In 1894 he acquired a business at 59 George Street which had originally been established by a Mr. Rawlings about 1850.

Stone Ginger Beer bottles made for George Milsom by the Bendigo Pottery are reasonably plentiful, however his earlier salt glazed stone bottles are as scarce as most pre-1900 ginger beer bottles and are the only type which lack the trade mark elephant, which was adopted by his predecessor Thrower; and generally used by Milsom. Apart from his bottles very little evidence of his successful business career remains, except perhaps his Launceston residence at 16 Maitland Street.

E. Rowlands (Full page article in A.B.C. Newsletter October 1981).(More page 41)

Extracts from History of Ballarat by William Bramwell Withers. Also a four page article on E. Rowlands is in the W. A. B. C. Newsletter of March 1992 Vol. 13 No. 8.

M. Mc Donald Aerated Water & Cordial Manufacturer, Madeline Street Carlton.

Mc Donald arrived in the colony at the beginning of 1858 and for many years had his ups and downs. In 1861 he went to New Zealand and was moderately successful. Glowing accounts of the Lachlan in N.S.W. induced him to try his luck there. It was bad luck and he found himself penniless and 600 miles from Melbourne and friends. It was a long tramp but a few weeks rest and a friendly advance from a relation, enabled him to return to New Zealand. This time at Dunstan, without much rest he proceeded to Fox's and the Shotover where several parties were getting plenty of gold. He was not lucky to get any himself, so in a week or two he left with a mate for Invercargill and after a while storekeeping at Winton, he started a business as a Soda Water manufacturer in Dee Street; Invercargill in 1864.

This business was successful and since then and up till 1904, he was successful showing his wares at Ballarat and Melbourne. Mr. McDonald also gained first prizes for Liquors and Cordials at the Industrial and Colonial Exhibitions at Melbourne and New Zealand. He attributed much of his success to the thorough knowledge of every department of his business and the use of the best Filters to be had in the world. He was one of the first in the Colony to use the Celebrated Pasteur Filter.

Ride of Benalla and Euroa

Account of the history in a full page, in the ABC Newsletter of February 1981.

Also another in the W. A. B. C. Newsletter of October 1984. Volume 6 No. 4.

Histories/Potteries/Manufacturers

Prev^ot E.J.

Manufacturer of cordials and aerated waters at both 120 Queen Street, Melbourne and 11 Madeline Street, Carlton. The factory at Queen Street was known as the 'Phoenix

Cordial Manufactory'. The company's registered trade mark included a representation of the legendary phoenix rising from the ashes. At the Victorian Exhibition held in Melbourne in 1861, the firm gained 2nd. Class certificates for 'lemonade' and 'soda water' and an honourable mention for their 'orange bitters'. The firm is first mentioned in the Sands and Kenny's Melbourne Directory for 1859, but this date is not necessarily that of the establishment of the company.

1859	E.J. Prev^ot	12 Madeline Street, Nth. Melbourne.
1860-1862	" "	120 Queen Street, Melbourne.
1863-1865	" "	" " " " / 11 Madeline Street, Carlton.
1864	" " & Co.	120 Queen Street, Melbourne.
1866	" " "	" " " "
1867-1871	Prevot & Co.	Queen & Madeline Streets.
1872-1877	" "	11 Madeline Street, Carlton.
1878	E.H. Prev^ot	" " " "
1879-1883	Pr'ev^ot & Bilton.	" " " "

Sands and Kenny's Directory for 1884 and those of the following years, do not refer to the company, so it could be assumed that this particular firm ceased production in 1883.

Karl Korju is accredited with this report and he lists these three bottles from his private collection :-

E.J. Prevost & Co.)
E.J. Prev^ost.) c. 1859 - 1866.
E.J. Prev^ot & Co.)

Mc Donald M.

Michael McDonald (Aerated Water Manufacturer) first mentioned in Sands and Kenny's Directory for 1880, at 18 Franklin Street, Melbourne. He continued at this address until 1883 and in the following year, took over the factory of Prevot & Bilton, at 11 Madeline Street, Carlton.

1880-1883	Michael McDonald	18 Franklin Street, Melbourne.
1884-1888	M. McDonald	11 MadelineStreet, Carlton.
1889	McDonald & Co. Ltd.	12-18 Madeline Street, Carlton.
1890	" "	11 Madeline Street, Carlton.
1891	" "	18 " " "
1892-1894	" "	12 " " "
1895-1905	McDonald & Co.	12 " " "

(Firm at the same address but streets were often re-numbered, which accounts for the differences.)

Histories/Potteries/Manufacturers

McDonald M.

The company was still in business in 1910, as their name appeared in the directory for that year. The firm probably continued for some years after 1910, but I have not researched later directories. The company's registered trade mark was a representation of a crown beneath which there were the words 'Trade Mark'. The bottles most commonly used by the firm appear to be 'codds' and 'Hamilton' patents and stone 'Ginger Beers'; of which there exists numerous varieties.

(This article also by Karl Korju.)

Character Jugs were made by the Bendigo Pottery.

The Lord Kitchener has a Rockingham Glaze. Circa 1915.

R. Harrison Aerated Waters and Cordial Manufacturer, 6-10 Spring Street, Fitzroy.

Has a large selection of Bendigo Pottery pieces.
(From The Encyclopaedia of Victoria, 1904. Full page story).

George Bollington 1898- ? Bollington Hop Beer Co. 171-179 Stawell Street, Richmond.

Aerated Waters and Ginger Beer maker. Maker of 'Orb' ginger beer. Detail in the 'Cyclopedia of Victoria, 1906'. Most manufactories are listed in this medium just after the turn of the 1900's. 'Cyclopedia is the fore runner of our modern 'Encyclopaedia'. Bollington had bottles from both Richmond and Geelong.

10 Rare Ginger Beer bottles are listed in the August 1982 ABR Newsletter with a description of the known bottles at that time. This listing is important because of the detail of production of the ten bottles depicted. The best example is as No. 5 Jos. Hatchett 750 made by the Bendigo Pottery, in 1923. The editor has only seen two. (Years later more than 20 were unearthed). Yet with No. 2, Billson 'open' stamp he knows of only 1 - so do I - but Billson had 121,248 delivered.

Moonee Valley Aerated Water & Cordial Co. Miller and Clauscen Streets, North Fitzroy.
Proprietor Mr. John Dunne. 1906.
From the ABC Newsletter of December 1982. (Two page story of that and Carlton Brewery of which Mr. Dunne was involved for 25 years).

Article on Ginger Beers and their Rarity in the ABC Newsletter of April 1981. This account gives amounts made and editor's rough estimate of their scarcities.

Histories/Potteries/Manufacturers

G. H. Billson Aerated Water Manufacturer, Brighton Road, Elsternwick was born at Blackburn, England. He came to Australia in 1848 and established a business at Brighton Road in 1890. The factory was situated in the City of St Kilda at Brighton Road near the well known nursery of Brunning and Sons. He had a range of Ginger Beer bottles many of which were Bendigo Pottery pieces.

The Bendigo Pottery Co. An article by Ken Arnold showing sketches of the early pottery stamps used by G. D. Guthrie & Co 1898-1912. (Three full pages with sketches of articles made by the pottery. ABC Newsletter February 1981).

W.A.B.C. Newsletter April 1979 Volume 1 No. 3

On page 4 there is a report of a Green Top Elliott's Ginger Beer bottle - broken.

Bendigo Pottery

Article by Isabel Wilson of the W.A.B.C. Williamstown. July 1980. Vol 2 No. 7.

The Bendigo Pottery was started by George Duncan Guthrie. He arrived in Australia in 1850 and he made some ginger beer bottles at Camperdown, Sydney, about 1853. By 1858 with two assistants, Guthrie was making everyday wares at Epsom, just outside Bendigo. At the Melbourne Exhibition in 1866, Guthrie won a medal for his collection of stoneware and in particular his ginger beer bottles, some of these were broken by the judges to assess the quality of the interior glaze. By 1880 the Bendigo Pottery was one of the busiest of numerous potteries in Victoria. Guthrie died in Bendigo at the age of 83 in 1910. His partner, E. J. Hartley, then became proprietor. Fire destroyed the factory in 1941 but it now has been rebuilt and is again in the top bracket of Pottery Manufacturers.

Victorian Differences

Full page article upon the differences in pottery marks on the Bennett of Richmond Ginger Beer bottles. Differences in stamps and pottery marks that can help 'date' the bottles. Article by the editor of the W. A. B. C. Newsletter, Bryan Reed. Vol 9 No. 8 March 1988.

Victorian Differences

Other pages listed in W. A. B. C. N/Letters : Vol 9 Nos. 9, 10, 11, 12, Vol 10 Nos. 1, 2, 3, 4, 5, Vol 10 No. 3 includes pottery article by Greg Hill (Pottery Enthusiast) and Bryan

Reed, Editor who also has another article within. Vol 10 No. 4 lists L. Nolan, Brunswick Pottery.

Histories/Potteries/Manufacturers
Pottery pieces issued - Ginger Beers

Last column ( ) = Less than complete specimens known.

Addicott F. F.	Frankston	Vic.	C	1,440	(10 gross) G. B's. issued 1921-1922.	(4)
Alpha Cordial Works Mildura		Vic.	C	26,640	(185 gross) G.B.'s issued Dec 1910-Oct 1922.	
Albury Brewery Co.	Albury NSW.		D	10,656	(75 gross) G.B's issued May 1906-Oct 1909.	
Barrett Bros.	Nth Fitzroy	Vic.	C	11,520	(80 gross) G.B's issued Oct 1915-Aug 1917.	
Bartlett J. & Co.	Rush. & Tatura		C	14,832	(13 gross) G.B's issued July 1906-July 1913.	
Bennett G. H.	Richmond	Vic	C	79,344	(549 1/2 gross) issued July 1906-Jul. 1913.	(12)
Billson G. H.	St Kilda	Vic.	C	121,248	(842 gross) G. B's. issued 1906-1914.	
Bollington G.	Richmond	Vic.	C	1,440	(10 gross) G. B's. issued 1906.	(7)
Bollington Hop Beer Co.	Geelong	Vic.	C7,	488	(52 gross) G.B's. issued Mar 1912-Nov. 1913.sc	
Border United Co-op.	Albury NSW.		D	3,864	(26 gross&80) G.B's issued Nov 1911.	
Boon Spa	Melbourne	Vic.	C	7,200	(50 gross) G. B's. issued Dec. 1921-Jan. 1922.	(8)
Bray W.L.&Co.	St.Arnaud	Vic.	C c\s	21,312	(148gross) G.B's.issued Sep1907-Dec.1925.	(0)
Brook A	Horsham	Vic.	C tri.	1,440	(10 gross) G.B's. issued Dec 1911.	(1)
Brown D. O.	Castlemaine	Vic.	C	864	(6 gross) G. B's. issued Dec. 1913.	(6)
Brown R.J.	Rochester	Vic.	C	720	(5 gross) G.B's. issued Dec 1906. Plain (no transfer)	?

Bruce W. & Sons	Bendigo	Vic.	C	7,920	(55 gross) G.B's issued Nov 1909-1912. '12 GB added	
Bryant & Shields Co.	Wangaratta	Vic.	C	6,336	(44 gross) G.B's issued Oct 1917. (buffalo)	
Burns P.	Maffra	Vic.	C	864	(6 gross) G.B's issued Oct 1911.	(7)
Butchart G.Jnr.	Mildura	Vic.	C	21744	(151gross)G.B's issued Dec1906-1931.Gb added 1914	
Butler V. E.	Maffra	Vic.	C	1008	(7 gross) G.B's issued Oct. 1912.	
Centurona Cord.		C	Vic.	1,440	(10 gross) G. B's. issued 1908-1910.	(1)
Chapman Bros.	Fitzroy	Vic.	D c\s	14,400	(100 gross) issued Jul. 1927-Sep. 1927.	(10)
Chiselett W.A.R.	Merbein	Vic.	C	3,744	(26 gross) G.B's issued Jan 1921-Sep 1922.	
Cohn Bros.	Bendigo & Swan Hill	Vic.	D	1,440	(10 gross) issued July 1929 only to S.Hill.	(0)
" "	" "	"	C	79,920	(555 gross) issued Aug 1902-Jul 1929.	
Colac Aerated Water Co.	Colac	Vic.	D b\l	1,440	(10 gross) issued May 1917.	
" " "	" "	"	C	2,880	(20 gross) issued Sep 1921. 'Geo Hay's'.	
Cole Chas. & Co.	Geelong	Vic.	C	25,344	(176 gross) issued Jan 1907-Sep 1918. blob top.	
Collis Dyason	Mildura	Vic.	C	1440	(10 gross) issued Oct 1923.	
Crystal Spa Co.	Hamilton	Vic. Tri	C	2,160	(15 gross) issued Sep 1908.	
Curtis S. H.	Maryborough	Vic.	C	72	(1/2 gross) issued Nov. 1925. 14 fluid ozs.	(3)
" "	"	"	C	72	(1/2 gross) issued Nov. 1925. 27 fluid ozs.	(8)
" "	"	"	C	144	(1 gross) issued Oct. 1926. 27 fluid ozs.	
Cowap A. V.	Launceston		Tas.	3,168	(22 gross) G. B's. issued Dec. 1906-Nov. 1910.	

Dandenong Botanic Brewery	Dandenong	Vic.	D	864	(6 gross) Mar 1924.	
Daniels	Yan Yean	Vic.	C	2,160	(15 gross) issued Oct 1906-Dec 1908.	(0)
Darby Bros.	Shepparton	Vic.	D c\s	3,024	(21 gross) G.B's issued Feb 1930.	
" "	"	"	C	12,312	(85.5 gross) G.B's issued Jan 1931-Sep 1933.	
Davis and Grant	Gisborne	Vic.	C			(2)
Deans A & Co.	Ararat	Vic.	C	8,784	(61 gross) G.B's issued Oct 1907-Oct 1918.	
Dixon J. & Co's.	Prahran/Melb	Vic.	C	7,200	(50 gross) G. B's. issued Oct. 1908.	(6)
Dixon P. G. & Co.	p/l W. Melbourne	Vic.	C	26,640	(185 gross) G.B's. Oct 1908-Dec1913.	
Downer Co.	Sebastapol	Vic.	D	2,880	(20 gross) issued Jul 1913-Dec 1915.	(0)
Durham Geo.	Terang	Vic.	C	1440	(10 gross) issued Nov 1906.	(4)
Eberhard & Co.	Clunes	Vic.	C	4,370	(30 gross) issued Oct 1908-Aug 1920.	
Egypta Pty. Ltd.	Melbourne	Vic.	C	28,300	(195.5 gross) issued Aug 1920-Jul 1921.	

Histories/Potteries/Manufacturers
Pottery pieces issued - Ginger Beers

Elliott G. H.	Carlton	Vic	C	75,672	(524 gross+16) G. B's. " Dec. 1906Jan.1940.t/t	(12b/t)
Franklin &Co Balaclava	Melb.	Vic.	C	10,800	(75 gross) G.B's issued Dec 1906-De1910.	(8)
Frankston Springs Col'wd	Melb.	Vic.	1906-13 C	102,240	(737.7gross) Dec 1907-Sep1912b/t	
Frankston Aerated Water Co.	Carlton	Vic.	1913-C	36,000	(250 gross) Jan 1914-Nov1934.	
Gamble H. J.	Melbourne	Vic.	C	2,880	(20 gross) Nov 1921.	(2)
Geelong Aerated Water Co.	Geelong	Vic.	C	7,200	(50 gross) Oct 1919.	(10)

Gibson James	Yarrawonga	Vic.	D	720	(5 gross) Dec 1906.	(8)
Glover Chas. J.	Bendigo	Vic.	C	1,152	(8 gross) Feb 1923.	(10)
Goodfellow Richmond	Melb.	Vic	C	1440	(10 gross) Oct. 1909.	(0)
Goulding C.R.	Prahran	Vic.	C	7,200	(50 gross) Jan 1915.	(4)
Gow J.	Footscray	Vic.	C			(7)
Gray G.	Campbells Creek	Vic.	C	1440	(10 gross) G. B's issued Dec 1913-Sep 1914.	
Green T. J.	Morang	Vic.	C	1,872	(13 gross) G. B's. issued 1907-1914.	(3)
Haustorfer H. E.	Horsham	Vic.	C	2880	(20 gross) G. B's issued Sep 1913.	(3)
Harrison R.	Fitzroy	Vic.	C	158,688	(1102 gross) G.B's issued Sep 1913-Jan 1939.	
Hatchett Jos.	Murtoa	Vic.	C	720	(5 gross) G. B's. issued Sep 1923.	(10)
Herron H. W.	Sale	Vic.	C	1,872	(13 gross) G. B's. issued Dec 1913-Apr 1920.	(8)
Heywood F. C.	Stawell	Vic.	C c/s	1,728	(12 gross) G. B's issued Jul 1927.	
Hosies Hotel	Melbourne	Vic.	C	1,440	(10 gross) G. B's issued Jul 1912- Oct 1915.	(2)
Hosken T. J.	Violet Town	Vic.	C	720	(5 gross) G. B's issued Dec 1907.	(1)
Hunter Bros.	Bendigo	Vic.	C & c/s	16,416	(114 gross) G. B's issued Dec 1909-Oct 10	(4)
" "	"	"	C incl tri		" " " " 26 fl ozs. & 14 fl ozs.	
Hunter Jos.	Horsham	Vic.	C	4,320	(30 gross) G. B's issued Jul 1912-Dec 1914.	
" "	"	"	C incl tri		" " " " 26 fl ozs. & 14 fl ozs.	
Jackson C. S.	Corowa	NSW.	C	2,160	(15 gross) G. B's issued Nov 1914.	
" Bros.	Corowa	NS W.	D	2,160	(30 gross) G..B's issued Feb 1918.	
" "	" "		C	4,320	(30 gross) G. B's issued Oct 1920.	

Jacobson & Co.?	Footscray	Vic.	C	8,640	(60 gross) G. B's issued Dec 1906-Dec 1914.	
Jacobsen's	Footscray	Vic.	C		extremely rare	(1)
Johnson F.	Riddell	Vic.	C	720	(5 gross) G. B's. issued Nov 1917-Jan 1918.	(3)
Jones & McEwan	Castlemaine	Vic	D bl/t c/s	2,880	(20 gross) issued Sep 1926.	
Lindner Dolph (Adolph)	Dimboola	Vic.	D	12,240	(85 gross) G. B's issued	
McDonald & Co.	Carlton	Vic.	C	6,768	(47 gross) G. B's issued Nov 1906-Feb 1915.	
McGavin J.	Corowa	NSW	D b/t	1,440	(10 gross) G. B's issued Jul 1912.	
McGaw L.	Maffra	Vic.	D	2,160	(15 gross) G. B's issued Oct 1921-Feb 1923.	
"	"	"	C c/s	2,880	(20 gross) G. B's issued Jul 1923-Sep 1924.	
McGee J.	Rochester	Vic.	C	2,016	(14 gross) G. B's issued Nov 1911-Nov 1914	
McMartin M.	Nhill	Vic.	C	720	(5 gross) G. B's issued Mar 1911.	(4)
Manallack F.	St. Arnaud	Vic.	C	15,264	(106 gross) G. B's issued Nov 1906-Jan 1926.	
Manger & O'Neil	Echuca	Vic.	C	33,840	(235 gross) G. B's issued Dec 1913-Jul 1929. b/t	
Mason S.	Wodonga	Vic.	D	13,104	(91 gross) G. B's issued Mar 1911-Aug 1920.	
"	"	"	C	1,728	(12 gross) G. B's issued Aug 1923.	
Medwin H. A.	Tongala	Vic.	C	216	(1.1/2 gross) G. B's issued 29th. Oct 1934.	
Melbourne Glass Bottle Works		Vic.	C	144	(1 gross) G. B's issued Feb 1907.	(0)
Mitting H.	Irymple	Vic.	C	1,440	(10 gross) G. B's issued Aug 1922.	(4)
Morrow G. A.	Wangaratta	Vic.	C b/t	288	(2 gross) G. B's issued Sep 1923.	(8)
" "	"	"	C t/t		? ?	(6)

Moonee Valley		Vic.	C			(2)
Murray & Meade	Albury	NSW.	D	1,440	(10 gross) G. B's issued Jan 1908.	
Nugent Jas.	Wahgunyah	Vic.	C	432	(3 gross) G. B's issued Nov 1909.	(8)
O'Neill Edward J.	Echuca	Vic.	C	576	(4 gross) G. B's issued Sep 1930.	(0)
O'Sullivan& Purcell	Carlton	Vic.	C	1,872	(13 gross) G. B's issued Nov 1910-Nov 1911.	(6)
Oswald D.	Eaglehawk	Vic.	C	1,440	(10 gross) G. B's issued Dec 1922-Nov 1925.	
Oswald J. H.	Corowa	NSW.	C	9,648	(67 gross) G. B's issued Oct 1908-Oct 1925.	
O. T. Ltd.	Prahran	Vic.	C	7,200	(50 gross) G. B's issued Dec 1913. (ex dixon)	(4)
Palling J.	Heathcote	Vic.	C	2,160	(15 gross) G. B's issued Dec 1907-Mar 1916.	(9)
Phibbs Bros.	Albury	N SW	D b/t	23,224	(161.3 gross) G.B's issuedApr1908Oct1919.	
Plummer Murphy & Co.	Sth. Melb.		C	288	(2 gross) G. B's issued Dec 1908.	(0)
Priddle Bros.	Queenscliffe	Vic.	C	1,440	(10 gross) G. B's issued Oct 1914-Oct 1918.	(8)
Pritchard G.	Bendigo	Vic.	C	1,440	(10 gross) G. B's issued Dec 1910.	(8)
Reed Bros.	Bendigo	Vic.	C c/s	7,920	(55 gross) G. B's issued Nov 1925-May 1929.	
Reeves R. V.	Hamilton	Vic.	C	5,760	(40 gross) G. B's issued Aug 1920-Apr 1921.	
Ride E.	Benalla	Vic.	C	18,000	(125 gross) G. B's issued Sep 1914-Sep 1924.	
Ride J.	Euroa	Vic.	C	7,488	(52 gross) G. B's issued Oct 1908-Dec 1915.	
Rochester A. W. Co.		Vic.	C	1,872	(13 gross) G. B's issued May 1914-Jul 1919.	(6)
Rogers Bros.	Hawthorn	Vic.	C	16,128	(112 gross) G. B's issued Sep 1906-Oct 1924.	
Rosel A.	Echuca	Vic.	C	7,920	(55 gross) G. B's issued Feb 1914-Nov 1920.	

Rowlands E.	Ballarat	Vic.	C	73,160	(508&5 gross) G. B's issued Jul 1908-Dec 1915.	
Rowley J. S. & Co.	Hamilton	Vic.	C	5,760	(40 gross) G. B's issued Oct 1908-Apr 1910.	
Schweppes Ltd.	Abbotsford	Vic.	D	79,200	(5,500 gross)G. B's issued Sep1915-Aug 1919.	
Skeyhill J. P.	Hamilton	Vic.	C	1,440	(10 gross) G. B's issued Dec 1913.	
" "	"	"	D	1,728	(12 gross) G. B's issued Oct 1915. b/t	
Sloan S.	Hamilton	Vic.	C	1,440	(10 gross) G. B's issued Jun 1921.	
Stacey T. G.	Nth. Carlton	Vic.	C	14,400	(100 gross) G. B's issued Sep 1912.	(1)
Stevens E. C.	Warracknabeal	Vic.	D	1,440	(10 gross) G. B's issued Mar 1909.	
Stewards & Hunter P/L	Bendigo	Vic.	C	3,600	(25 gross) G. B's issued Nov 1914.	
Thornley & Howlett	Sale	Vic.	C	1,628	(11.2 gross) G. B's issued Feb 1920.	
Thornley W. J.	Horsham	Vic.	C	11,232	(78 gross) G. B's issued Nov 1919-Nov 1923.	
Thornley W. T. & Co	Sale	Vic.	C	4,464	(31 gross) G. B's issued Aug 1911-Jul 1915.	
Trait J. H.	Geelong	Vic.	C	3,600	(25 gross) G. B's issued Oct 1913-Jan 1914.	
Walker J. A. & Co.	Wonthagga	Vic	C	576	(4 gross) G. B's issued Nov 1911.	(1)
" "	" "	Vic	D	864	(6 gross) G. B's issued Aug 1920.	(3)
Ward&Cress (cross)	Yarrawonga	Vic.	D	3,312	(23 gross)G.B's issued Aug 1915-Nov 1921.	
Waterfield T.	Horsham	Vic.	C	5,616	(39 gross) G. B's issued Aug 1910-Sep 1914.	
Watson D. S.	Albury	NSW.	D	4,320	(30 gross) G. B's issued Oct 1906-Oct 1908.	
Whittaker W. & Sons	Dunolly	Vic.	C	864	(6 gross) G. B's issued Jun 1922-Jul 1923.	
Wilcox Bros.	Dandenong	Vic.	C	1,872	(13 gross) G. B's issued Nov 1910-Oct 1915. b/t	(6)

Willis H.	Cressy	Vic.	C	288	(2 gross) G. B's issued Nov 1910.	(0)
Wilmot G.	Colac	Vic.	D	3,744	(26 gross) G. B's issued Apr 1910-Dec 1914. b/l	
Wilson J. F.	Albury	NSW	C	3,672	(25.5 gross) G. B's issued Jan 1932.	
Young D. C.	Albury	NSW.	C	2,880	(20 gross) G. B's issued Nov 1906-Oct 1908.	
Yoxall J. P.	Wangaratta	Vic.	C	7,200	(50 gross) G. B's issued Nov 1906-Feb1910.	
Dolphin O.	Nagambie	Vic.	C		(Ginger Beer)	(2)
O. T. Limited	Prahran	Vic.	C	7,200	(50 gross) G. B's. issued Dec. 1913.	(5)
O'Sullivan Purcell	Carlton	Vic.	C	1,872	(13 gross) blob/ top G.B's. Nov. 1910- Nov.1911.	(6)
Rogers Bros.	Hawthorn	Vic.	C	16,128	(111 gross+44) between Sept. 1906- Nov.1925.b/t	(4)
Rowland E.	Melbourne	Vic.	C		Impressed on shoulder. 10 ozs. internal thread	(1)
Wilding Henry	Queenscliff	Vic.	C		(6)	
Kempthorne Presser & Co	Christchurch N.Z.				1910 10oz D int. 144 (1 gross)	

Known Ginger Beer bottles with the C.A.P. stamp. (Cornwells Australian Pottery?)

Bennett J.H.	Richmond		(H. R-Pelling collection)	
Harrison R.	Nth Fitzroy		" "	
Rowlands	Ball,Syd,Melb.	(C.A.P.)	" "	
Trait J.J.	Geelong		" "	Ltg.
Ride E.	Benalla		(Longford ")	

Impressed G. B's. Known of. E.W. Jones Forest Creek D 1850's.

Histories/Potteries/Manufacturers

Ginger Beer Bottles Mintage Figures (less than 1,000 made)

D.O. Brown	Castlemaine	Vic.	1913	Ch	864	(6 gross)
R.J. Brown	Rochester	Vic.	1906	Ch	720	(5 gross)
J. Burgess	Pt. Pirie	S.A.	1914	D	432	(3 gross)
P. Burns	Maffra	Vic.	1911	D	864	(6 gross)
V.E. Butler	Maffra	Vic.	1912	D	1008	(7 gross)
A. Castres	Charters Towers	Qld.	1933	Ch	624	(4 gross & 4 dozen)
Catties	Renmark	S.A.	1922	D	288	(2 gross)
S.H. Curtis	Maryborough	Vic.	1923-30	Ch 14oz	72	(1/2 gross)
" "	"	"	" "	Ch 27oz	216	(1. 1/2 gross)
Bot. Brewery	Dandenong	Vic.	1924	D	864	(6 gross)
E.R. Fielding	?	?	1927	D c/s	720	(5 gross)
James Gibson	Yarrawonga	Vic.	1906	D	720	(5 gross)
J. Hatchet & Co.	Murtoa	Vic.	1923	Ch	720	(5 gross)
Heath & Co.	Walleroo	S.A.	1914	D	720	(5 gross)
T.G. Hoskin	Violet Town	Vic.	1907	Ch	720	(5 gross)
T. Johnson	Riddell	Vic.	1917	Ch	720	(5 gross)
F.L. Kolosche	Loxton	S.A.	1921	D	720	(5 gross)
Mc Mahon	?	W.A.	1914	D	720	(5 gross)
M..Mc Martin	Nhill	Vic.	1911	Ch	720	(5 gross)
Mc Swiney	Rochester	Vic.	?	Ch	432	1 Gallon
H.A. Medwin	Tongala	Vic.	1934	Ch	216	(1. 1/2 gross)
M. G. B. Works	Melbourne	Vic.	1907	Ch	144	(1 gross)
Moore	Norwood	S.A.	1908	D	720	(5 gross)
Moore Bros.	"	"	1923	D	720	(5 gross)
G.A. Morrow	Wangaratta	Vic.	1923	bl/n Ch	288	(2 gross)
Noonan Bros.	Broken Hill	N.S.W.	1913	D	720	(5 gross)
J. Nugent	Wahgunyah	Vic.	1909	Ch	432	(3 gross)
Edward J. O'Niell	Echuca	Vic.	1910-11	Ch	576	(4 gross)

Pearce	Devonport	Tas.	1905	D	288	(2 gross)
Phillips & Son	"	"	1925	D c/s	720	(5 gross)
Plummer & Murphy	Sth. Melbourne	Vic.	1908	Ch	288	(2 gross)
Shamrock A.W. Co.	Perth	W.A.	1926	Ch c/s	720	(5 gross)
J.T. Shepherd	?	?	1918	D	720	(5 gross)
Spicer & Detmold	?	?	1924	16oz Squ Neck	432	(3 gross)
Starkey	?	N.S.W. ?	1914	D c/s	288	(2 gross)
Tetlow	?	?	1911	D	864	(6 gross)
J.A. Walker & Co.	Wonthaggi	Vic.	1911	Ch	576	(4 gross)
" "	"	"	1920	D	864	(6 gross)
Wattle A. Waters	?	?	1921	12oz D	864	(6 gross)
W. Whittaker & Sons	Dunnoly	Vic.	1922-23	Ch	864	(6 gross)
H. Willis	Cressy	Vic	1910-15	bl Ch 10 oz	288	(2 gross)

Histories/Potteries/Manufacturers

Facts and - doesn't Figure?

Browsing through the Bendigo Pottery book by Paul Scholes, I honed in on the known list of issues that were delivered to the various ginger beer producers. It would seem that some of the more common 'scarce' bottles such as Egypta Pty. Ltd. Melbourne, Victoria, of which there were 28,000 made in 1920-1921 (that is 196 gross and 76) are equally hard to come by as the Dandenong Botanic Brewery, Victoria dump; of which there were only 864 (6 gross) made. Perhaps this un-equality came about because most of the Egypta bottles were destroyed, while the Botanic bottles were un-used and therefore stored away.

By the same token, how is it that H. A. Medwin of Tongala Victoria ginger beers, of which 216 (1. 1/2 gross) October 1934 were made, are easier to come by than J. Nugent

Wahgunya, 436 (3 gross) November 1909? Could it be that the Nugent bottles of 1909 had an extra 25 years to become lost, stolen or destroyed? And how does that compute with the 864 (6 gross) 1911, P. Burns of Maffra, Victoria of which there are only four or five known?

It seems ludicrous that S. Sloan of Hamilton Victoria, with 1440 (10 gross) issued June 1921, are so common with such a small total - compared to Egypta's 28,000 and yet O'Sullivan Purcell of Carlton Melbourne Victoria, with a higher than Sloan output of 1872 (13 gross) November 1910-1911, are so scarce that I have only heard of the one! How does one account for it. Perhaps some drink-makers destroyed all of their containers when they ceased operations so their competitors could not use their defunct containers - and others did not - who knows?

Another point to ponder - just how common are the 'Plain' ginger beer bottles? Admittedly, in the early 'Gold Rush' days they were not transferred, but most did have a Pottery Mark; such as Dahlke's, Field, etcetera. These are easily identified if only by their composition. Rough clay, salt glaze and quaint hand made tops. Not many plain ginger beers issued after transfers became fashionable were to be seen. Scholes lists only four, all of which would have to be scarce bottles - if they could be identified. For a start, many could have the oval Bendigo Pottery Stamp with Coy. Ltd. Which dates from 1898 and the Pinnacle Brand from 1910. Ginger beers from this era were also stamped Mauri Bros. and Thomson.

1440 (10 gross) of plain ginger beers were made for T. H. Faulding of Perth in 1909, these were the only plain Dumps listed, perhaps that is why there are not many here in Victoria; from the Bendigo Pottery anyway! There are fewer still of the plain Champagne Type ginger beer bottles. Only three were listed. They were :-

R. J. Brown Rochester Victoria. 750 (5gross) December 1906.

Melbourne Glass Bottle Works Victoria. 144 (I gross) February 1907.

These would have had the Bendigo Coy. Ltd. - Pinnacle and M&T Stamps; if any.

With Daniels of Yan Yean Victoria, 2,160 (15 gross) October 1916 - December 1918, it is almost certain that this huge issue would have many impressed with the Pty. Ltd. oval Bendigo Pottery stamp. Where are they all - and how does one distinguish the one from the other?

Mark my words - soon a study will be made and an answer found - then watch the prices soar for those, as yet, unwanted 'common' plain ginger beers. (Not to be confused with Stout bottles). Howard Reede- Pelling.

Histories/Potteries/Manufacturers

Victorian Differences

Article in the W. A. B. C. Newsletter of the differences in the Bendigo bottle of G. H. Bennett, ginger beer bottle as against its counterpart made in England. Vol 10 No. 9.

Whisky Jugs

An article in the W. A. B. C. Newsletter of February 1990 issue Vol 11 No. 7, depicts two whiskey jugs of local make. The question posed, is there anyone who knows if the Bendigo Pottery produced these? The same issue has the British registration diamond for glassware.

Boon Spa Pty. Ltd. Mary Ann Jacobson 1893-1920.

When the proprietor of the Footscray Enterprise, Dandelion Ale and Aerated Water Manufactory died in 1893, his wife continued as proprietor of the business. In 1898, Mary Ann shifted the firm to Geelong Road and became joint proprietor with Johann Jacobson. The factory was then trading as Jacobson's Cordial Factory. The horse shoe trade mark was adopted in June of that year. A new factory was opened in 1914 and by 1917 Mary Ann was also trading as Simla Cordial Works, Footscray. Mary Ann was one of the six shareholders when Boon Spa Pty. Ltd. was registered in 1920. It was situated at 283 Collins Street, Melbourne from

1920-1925. Presumably, Mary Ann was associated with the company until it was sold to a former employee, George Sayer, in 1937. The horse shoe trade mark was used on most Jacobson and Boon Spa bottles including marbles, ginger beers and internal threads.

Frankston Springs Miss D. Robertson 1902 - 1908.

In 1897, this company's premises were at 137-139 Islington Street, Collingwood. Quite a few women were associated with the firm. A Mary Wilson was employed as a cordial maker and was later succeeded by Mrs. Eliza Robertson. In 1902, a Miss D. Robertson was the proprietor of the business. (Presumably the daughter of Eliza). The business changed addresses a couple of times and was finally sold to George H. Elliott in 1908.

Curtis, St. Arnaud Dinah Sophia Curtis 1887-1902.

Dinah Sophia Curtis managed her husband's cordial factory in Napier Street, St. Arnaud after his death in 1887. The business prospered under her control and she was making deliveries as far a field as Ballarat. Sadly, her success was short-lived, for she died in 1902 and the factory was sold to William Bray.

Histories/Potteries/Manufacturers

Hosies Hotel 1872 - 1917 Approximately.

James D. Hosie began his first business at Melbourne in 1872 as an Estate Agent. An enterprising man, he owned several cafe's and bars including Cromwell Arms Hotel, Music Hotel & Cafe' in Victoria Street, Hosies Pie Shop in Bourke Street, and Hosies Hotel on the corner of Elizabeth & Flinders Streets.

To supply these restaurants, he became a wine and spirits merchant operating from Union Lane in the city of Melbourne. Pictured is a very rare Ginger Beer bottle, marked 'Hosies Hotel', J. B. Mc Arthur. Mc Arthur was the proprietor approximately 1917. A 13 ozs. marble bottle embossed

'Hosies Hotel' is also known to exist. The sauce bottle pictured is embossed 'Rubira & Barbetta Hosies Hotel and Restaurant'. This partnership was formed in 1888 to purchase Hosies Pie Shop in Bourke Street. This partnership only lasted until 1891 when Rubira was the sole proprietor. (Article and pictures in the W. A. B. C. Newsletter of September 1992 Vol 14 No. 3.)

R. M. Goodfellow & Company ... Ballarat

Mr. R. M. Goodfellow commenced business as an Aerated Waters and Cordial Maker in Ballarat in 1880. In 1889 a Mr. R. Fleming purchased the firm and carried on the business as proprietor and manager, trading as R. M. Goodfellow and Company, Ballarat.

Warrenheip was a prime location for quality mineral water and by 1903, Fleming was transporting 400 gallons daily to his factory located only a few hundred yards from the centre of the town; alongside of the railway line. At this time 37 hands, 12 carts and twenty horses were employed at the factory; a building measuring 200 feet by 70 feet and 50 feet high.

Goodfellow and Company used a variety of bottles of which most were branded with the distinctive Horse head Trade Mark. The types of bottles used ranged through stone ginger beers, blob top sodas, crown seals, internal threads and soda syphons. (Imported from Britain).

(A two page atricle with pictures appears in the W. A. B. C. Newsletter of July 1993 Vol 15 No. 1).

City Brick Company Pty. Ltd. Hawthorn.

Mr. Frederick Spear is mentioned in a full page article on Brick Making, in the W. A. B. C. Newsletter, of August 1993.

Jos. Hatchett Murtoa. 1903 - 1920.

Article in W. A. B. C. Newsletter of August 1993 with sketches.

Histories/Potteries/Manufacturers

G. H. Elliott. Carlton.

Article on the above named person in the W.A.B.C. Newsletter of August 1994, Vol.16 No. 2.

E. J. Kimpton Abbotsford.

Mr. Edward Kimpton was a native of Lidington, Cambrideshire, England. He arrived in Victoria in November 1853. Kimpton first lived in a tent on Batman's Hill and commenced work by assisting to load small vessels at the wharf. He was employed in a lemonade factory and soon afterwards hired a water cart and horse and carted water until he had saved enough money to purchase a team of horses and a dray to cart goods to the goldfields, receiving up to twelve pounds per ton for carriage from Melbourne to Bendigo.

Two years later he joined his brother in a farm but dissolved this partnership after about a year and a half, when he bought a farm himself at Laancoorie and ran it for about 12 years. Kimpton then leased the farm and returned to Melbourne and bought into an established grocery store in Toorak Road, South Yarra. He eventually purchased and rebuilt the property in 1876, carrying on the business until at least 1888. E. J. Kimpton was in partnership with a Mr. Wilson in the lemonade trade from 1893, shortly after taking sole control of the business and trading from Park Street, Abbotsford until 1903.

E. J. Kimpton, Park Street, Abbotsford bottles. (All rare). Pictures and story in the W. A. B. C. Newsletter of November 1994. Vol 16 No. 5.

Jacobson's 1886 - 1920.

1886	Johann Jacobson established a cordial and aerated water factory in Paisley street, Footscray, with no competition in the immediate district.
1888	Employed 12 people and used steam power.

1893	Death of Johann. Mary Ann Jacobson takes over control of the business.
1898	Trade Mark depicting a horseshoe applied for.
1917	Mary Ann registered the trade mark of 'Simla'.
1920	Company formed with Mary Ann, Alexander and Sylvester Jacobson and others as shareholders on the Boon Spa Company.

J. Gow Footscray 1900 - 1930.

The J. Gow Cordial and Aerated Water Company was in operation between 1900 and 1930, in Nicholson Street, Footscray. Few bottles have surfaced from this factory, chiefly this :

Ginger Beer with J G in monogram. Taylor Pottery.

Histories/Potteries/Manufacturers

Corowa's Stonies

Watson & Young, Corowa.

It is not quite certain if this firm actually brewed in Corowa, but there was certainly a distribution operating from this address. They were in operation pre 1893 through to 1908. G. B's used were an internal screw by Bendigo Potteries and an attractive cork top by Denby Potteries - unusual in that the brown glaze extended down over the shoulder to cover half the bottle.

D. C. Young, Corowa.

Commenced in 1908 using a champagne type by Bendigo Potteries. Of the 4,112 (35 1/2 gross) bottles there are very few known survivors. Only about 8 in mint or near mint condition.

J. Mc Gavin, Corowa.

Commenced in 1912 using a small, blue blob top stony of poor quality glaze by Bendigo Potteries, some were made by Pinnacle Brand also.

C. S. Jackson, Corowa.

Entered the fray in 1914 with a cork topped champagne type made by Pinnacle Brand, this firm merged to become :-

Jackson Bros., Corowa.

This new firm commenced by using a lightning stoppered dump in 1918, then a cork stoppered champagne type in 1920. Both bottles were by Bendigo Pottery.

A. E. Jackson, Corowa.

Son of C. S. Jackson. He introduced a crown seal made by Fowlers in 1925.

Histories/Potteries/Manufacturers

J. H. Oswald, Corowa. Edwards Street factory. (Part still there)

The giant of the locals. To the delight of collectors, he used four different styles and six different bottles. Opening in 1908 with an internal thread by Bendigo potteries, he then changed to a lightning stoppered dump made by Price - Bristol, a beautiful bottle that is honey-coloured glaze to the shoulder with light blue print. Continuing to spread the wealth, he now had a cork stoppered champagne type made by both Bendigo and Fowler Potteries. Both Oswald and Jackson used the same style of stamp on their champagne and crown seal bottles made by Bendigo and Fowler.

Wahgunyah Factories

R. Savage & Co.

Federal Brewery commenced operations in 1897 and used an internal thread made by Bendigo Pottery.

James Nugent, Wahgunyah.

Commenced operations in 1909 using a cork stoppered champagne type by Pinnacle Brand. This bottle is unusual in that it is one of the few stonies with brown print. James

Nugent also ran a dairy in Wahgunyah. These milk bottles are very scarce.

Rarity of the Corowa - Wahgunyah bottles.

1. D. C. Young (Champagne)
2. Watson & Young (Champagne)
3. James Nugent (Champagne)
4. R. Savage & Co. (Internal Thread)
5. J. H. Oswald (Internal Thread)
6. J. Mc Gavin (Blue top Dump) (2 = Bendigo and 1 Pinnacle)
7. C. S. Jackson (Champagne)
8. Watson & Young (Internal Thread)
9. J. H. Oswald (Crown Seal) Fowler
10. Jackson Bros. (Lightning Stopper)
11. J. H. Oswald (Lightning stopper)
12. J. H. Oswald (Champagne) Fowler
13. Jackson Bros. (Champagne)
14. J. H. Oswald (Crown Seal)
15. A. E. Jackson (Crown Seal)
16. J. H. Oswald (Champagne)

Story and Photo's, North East Bottle Club Newsletter, issue No. 1 1984 / 1985.

Histories/Potteries/Manufacturers

Rides of Benalla, Euroa and Yarrawonga.

Full page history in the North East Bottle Club Newsletter. No. 2 1984 / 1985.

Billson's of Beechworth.

Full page history in the N. E. B. C. Newsletter. No. 3 1984 / 1985.

Schweppes

Stone bottle of Schweppes with address on it depicts that the bottle was in service as early as pre 1832. Cavendish

Square with a J. Bourne Codnor Park Pottery mark on the reverse.

Mr. E. Rowlands

Three page article on the Rowlands Empire can be found in the August 1985 edition of the W. A. B. C. Newsletter.

Two pages article on the Rowlands and Lewis Cordial Maker, in the M.H.B.S. Newsletter Extracts, September 1972 - August 1973; including a sketch of the farmer & miner trade mark. Article by Karl Korju.

Plummer and Murphy, Aerated Waters, South Melbourne.

In response to my request for information on J. Plummer bottles in the last newsletter, several members have given me some information for which I am grateful; including the following notes from James Lerk. (James Lerk is an acknowledged history buff from Bendigo, who has a great interest in ancient bottles.)

The firm was established in 1874 by Joseph Langdon Plummer, starting with ginger beer manufacture. After the death of J. Plummer Snr. in 1891, the business was carried on by his four sons until the partnership was dissolved in 1893. Two of the sons, Alexander and Charles Plummer, with James Murphy; then established in 1894 the firm of Plummer Murphy and Company.

Above are sketches at half-scale, of the trade marks embossed upon the two Plummer bottles I have. Left: On a 10ozs. Lamont made by Kilner Bros. Right: On a 10 ozs. Codd patent, four-way, made by Melb. Glass Bottle Works. (Sketches supplied)

Article by Jim White in the M.H.B.S. N/Letter Extracts Sept. 1972 - August 1973.

N.B. Sketch No. 2 is the exact replica of the transfer on the Ginger Beer bottles from this firm.

Histories/Potteries/Manufacturers

Port Melbourne Glass Works

Several glass manufacturing works were well established in Melbourne as early as 1870. However, quality bottes were not being produced until the early 1880's and certainly 1900 Melbourne bottle users were no longer reliant on imports from the British glass works.

On the Yarra bank Emerald Hill, South Melbourne and Port Melbourne areas, the largest glass bottle manufacturer was possibly that of the two factories operated by Messrs. H & Lambton Le Breton Mount; near the old South Melbourne Gas Works. One factory was for flint glass, the other for glass bottles.

Mr. L. Mount played a major role in helping to establish the footing for the Melbourne Glass Bottle Company which was later to become Australian Glass Manufacturers (AGM), or more recently ACI. Mount can also lay claim to an early bottle patent closure known as the 'Mounts Patent'. The bottle had four triangular indentations on the shoulder and is sealed by a patent ball stopper. Unlike the Codd's patent, the bottle has no ridge to stop the ball from falling and breaking against the bottom of the bottle.

Possibly the last glass works to operate in this area would be that of Paterson Brothers, 'Caledonian Glass Bottle Works'. Not much is known of this firm. They were established in the mid 1890's and ceased operation shortly after 1900.

An entry in the Sands & Mc Dougal Post Office Directory of 1900, lists the firm as:

Paterson Brothers. Caledonian Glass Bottle Works, makers of all kinds of bottles.

Aerated Water bottles a specialty. Princess Street, Port Melbourne.

Of interest in this entry is the 'Aerated Water bottles a specialty'. Of all the bottles recognised as being of Caledonian Glass Bottle Works, the only types I have seen embossed are marble bottles. These bottles are usually embossed around the side towards the reverse base of the bottle. The factory was situated at the corner of Beach Road and Paterson Street, Port Melbourne. This site was excavated some time ago. All evidence of kilns and buildings has gone with time. What could be found was molten glass from the kilns and a few broken bottles, (not from the factory as all broken bottles would have been melted down). Of interest were the number of Hogben Patent stick closures and Lamont type stoppers. I have not actually seen either bottle type embossed from Caledonian GBW. I do not believe they made these types of bottles as they are of an earlier origin.

Sand in the Port Melbourne area is especially suitable for glass making. I read of the Graham Street glass works excavating sand near the lagoon. Paterson's works were on a large piece of land, they may have had their own sand pit or certainly it would have been obtained locally. R.B.

(R.B. Would have to be Ron Barry, editor of the W.A.B.C. Newsletter, from which this page was taken. There are a couple of sketches of a Mount's Patent included. August 1995, Vol. 17, No. 2.)

Histories/Potteries/Manufacturers

Convict Bottles

Nichodemus Dunn was listed as a Ginger Beer brewer at Castlereagh Street, Sydney, from 1842 - 1851.

Yoxall J. P.

John Proudlove Yoxall was born on the 4/10/1863 at Beechworth, Victoria. He was one of twelve children, having five brothers and six sisters. J. P. Yoxall married Alice Allen at Beechworth on the 28/3/1887. They had nine children, five girls and four boys, all born in Wangaratta between 1887-1909. The earliest J. P. Yoxall was known to have been operating in Wangaratta, is 1888. It is believed that he learnt his trade from Fred Allen, brewer, Beechworth. He opened his first brewery in Spearing Street, Wangaratta, then moved to the corner of Rowan and Swan Roads, Wangaratta. He also operated breweries in Rutherglen and North Fitzroy. He had ceased operating all of these breweries by approximately 1925, when he moved to Hepburn Springs where he bottled mineral water direct from the springs and sold it to Hepburn Spa. The three that made up Yoxall Brothers were :-

John Proudlove Yoxall
Samuel Marshall Yoxall
Beechworth Yoxall.

J. P. Yoxall died at Hepburn Springs in 1936.

P.S. Yoxall had a large variety of containers for his products including glass bottles of Hamilton Patents, Flat-foot Hamiltons, Alleys, Lamonts and Soda Syphons.

A full description of Yoxall bottles is reported in the N.E.B.C. Newsletter, No. 5.

W . Leak & Sons

William John Leak was born at Nunburnhilm, Yorkshire, England in 1831. William and his family left Liverpool on 2nd. December 1864 on a cargo steam ship called the Florence Nightingale and arrived in Victoria on the 4th. Of April 1865. On his arrival he took a temporary job as a butcher in Clarendan at Emerald Hill (now South Melbourne). In 1869 the Leak family moved to addaginnie, South East Victoria. In 1870 they moved to Oxley where they opened their first cordial factory in King Street. This factory remained operational until 1882 when they decided to move manufacturing to Bridge Street, Benalla where the business remained in the family until 1929.

The essences of all Leaks Cordials came from England and Germany. The good quality of their drinks was helped by a semi mineral well that was 15 feet from the curb of their premises and 40 feet deep. The Leaks drinks must have been popular for not only did they supply Benalla and Oxley, but they opened a factory on the corner of Warby and Riley Streets, Wangaratta in 1891, which ceased operation in 1916 and was managed by John Leak. (son) (Continued :-)

Histories/Potteries/Manufacturers

Leaks & Sons

In 1905 the Leak operation took over the Tungmah Cordial factory from a Mr. Cornish and used it as a depot until it ceased operations in 1909.

Leaks had a variety of containers including :- G.B's., Lamonts, Alleys, what are believed to be a 'Leaks' patents (similar to a Hogben's), Hamiltons and a variety of Soda Syphons.

A full report with diagrams in listed in the N.E.B.C. Newsletter No. 6.

U.K. Potteries

Port Dundas, Kennedy, S. Green, Bourne, Doulton, Taylor etcetera.

Convict types Ginger Beer Bottles

Leak, Fowler, Field 1840's, Mashman, Lithgow 1873-1896, and Amateurs.

Early Australian Potteries

Alfred Cornwalls 'Brunswick Pottery'	1859-1964.
Luke Nolan's 'Gillbrooke Pottery'	1861-1909.
Graham Ferry's 'Brunswick Terra-Cotta Pottery'	1890-1926.
Hoffman Pottery Company	1893-1968.} G.B's.
Victoria Pottery Works	1890-1906.

Most Ginger Beer bottles made by :-

Govancroft, Glasgow	C/s 1920-1940.
Fowler of Sydney	Possibly 1837- 1839, up until the 1940's.
Gutherie of Bendigo	G.B's not known but he started Bendigo Potteries 1857-now.

Bendigo Pottery	D, Ch, Internal threads, C/s etcetera. 1857-1937.
	Still operating as a pottery to the present day.

Dahlkes Pottery and Filter Works, Melbourne. 1872.

Footscray Pottery (Chesterfield Pottery Works) 1871-1872.

Agencies :- Mauri Bros. and Thompson.

Pinnacle Brand. (Bendigo Pottery) 3 types. ('Pinnacle' was a brand name by Fowler, as they shared pottery pieces, no doubt this was usurped by Bendigo.)

J. Gow Footscray (P.W. Taylor Pottery, London. Hop Exchange. (I2) 6 Mint. G.B's.
Jacobson Footscray 1926-1950. (20) 8 Mint G.B's.

Histories/Potteries/Manufacturers

Egypta Drinks

Egypta Products Pty. Ltd., Nicholson Street, Fitzroy appeared on the scene in 1922 and are not listed after 1924.

My Egypta bottle is small, brown with a crown seal and the mark is 'curly' A.G.M. It also carries the embossing, 'Pure Water Process Pty. Ltd. Melbourne'.

This article is listed on the top of page 24 of the M.H.B.S.Newsletter of Nov. - Dec. 1982. It was written by J.L. Scott-Kemball.

N.B. There are three known ginger beer bottles by this firm, there are two from the Bendigo Pottery and one from Fowler (Melb.)

J.W. Wilding

J.W. Wilding was one of the earliest soldiers in the fort at Queenscliff. (Victoria) He signed in on 18 July, 1882 and was No. 104. He was discharged at his own request on March 31 1892. He came from India and signed on as a wool sorter. He died on 13 December 1913 and in his obituary it says he was a cordial manufacturer and he fought in the Maori War.

In a map of the Fort 1905, it shows a cordial factory on the far wall near the keep. He was in charge of three soldiers working in the Soda Water factory.

The trade mark on the Wilding bottles is from the buttons on the old uniforms. There are two moulds of the Artillery bottle - one has spots on the bomb. The ginger beer bottles are from two pottery firms. A member of the family confirmed that Wilding bottled ginger beer under two names, Henry and J.W. Wilding.

The glass artillery bottles were never sold in the shops but were given to the soldiers to encourage them not to drink rum.

A two page story with sketches of the Wilding bottles on one page are to be found on pages 5 and 6 of the M.H.B.S. Newsletter of Nov/Dec. 1982.

Plummer Murphy & Co.

A three page article on the Plummer glass bottles with nine first class sketches, is reported in the M.H.B.S. Newsletter of November 1975. This article is by Jim White

Histories/Potteries/Manufacturers

G.D. Guthrie, potter, Camperdown, Sydney. Article by Paul Davis.

When George Duncan Guthrie came to Australia, he came to Sydney. In 1851 he went to work for Enoch Fowler. They were both Masons and Guthrie would have learnt a lot from Fowler. He then set out on his own and established a small pottery at Camperdown. The competition was very strong as he was competing against Fowler and Thomas Field who already had well established businesses. Fowler suggested that Guthrie might go to Victoria and told him where there were good supplies of clay where Fowlers were bringing it in from Victoria. Enoch Fowler made a gentleman's agreement not to sell his wares in Victoria, if Guthrie would do the same should he become successful. When Mr. Guthrie produced a water filter called the Abbott Filter, he informed Mr. Fowler who then produced the same filter in Sydney, called the Abbott but stamped Fowler. A lot of Bendigo and Fowler Pottery bear a remarkably same resemblance. Fowler at one stage even used the name 'Pinnacle'.

Potters and Potteries in Sydney & N.S.W. 1803 - 1900.

Fowler Enoch		1837 - ?
	Parramatta Street	1839
	" " & Glebe	1847
	Camperdown	1863 - 1871
Fowler Robert	"	1837 - 1900
Gardner John	Fitzroy Street, St. Leonards E.	1888
Gibson John	Herbert Street, Gore Hill, N. Willoughby	1887
Goodlet & Smith	Surry Hills Pottery, Riley St. Surry Hills	1867 - 1900
Grimly Arthur	Sydney District	1847
	Cambell St. Camperdown	1871
Grimly Charles	Cambell Street, Camperdown	1877
Gulson Frank	Albury	1886 - 1887
" "	Goulburn	1889 - 1899
Hall & Silcock	Waratah	1889 - 1890
Hart & Gallagher	New Canterbury Road, Petersham	1886 - 1891
Hewitt George	187 New South Head Road, Paddington	1888
Hillcoat Anthony	East Maitland	1872 - 1895
Hillcoat W.J.	Victoria Avenue, Chatswood	1900
Hilton & Barker	Highgate Street, Auburn	1894 - 1895
Hind Robert L.	320 Oxford Street, Paddington	1888
Hind William C.	120 Oxford Street, Paddington	1888
Holroyd & Rinder	Sherwood Pottery	1887
Hughes Samual	Merewether	1867 - 1895
Hutchins W.F.	Great North Road, Five Dock	1888
Ireland W.H.	142 Dowling St. Woolloomooloo	1873
" "	George Street Markets	1888
Irrawang Pottery	Near Raymond Terrace	1834 - 1852
Isaac George	Burwood Road, Glebe	1888
Johnson J.	Cockle BayPottery	1813

Histories/Potteries/Manufacturers

Potters and Potteries in Sydney & N.S.W. 1803 - 1900.

Kippax Bros.	George Street Markets	1888
Leake Jonathan	Market Lane, Elizabeth Street	1828 - 1839
Leiper Edward	Longueville Road, North Willoughby	1888
Leiper Robert & }	" " " "	1889 - 1890
Mundle George }	" " " "	" "
Leiper Samuel	" " " "	" "
Liebentritt F.	Cumberland Pottery& Tile Works	1863
	near Enfield	1893 - 1898
	Bankstown	1897
Liebentritt F. & Sons Cumberland Pottery & Tile Works, near Enfield	1898 - 1900	
Lion Tile Works	Enfield	?
Lithgow Pottery	Lithgow	1879 - 1900
Longueville Pottery	62 Hunter Street	1898 - 1900
McDermott Charles	20a Oxford Street, Paddington	1888
McIntosh F.	498 George Street	1875 - 1877
Marshall Henry	East Maitland	1898 - 1899

To be continued...

Some Early Australian Potter s

A two page article on Enoch Fowler listing his early start and the clays he used, is to be found in the August 1974 edition of the M.H.B.S. Newsletter. Also a small item regarding T. Field, Potter of Sydney including sketches. Pages 6 and 7. Article by Karl Korju.

Page 9 of the same edition, has a one page story of Phibbs Bros., Albury and Tallangatta with three sketches. This article is by Phillip Atkins.

Lionel Charles Phibbs came from Adelaide in 1875 and settled in Albury where he operated a cordial factory. He died in 1902 and two of his three sons took over the business. Late in 1902 they changed the name to Phibbs Bros.

Histories/Potteries/Manufacturers Impressed

Rowlands and Lewis 1873 - 1880 Melbourne

1 Rowlands & Lewis }
2 Rowlands andLewis }
3 Rowlands & Lewis }
4 Rowlands and Lewis }

Farmer & Miner } a/o/w &a/t D
E. Rowlands } t/t Ch
1854 - 1873
Ballarat E. Rowlands Pty. Ltd. } 1906 - 1917
a/t D t/t Ch = large range }
Lewis retired}
E. Rowlands t/t D Sydney 1884 ?

Potteries used :- Bendigo, Bourne (Denby England), Fowler Sydney, Taylor (London).

6/1/1880 = F & M trade mark
Sydney = 1884
Katoomba = 1888

Rowlands died 1894.

Paulson & Stanton Late 1850's. Campell's Creek, Midland highway, 5 k's Sth. Castlemaine

P.G. Dixon Coy. Ltd. 1851 - 1943 t/t. Impressed 1882 - 1898

G. Bennett 1854 partner with Timothy Lane, impressed bottles. Melbourne 1884 - 1915.
(Richmond)

R. Harrison 1866 - Melbourne

John Mills 1830 Main Brewer, own pottery, Melbourne

Dahlke's 1872 - 1888 Melbourne

J. Williams 1850 - 1860 Fryers Town and Vaughn, s/w of Castlemaine

F.G. Beard 1853 Bendigo

O. Dolphin Nagambie impressed at shoulder t/t internal threads, tonic ale, ginger beer.

Darby Bros. Rushworth impressed at least seven types D, also t/t ch including a dump.

G.H.M. 1857 - 1861 impressed at base, George Hugh's, Melbourne. (Chemists)

Wolton & Wigg Rushworth Victoria, impressed

Waters W.M. & J. Pleasant Creek, Stawell. impressed at base (2) at shoulder (1).

Histories/Potteries/Manufacturers

Impressed

W. Frane Before 1857 Pleasant Creek (Stawell) at least 3 types.

R.G. Urquhart Richmond, Victoria.

Grant Menon Whroo, Victoria. } 6 - 8 varieties. Also J.G. Menon Whroo.

Bruce & Sons 1891 - 1900 Bruce & Sons
B. B.
Bendigo

Jenson Huston Ballarat a/pale/blue 2 types :- Jenson & Huston, Jenson
&
Huston.

Footscray Pottery 1871 - 1872 imp. mid bottle scrolled down, small print.

Capel 1835 Melbourne, convict type.

S. Mason Wodonga Victoria, 7 types, mostly impressed at shoulder.

J.F. Liston 1860 Tarradale, Victoria.

J.F. Liston & Nize 1866 Sale, Victoria. Soda water, lemonade, ginger beer. Bottles of glass and stone. G.B. 75% of trade.

17 St. Kilda Baths

I remember when I was only twelve that I was first introduced to the St. Kilda Sea Baths. It was an eye-opener for me as I was just out of the Canterbury Boys Home, where quite strict regimen was implemented and good manners and courtesy were drilled in to all of the eighty or so boys there. It was a Church of England religion and there was fifteen minutes of religious instruction every day accept Sunday; where we had an hour in the morning and then another hour in the afternoon of it. My friend John Mitchell, who lived across the road from me in Kooyong Road, Caulfield, was the instigator who talked me into accompanying him to the baths one Saturday afternoon. Oh boy! It was sure a new experience for a naïve 'home boy'. At week-ends there was mixed bathing only in the ladies section of the swimming facility, which was separate from the men's section – divided by a high concrete wall. In the ladies section I believe all swimmers wore their bathing costumes – not so the men's section, one was able to bathe nude there. Costumes were not compulsory to wear. Men's bathing was for men only; women were excluded because of the liberty given to nude bathing. As a child I was very surprised at seeing men and boys without cover for I came from a very strict church upbringing. It took me about two years to overcome my inhibitions and swim nude. When I was eighteen, some of my ice hockey mates and I would strip off after skating of an evening and 'skinny dip' outside the baths in the public section of the beach; but I am getting ahead of myself. When I was still but a boy of twelve years of age, John and I would swim every week-end and some after school times at the St. Kilda Baths. We had a ball – skylarking as kids will – diving off the different heights that were available to us, such as different height diving boards of which there were six about the diving area; as well as diving off the various height platforms and railings about. The swimming area was larger than an Olympic Swimming Pool and the added significance of a sea that fights back at one, waves which at times were frightening to be amongst as you could be washed against the restraining surrounds or under the various super-structures that were the baths – even on a rough day one could be washed under the buildings themselves. As a teenager I lost a set of lower dentures in the swirl of the eddies and huge waves, the dentures could not be found in the torrid under wash. As a child it was great fun duck diving for sea shells on the bottom in the deep water. The depth of water rarely got above nine feet in depth at the diving end and petered out to the sand at the shore line.

Chasey was the main game played at the St. Kilda Sea Baths, although when one became a member of the swimming club which was based there – The St. Kilda Swimming Club – then activities such as racing each other was organised. We children were not ready for that, there was too much playing about to be done at our young ages. It was ever the way that to get away from another play-mate, we would swim across the baths from one side to the other, then race away to hide. There were a few good hiding places in the bathing area for adventurous scallywags like us. On the right side of the bathing area was a little two-roomed glazed shelter from the wind – which could be icy at times – this was really a change room for those bathers who were a little reticent about bathing nude themselves, but we youngsters always referred to it as the 'poofter's' rooms as we seemed to ever encounter ogling strangers there. Mostly we gave it a wide berth, except when we needed to hide. There were about four showers on the side platforms at the pool; these were cold showers to wash away the salt water before getting into one's 'civvies' – every day clothes – prior to going home. I recall that during my childhood days, before I took up ice skating and hockey at seventeen, I rarely got home before nightfall after a day at the St. Kilda Baths. We youngsters wanted to get our three pennies worth of swimming. I earned sixpence for mowing the lawns at home, this allowed me the privilege of the threepence admission charge and if one was lucky – threepence for a pie for lunch – which allowed us to stay for the whole day; and did we enjoy it! Beneath the building at the end of the baths on the left side was the superstructure which supported the Melbourne Swimming Club, there was a row of eight or so supports – three deep – and they had cross supports just at or below the water-line. These would normally have become encrusted with mussels or shell life but as the children were forever using them to swim to and then climb upon; they never had time for the shell life to form. Later this was used by me and the multitude of others to climb on and to swing from the one to the other; whilst being chased. The Life Saving Club and the Swimming Club was high above water – about eight feet – and the offices had two rooms; then there was a stair way which the members could use to get to the sun deck where the members could sunbathe. This had a high wall on the ladies side and a low safety rail on the men's side. As a teenager I and others used to dive from this twenty-five to thirty foot high wall into the open sea on the ladies side – where we would either clamber into the ladies section or swim around to the men's section and either climb the concrete wall to get back in, or squeeze through one of the gaps in the concrete wall which – if you knew of them - a child could get through and so resume the day's activity.

If one chose to dive off the lower wall into the men's section, you had to be a good diver, for diving was not just off the railing but the body had to clear three or four 'steps' as it were. These were about eight inches wide and about the same distance from each other. The lower step would have been two feet from the high water mark and if one swam under them on a rough day, well that person would risk having their head smashed against them as the wave took them. So, two feet from the lowest step, then four steps of eighteen inches plus the width of the planks (about two inches), would be eight feet ten inches, then the railing on the floor level at about four feet; then the building height of approximately ten feet then the balcony height of another four feet. In all, the height of diving into the men's pool from the balcony railing would be about twenty-two feet eight inches. And that was into a nine feet depth of water at high tide. This was higher than the high tower at the deep end of the swimming pool, which had a lower deck of twelve feet and a higher deck of fifteen feet. Add to that, from the balcony railing into the men's side a diver had to dive out from the building, across the floor level passageway, then out further over the stepped planks; a distance of approximately ten feet out from the building. Only very good (or foolish) divers were able to accomplish this feat. For five years (1942 – 1947) was I more than a weekly visitor to the St. Kilda Baths. I did often attend afterwards but very intermittently, as I then took to ice skating and skated in one form or another for sixty plus years. I look back at those five years as amongst the best years of my life (which at this time of writing has extended for eighty years). The St. Kilda Baths is no more now and the foreshore has returned to something of a scenic feature; however we oldies can remember the fun times of learning and camaraderie that ensues whilst we were able to enjoy the baths. One thing that was surely missed was the reaping of mussels from the surround shark-proof walls. They were anything but shark proof as there were gaping holes here and there that we daring divers found under the water. A favourite pastime of many adults was the daily harvest of fresh mussels that grew on these walls. Indeed there was a report in the mid to late 1940's of one harvester being killed by a sting ray – he was speared in the chest while harvesting – we youngsters took note and kept away from this dangerous area. I and many of my ilk really miss The St. Kilda Sea Baths.

18 St. Moritz Ice Skating Palais

The St. Moritz Ice Skating Palais first started about 1937; it was a dance hall and was converted into an ice rink with the proprietor being a Mister Harry Kliener. His second in command was a Mister William (Bill) Normoyle, who managed the rink with a very firm hand. When this writer first became involved in the rink, I was just seventeen years of age. Entry cost 11d including skates and that was in 1947 and I skated at the rink until it closed in the late 70's to early 1980. There were five ice hockey teams based there at that time, they were: Red Arrows, Monarchs, Demons, Tigers and the Pirates. I joined the Red Arrows and was with them for half a year. They disbanded in 1953. I then joined The Monarchs for three months and was enticed to defect to The Pirates where I ended my ice hockey career. I skated with The Pirates until 1959 when, by doctors' orders, I was advised to give it up as skating so intensely was detrimental to my health. I had contracted osteoarthritis. I gave away ice hockey but continued to skate socially as my lady-friend at the time was still most interested in it. During my ice hockey years I had become Vice Captain for two years and another two years as the Captain, until I ceased playing. Amongst my peers were a few very notable people, to name a few.

Lindsay Fox – a strapping young six foot plus defender.
Johnny Nicholas – an ex-Victorian Diving champion and his mate -
Roddy Husten – a diminutive little fireball of energy who was the Pirates first-liner. (Later of the Demons.)
Clarrie King – was our very successful Goalie. He became Lord Mayor of St. Kilda.
Peter Kavanagh – was the 'B' grade goalie and often stood in for the Seniors, he became a Disc Jockey for a couple of Melbourne Radio Stations. 3AK and 3KZ.

There have been many other notable people involved with ice hockey, not only from my team –The Pirates – from others teams.

Kevin Gronow – of the moving van people, he lived in East St. Kilda where his folks ran their business.
Brian Bullen – who ran a used car business amongst many others.

Then of course there are the Speed Skaters of whom one stands out for me, his name is Colin Coates. Colin came to my notice first as a ten-year-old, it was during the interval in an ice hockey game, we had a fifteen minute breather during half time when the crowd were entertained for fifteen minutes by the speed skaters. Young Colin was struggling to keep up with the older, more experienced skaters in the race when he just happened to exit the ice after his race at the doorway where I was resting. I called him over as I had noticed where he was going wrong with his strides. I made a few suggestions to him about rhythm around the corners and the boy showed a keen interest, he wanted to learn. So I arranged with him, for me to come to his practice sessions the next morning and give him some pointers. Early Saturday we got stuck into some serious training. He was a good student and learned well. Colin went on to become Australian Champion and then to represent Australia in no less that seven consecutive Olympic Games – a world record at the time – he never became a world champion or even placed for that matter; but he did compete with our colours and with dignity. He was the Winter Olympics Team Captain. I was very proud to have been associated with him. Colin had more recognition in Holland and other countries than here. Other notable Speed Skaters were:-

Colin Hickey, Victorian Champion - Eddie Spicer, Victorian Champion - Colin Cusden, Dave Morgan, Peter Pinsent, Wally Truscott, Ken Rattan, Ken Lee, Alex Figgins.

Ken Lee was also a great ballroom dancer – on ice – and instructed too. In the very early 1950's, the St. Kilda Ice

Skating Rink was taken over by the two who would have the most affect on my skating days. Ted Malony and Jack Gordon. Ted Malony had a brother Jack who had an ice skating shop in Kings Road, Melbourne, where a lot of the ice hockey boys got their equipment. Jack Gordon was the main resident skating instructor at the St. Moritz Ice Skating Palais. Of a Saturday evening there was always a night of dancing with many exhibitions. Some of the solo Artists were :-

Nita Solomon, Nola Wood, Pat Weeden, Tim Spencer, his sisters Faye and Shirley; these last three I had the honour of teaching to skate when they were children. Tim, (real name Harry after his father) was nine, Faye was seven and Shirley was five when they gave an exhibition of acrobatics on a rubber mat that was spread across the ice rink. This was an added attraction to the normal; routine of skating exhibitions. Their gig ran a period of ten minutes and was usually performed in town halls, the Tivoli, Play Houses and Football Clubs – sometimes three shows a night. As a spectator I was amazed at their agility and mentioned to a bystander that their balance was impeccable and they would easily learn to skate. The bystander said. "Do you really think so?" I said "Of course, they are naturals. "Okay!" He said. "You have the job!" I was amazed to find that the bystander was their father and that he had just got a job at the ice rink as a carpenter.

As the three grew up their expertise as skaters grew and they gave many an exhibition at the rink. Tim became a notable ice hockey player and represented Australia in the 1960 Olympic Games at Squaw Valley, USA. When he was ten years of age Tim did a standing somersault with half twist on ice, he was the first person ever to accomplish this feat.

The Saturday nights were special events with this type of schedule.

8 Pm. Dancing. Waltz, Fox Trot, Blues, Tango, Waltz, Quickstep.

Exhibition. Carmel Dockendorf.

Dancing. Waltz, Swing Ten Step, Tango, Rocket Fox Trot.

Exhibitions. Jacqueline Mason, Ray Ashton.

1.25 GENERAL SKATING.

9pm. All skaters are requested to be on the ice, at sound of gong, all skaters to stand still. Prize given for lady and gentleman on the secret spot – usually spotlighted.

Dancing. Waltz, Swing Ten Step, Tango, Fox Trot.

9.20 General Skating.

Ray Dean and his orchestra – Vocalist – Lewis Gould.

GOD SAVE THE QUEEN.

This programme was on Saturday Night 29 May 1954.

After my ice hockey career was over I was enticed to become a 'Floor Walker', this entailed keeping the larrikins in order and stopping any tomfoolery which could be injurious or a hindrance to the general skating public. For this service I was rewarded with a nominal payment of TWO SHILLINGS – twenty cents – and free admission. I was also a regular floor walker at the Glaciarium on the outskirts of the City of Melbourne. At the ice rink I regularly gave exhibitions of fancy skating such as the Chop Sticks, Grapevine, Rubberlegs etcetera. My expertise in that area was of the utmost extreme and I had no competition as few people could manage what I had practised and mastered. I have written an Instructional Manual covering most of the intricacies involved the likes of which I can not imagine being repeated. Rollerblading has added new movements and they too, are involved.

One of the features that came about at the St. Moritz Ice Skating Rink which was frowned upon and not encouraged; was Wall Skating, this I perfected on the rather low sidewalls surrounding the ice rink. There was a metal kick strip entirely surrounding the ice rink to save the wall from being chopped to pieces with the steel blades of the skates. This metal strip about eight inches in height was a challenge to wall skating as it caused the metal blades to slip. This slipping could be over come by an expert skater and so it was with me. Most pupils that I have taught to Wall Skate actually lifted their skates and plonked them on the wall higher up; this is NOT the way to do it. One must slide the skates all the way up the wall attacking the wall on an angle both ways i.e., forty five degrees angle to the floor AND forty five degrees angle to the wall. So one approaches the wall from the side whilst turning and the angle of approach makes entry to the wall smooth and also the exit from the wall. This must be practised and ONLY attempted by an EXPERT SKATER. Square dancing was introduced to ice skating in its heyday and proved to be most popular in Melbourne. Another outstanding performer at the St. Moritz Ice Rink was a small chap by the name of Ernie. I never knew what his surname was but Ernie could skate around the entire rink doing the 'Spreadeagle', this involves the skater skating sideways (crab fashion) with one skate forwards and the other skate backwards. His expertise was so good that he did the outside spreadeagle, that is, circling the rink backwards and also with his hair touching the ice. I have never seen anyone who could duplicate this feat and I doubt that I ever will. Of course, the fact that Ernie stood all of four feet two in height (including skates) may have had something to do with his nightly performance. There were many outstanding skaters to be witnessed doing a mountain of highly skilled things but one cannot recall them all. In the 1950's there was an Annual Ice Review, sometimes called a Mardi-Gras and the Ice Shows had all the glitz and glamour of a stage review. In 1953-1955 the Glaciarium was charging 11d. and 2/3d. with skates. St. Moritz had season's tickets that were available from March – October for the winter season at 9 pounds, summer season October – March for seven pounds; these were for night times and Saturdays only. About the time we changed our currency from Stirling to dollars and cents, the admission price was

1s and 11d. With tax it became 2s 3d.I seem to remember my last skating days at the St. Moritz that entry was charged at $2 or $3. St. Moritz Ice Skating Palais is sorely missed, gone are the hey days of ice skating in Melbourne. The other ice rink at the time was the Glaciarium, on the outskirts of Melbourne, it had four ice hockey teams against whom we played. Their teams were:- Hakoah, Black Hawks, Raiders and Bears.

P.S. In 2010 fabulous TWIN ice skating rinks have been erected in the city. Howard Reede-Pelling. 1995.

19 Dum - Dum 9-2-2006

Demitri was just so cute that one could see no wrong coming from this sweet little cherub. His mother absolutely doted over him and he was the apple of his father's eyes, even all of his relations were entranced by his baby looks and that cute little innocent face. Yes, Demitri possessed all of those qualities that endeared him to people and even strangers were apt to turn their heads in wonder at his Adonis - like features. But - that is where the innocence stopped - for Demitri was anything but an angel. Not that the five-year-old was bad or even intended those things that happened, it is just that it would seem everything which could or would go wrong; they just appeared to happen. Oh it was not Demitri's fault - like when he wanted a particular piece of wood with which to play - well he just tugged it away and used the stick to play with. It was not Demitri's fault that the stick happened to be holding closed the chute that the chicken feed was stored in. Of course once the stick came away then the chute opened and the chicken feed spewed out all over the ground. And Demitri did the right thing and told his mother that the chicken feed was leaking. Mother came racing out and began cleaning up. She said to the child "Oh dear, Dimmy, you are such a Dum - Dum, what am I going to do with you?" Well, Demitri wondered why mummy would want to do anything with him, so he just continued to play with the stick. Unfortunately Demitri's puppy Chuff - Chuff wanted to play with the stick too and raced over and took it from Demitri. Well of course the boy wanted it back and chased Chuff - Chuff to get his stick back. The chase went under the clothes line and the stick tangled in one of mummy's sheets, the sheet tugged free from the clothes line and was dragged through the grass and dirt with Demitri getting tangled within it. Demitri chuckled, for this was fun and the puppy thought it was too; he deserted the stick and began romping with the boy inside the sheet. In the turmoil mummy came across to untangle Demitri in case the boy choked and daddy entered the gate in the midst of all the commotion. Chuff - Chuff thought it was just part of the game and kept tugging at the sheet, knocking daddy's brief-case as he played. It was very unfortunate that daddy tripped over his brief-case and ended up in the middle of it all. Chuff - Chuff pounced upon daddy's hat and ran off with it to disappear behind the house. When the sheet was free and Demitri got up, his daddy was still dusting himself down and mummy was attempting to take the sheet in to be washed again. Daddy looked all about him but could not find his hat, Demitri looked too but he was not interested in daddy's hat so he wandered off to find Chuff - Chuff. The puppy went under the house to bother the hat in private so Demitri crawled under there too. How Chuff - Chuff got into the crevice near the fireplace was not the boy's concern, what worried him was how he would get out himself, because he was not as small as Chuff - Chuff and his little body became stuck. After screaming for daddy to come and get him out, the boy wondered why daddy was cross and he was all wet too. Demitri did not know that daddy was in the shower but it was not his fault. The boy was made to stay indoors and have a glass of milk, and then he had to lie down and have a little nap. Demitri liked meat balls, so when mummy made some for the evening meal of course he shared a meat ball with his puppy. Chuff - Chuff liked meat balls too and demanded more. Mummy said 'no' as Chuff - Chuff had his can of dog food already and the meat balls were for Demitri's meal. The pleading look upon Chuff - Chuff's face was too much for the child, so he sneaked a meat ball under the table to his pet. That it hit mummy's leg on the way to the floor was not noticed by the child but mummy knew. He wondered why mummy berated him and shooed Chuff - Chuff out. Mummy said it was bath time about an hour after the meal; Demitri was keen to have a bath because he liked to splash the water about. It was not his fault that the soap fell to the floor and mummy stepped on it. Her shriek was answered by daddy and he came to help mummy up off the floor. After he was dried, Demitri ran to the heater while mummy got his night attire, it was a serviette that caused the trouble. The boy found it on the side table by a glass of wine daddy had been drinking whilst he read the paper. Demitri was lighting it from the heater when mummy returned with his pyjamas. That he had his hand slapped and mummy was very cross, made the boy whimper.

He was right away put to bed and the light turned off. Sleep would not come so Demitri slipped out of bed and began playing with one of his toy cars, that the siren worked as the car moved did not worry the boy; however mummy came in and took the toy away and put Demitri down again. Dire threats that he would be smacked if he got out of bed again, ensured that the child would stay put this time. He looked about for something to amuse him as he was not sleepy, there was a large picture of a teddy bear on his blanket; Demitri got to playing with it. Deciding that he did not wish to sleep with a huge bear, the boy began stuffing it over the side of his bed. When most of the blanket was over the side, the weight took the rest of the covers off him too. Demitri just lay there without any covers over him, he tried to sleep; it was getting cold so he cried for mummy. She came in and put the bedclothes in place again - this time Demitri slept. Morning found him up before anyone else, he ran into his parent's room and jumped up and down upon the lumps that were his sleeping parents; they woke. Mummy was used to this behaviour and put her dressing gown on and began preparing breakfast. Demitri wished to help and began eating the toast before it was cooked. Mummy got his cereal ready and made him sit at the table and eat it, Chuff - Chuff began scratching the door to come in so Demitri got down from the table to let him in; that he pulled the tablecloth away a little was not his fault. The glass of milk mummy put there for him spilled upon the floor. Mummy was cross and said that Chuff - Chuff was not allowed in until Demitri had eaten all of his cereal up. While she was cleaning up the spilled milk, Demitri had to sit still and finish his breakfast. Daddy came in with the morning paper and sat at the table to read it, but Chuff - Chuff had slipped in the door when daddy opened it and was sitting at Demitri's feet; wagging his tail profusely. Mummy was too busy and ignored the puppy; Demitri put the lull in mummy's concentration to good use and spilled a spoonful of cereal on the floor for his little playmate. This was what Chuff - Chuff was waiting for and he wagged his tail as he excitedly lapped up the mess. Daddy kissed mummy and Demitri goodbye and went to work; this gave Demitri an excuse for leaving the table to wave goodbye to daddy. Mummy began cleaning the house and Demitri helped. As mummy stripped the beds, her little helper picked up the pillow slips and took them to the laundry. He felt that he was doing a good job too, even to putting them in the washer. Of course the washer was too high for Demitri to reach so he stuffed them in the toilet bowl instead. Mummy gave him some of his toys out of a cupboard and placed them on the floor of his rumpus room. Demitri played for a while then got bored and looked for something else to do. Mummy came in from the laundry to see why it was so quiet; Demitri was silently pulling the petals off mummy's prize roses that were in a vase on the coffee table. That the room was a mess of petals did not seem to worry the boy and he could not understand why mummy was making such a fuss. It was time for Demitri to go to kindergarten. Mummy strapped him in his seat-belt in the back of the car and drove there. Again mummy called him a Dum-Dum for getting his seat-belt and a toy snake he insisted on bringing with him, tangled with his zipper tie of his jacket. Mummy took a long time getting the three pieces untangled. How much fun it was to get with his playmates again, Demitri and Annie raced over to where Tommy was playing in the sand-pit. Tommy had filled a small bucket with sand so Demitri helped by spilling it out again. Annie said he should not do that because Tommy had worked so hard to fill it. Demitri began filling the bucket again for Tommy. When it was full Tommy spilled it out for Demitri, they all went to the tyres that were made into swings. There were only two swings but there were three who wanted to use them. After a little pulling and tugging they all went over to the tunnel to play. It was just high enough for five-year-olds to crawl through, two went in one end and Dimitri went in the other end; they met in the middle and there was an argument about who should back out. They all did. When it was time for mummy to pick Demitri up from the kindergarten, he did not want to leave but mummy threatened to smack him if he did not go home willingly. The bribe of an ice cream after lunch soon moved him.

That Demitri behaved himself on the way home was only a teaser, for so soon as he left the car and raced inside the front gate; Chuff - Chuff came to greet him. While mummy was locking the car into the garage, trouble began. The puppy, eager to have his little playmate back, jumped up to Demitri over-balancing the boy. That Demitri fell into mummy's garden of phlox plants was just part of the game to Chuff - Chuff, he worried the child's hair and jumped all over him. Of course mummy was appalled at the damage to her phlox plants but was more upset that Demitri would have to be cleaned up again. It was when he had been cleaned again that the boy found another way to be a nuisance to mummy, the soft rubber play-ball that Chuff - Chuff was in the habit of chasing about the lounge-room, was what caught the boy's eye. He picked it up and rolled it along the passage for Chuff - Chuff to chase. Daddy had taught him not to throw balls in the house so Demitri had to roll it, that the ball came to rest beside the umbrella rack in the hallway was not the boy's fault; it was very unfortunate that the puppy brushed against the rack and made everything come off with a very loud clatter. Mummy raced to see what the noise was and picked the things up, by which time the two who were the cause of her extra toil were in the kitchen. Everything was quiet when mummy came in and beheld the pair of them sitting on the floor amongst the flour that had spilled from the packet that Demitri managed to knock off the shelf. They tasted it and had flour all over themselves. An exasperated mummy smacked the back of Demitri's hand and put Chuff - Chuff outside. Another trip to the bathroom to clean the boy up again and then he was made to have a nap and be quiet for an hour or so, to give mummy a breather and have a cuppa. After a snack for lunch Demitri and mummy were sitting in the lounge room and mummy was reading a picture book to her son to keep him occupied, when the doorbell sounded? It was mummy's sister and her little daughter Susie, they often popped in for an hour or so and the children were ecstatic to have each other to play with. While they romped around on the floor the adults caught up with each others news. Chuff -Chuff was scratching at the door to come in but was largely ignored. The two children were enjoying each other's company. Susie saw the large decorative rug over the lounge suite settee and decided it would be a nice coat. While she was trying to get it Demitri helped, it would cover them both. An argument started about who had the right to wear it first. Susie said it was her idea but Demitri claimed it was his rug. Auntie Janice said that neither of them should have it as the rug belonged to the settee, she took it from them and they were sent to Demitri's room to play with his toys. Susie and Demitri played together well for about ten minutes, when the parents in the lounge heard the wails of Susie coming from Demitri's room.

"Here we go again!" Demitri's mother exclaimed. "Ugh - huh!" Said Aunt Jane.

END

Howard Reede-Pelling.

20 Komik Kuts

Smiler came from a very impoverished family. His father was always out of work and his mother was forever on the hand-out line, in an effort to support her family. Smiler had an older sister and a younger brother who was always getting into mischief. The sister, Karen, never stopped dreaming of her 'phantom lover'; no she had no boyfriend as yet for she was barely fourteen. Young mischief-maker Kelvin, at only seven, being the baby-faced type; was forever being spoiled by all. Smiler's name was Bryan but because he had a habitual grin upon his face - well - Smiler became obvious. Being the middle child of this unfortunate family, Smiler had only just turned eleven and imagined that he was now the man of the family; if ever his useless dad was away or ailing. There was a playmate at the back of his home that Smiler seemed to always play with. David was a little older than Smiler, by two years, however they played together quite well but David's mother was a little frustrated with her boys' playmate, as he did manage to get into quite a bit of trouble when he came visiting. Being a naturally playful child, Smiler was ever up to mischief. One day while they were playing billiards on David's table, Smiler, who was not at all interested in the game, hid one of the coloured balls from the game and refused to say where he had it hidden. David took his game seriously and was wild with Smiler and locked him out of the house, telling him to go home if he could not be sensible. Smiler, forever the clown, refused to go and climbed upon the roof. He managed to remove a couple of tiles quietly and climbed through the hole available. Walking the rafters he found the manhole and, hanging by his hands through the manhole, dropped silently on to the lush carpet. He unlocked the bathroom window before he made his presence known to David. That young man was suitably surprised to find that Smiler had somehow got back in the house. Smiler said he just wanted to return the ball and retrieved it, giving the ball back to its owner he thought would settle the matter. David was still miffed and told Smiler that it was too late; David did not wish to play any more as the game was spoiled. Out went Smiler once more. With a very broad grin Smiler hurried to the bathroom window he had unlocked and climbed into the house once again. Knowing that David would put him out through the back door, Smiler unlocked the front door this time before he was again accosted. David's mother found him going towards David's room and said.

"Oh! I thought that you went!"

David came out of his room with an exasperated expression upon his face.

"You again, how did you get in this time? Dad replaced the manhole cover."

"Ah, be nice David, I won't hide your ball again - true!"

David relented and invited Smiler into his room to play with his toy cars. It was nearing lunch-time and as there was little food to be had at home, Bryan said "Yes please" when David's mother invited the boy to have some with them. He would not be missed at home because if he was not there, the boy would miss out - if there was at all anything left to eat - and he often ate at David's house. Smiler was not at all a bad boy, it is just that he had the devil in him and neighbours soon became aware of it and tolerated the young scamp. It was a most unfortunate incident that caused a little more turmoil for the house of David. That his boiled egg was just too hot to handle, became obvious to Smiler as he let it drop from his egg-cup when he attempted to crack it; the wayward egg rolled down his leg and disappeared under a tea-poy. Smiler went to retrieve it and in doing so, upset the laden tea-poy. A bowl of sugar and the jug containing a little milk was scattered all over the floor. "Oops, sorry!" Was frowned upon as the mess had to be cleaned up. All unperturbed, Smiler sat at the table again and finished his lunch. David was wont to rebuke Smiler after lunch and in the privacy of his room. "Mum was not too happy with you Smiler, making a mess for her to clean up. You should have gone when you were first kicked out and then it would not have happened."

"Aw, I didn't mean it, the egg was too hot and I dropped it! Hey, have you got any new comics?"

"Yes, there's a Mickey Mouse one and the new Superman one - I'll get them for you - you just sit here nice and quiet while you are reading them. I want to work on my model aeroplane!"

They went about their various pursuits and peace reined temporarily. It was whilst Smiler and David were peacefully going about their temporary pastimes, that Smiler's mum could be heard calling for him. He left the comics where they were and answered the summons. His mum needed him to go to the shops for some milk. Normally it was a mundane every-day task for him; today however, there was a difference. Joey, the big kid from three doors up, happened to be playing with his dog in their front yard. As Smiler trundled past, the big kid saw him and yelled.

"Where are you off to Smiler?" Of course the younger boy told him and Joey said. "Hang on, I'll come with you."

Well, he was not a bad sort of teenager, and Smiler waited. They were walking along to the shop when Joey asked.

"What ya got to get for your mum?"

"Just a bottle of milk."

"Ay, look what I have!" He produced a coil of very fine copper wire; he said it came from a wireless set he was dismantling.

"What is it?" Smiler asked. Joey explained just what it was, saying:-

"It is so fine that it is almost invisible when it is strung out."

Immediately Smiler recognised a good use for it.

"Ay, when I take the milk home, what say we string it from one door knocker across the road to another one? That way the neighbours will not know who is knocking at their doors - ay - what do you reckon?" He looked up to his older mate with interest.

"Crikey yeah, that might be fun."

And so it came about that when the milk was safely delivered home, the two went about their mischief. The ploy worked well. With a couple of gentle tugs on the wire, the front door of the one house was opened. Looking about, the occupier shook her head and closed the door. The action caused the knocker to activate the opposite house door knocker, that person came to see who was at the door. The same thing happened and the two silent onlookers were having a hilarious time. As one person answered the door they would activate their neighbour's knocker. It became a frustrating thing for the two opposite neighbours but it all came adrift when a motorcyclist roared his machine along the road. The very thin wire was unnoticed by the cyclist and it caught him across the chest of his leather jacket. With a surprised shout he felt the pressure as the wire snapped. Luckily, the motorist was not overly affected by the incident and continued on his way. As the consequent sudden tug caused both doors to be knocked on together - both neighbours came out simultaneously. They realised that a prank was being played upon them and waved fists angrily. The two mischief makers beat a hasty retreat.

"Gosh, we won't be doing that again!" Joey said in awed tones. "We could have killed that motorcyclist if the wire had taken him around the neck!"

"Yeah!" Smiler agreed. "It could have taken his head off!"

But the wire trick had worked well, so that evening, just as dusk was setting in, the young scamp was at it again. He had learned his lesson about the dangerous practice of stringing things across the road, so diverted his attention to the footpaths. Yes, Smiler was baiting passers by with the wire trap only this time he was using string. He tied some string from a lamp post across the footpath to a picket fence, with the string going under one of the cross bars and then up to the overhead cross bar, where he attached the string to an empty bottle. Smiler hid behind a nearby bush and awaited a passer-by. He heard footsteps approaching and waited expectantly. The pedestrian unwittingly walked into the string barring his path and the tug of the string brought the empty bottle crashing down with a horrific clatter of broken glass, scaring the daylights out of the said pedestrian. Smiler could barely suppress his chuckles and remained silent until the pedestrian had departed. When the way was clear the boy came out of concealment, surveying the mess, he thought he had at least better clean it up. Smiler picked up the larger pieces of glass and put them in the gutter, the rest he just kicked out of the way. Upon arriving home the boy was surprised at the agitated way his parents were behaving, he heard his father complain.

"I'll wring the little blighter's neck if ever I find out who did it!"

Smiler discreetly remained quiet. No doubt his father was the pedestrian. The next day, Smiler was again seconded to go to the shop. On his way there, right in front of him lying on the footpath; was a ladies purse. Well, Smiler could not believe his good fortune. However the purse was empty.

"Damn!" Said the disappointed lad and threw it away.

After only a few steps he had a brainwave, retreating he again picked up the empty purse a broad grin covered his features. When the message was safely accomplished, Smiler got another piece of string and tied it to one of the closure bits of metal on the purse. With a huge grin he hid behind a bush again and holding one end of the string, heaved the empty purse onto the road. He awaited a passing motor. Two cars passed before a driver saw the purse. The motorist pulled over to the side and went to look at the purse. Just when he bent down to pick it up, Smiler tugged the purse away. The motorist must have thought that the wind was responsible; he had another go at it. This time it was tugged further away and the motorist twigged that he was being made to look ridiculous. Shouting "Bloody kids!" he returned to his vehicle with a rather agitated face, looking about for the culprit. Smiler remained hidden. He caught two more motorists with the jape before another one was too quick and stood on the purse before he attempted to pick it up, no doubt expecting some sort of a trick. The string broke and the motorist took off with the purse. Smiling to himself the little imp sauntered home. Kelvin was playing with a ball when Bryan got back home; with nothing to do Smiler thought he would play with his little brother for a while. It so eventuated that the ball just happened to bounce in his direction as he entered the back yard. Smiler picked it up and threw it towards the back fence. Chuckling at having an older brother to play with, Kelvin took off after the wayward ball, find it he could not. Smiler had only pretended to toss the ball, young Kelvin was unaware that his older brother still had it in his hand; the teaser hid the ball behind the lemon tree as Kelvin was seeking it, but of course it just was not to there to be found. Smiler assisted his little brother pretending to help find the ball.

"Ah gee, now you have lost it!" Kelvin moaned.

"Never mind Kelv' I can find you another one." With which statement Smiler retrieved the initial ball from behind the lemon tree.

"Oh - bewdy - do you want to play five-stone with me?" The youngster asked, hopefully.

"No, I think I can hear Mum calling me." Smiler grinned as he went inside.

It was holiday time and all of the young rascals were away from school for the holidays, this left most of them nothing to do but get into mischief. Smiler and his ilk were no exception, therefore one day three or four kids from the local streets were mucking about in the shopping area looking for some mischief to get up to; as usual they found it. The local cheap goods shop was their primary target as the children knew there were shanghais to be bought there, they were only a penny each but none of these little urchins had a penny; so they hatched up a plot. The youngest of them was someone's little Brother Stephen. So it was that he was seconded into the mischief. The boys were well aware just where the sling-shots were kept in the store, Stephen was induced to wander along the aisle until he was near the goods in question; then, instructed and coerced from the doorway of the shop - he grabbed a handful and hurried out. Unnoticed by the storekeeper because he was a very junior child, he nipped around the corner with his booty. Every little ragamuffin there managed to get a slingshot. Elated, they headed for the local park. For the next two or three hours all the animal and bird life in and around the park had a torrid time of dodging any missile that the lads could find. When there were no other targets for the boys, they reverted to knocking the flowers off the stems and even butchered the very leaves from the plants. When a policeman cycled past on his bicycle, the youngsters made a hasty retreat. Left alone one day with nothing to do (David and his folk had gone visiting) Bryan, with slingshot in his pants pocket, was walking past the local iron monger's. There on the footpath displayed for sale, was a Hessian bag full of staples. These were the sort that were used to staple wire to fence posts. There were many farms about the district, so of course, without getting out of step as he passed by; Smiler grabbed a handful of the staples. Very satisfied with his pocketful of dangerous little missiles, the young scamp hurried along the road. Very soon he came across an abandoned gravel dispenser - it was empty - a golden opportunity. Before long Smiler was safely hidden within the cumbersome machine (which he used as his fort) and surveyed the countryside. A lady came out of her house and began pegging the washing upon the clothes line. She propped it high and then went inside. Smiler looked at the tin roof which was within range of his slingshot, and let fly with a barrage of staples on the tin roof. Inside the house the racket must have been disturbing. Smiler chuckled to himself as the occupants came out to investigate, of course there was nothing to be seen; they returned inside. Smiler let them have one more rally and then deemed it enough. Thinking that if he kept it up the people would be really annoyed and search everywhere for the culprit. The boy did not wish to be penned down for a long while, so he desisted. After fifteen minutes of patiently waiting, Smiler deemed it safe to alight and make a hasty retreat. He did so successfully and again went to the local park. The gardener was there working away at one of the flower beds when the boy casually walked past. Noticing him, the gardener called.

"Hey Son!"

"Yes Sir?" The boy asked innocently.

"Did not happen to see any kids destroying my plants did you?"

"No Sir, I have only just entered the park Sir!" The man "Harrumphed" as Smiler beat a hasty exit and went home. About a block from his home a schoolmate was hanging over his fence with nothing to do, Smiler came up to him and said.

"Hi Jack, what's doing?"

"Nuthin', coming in to play?"

Well Smiler had nothing else to do either, so they went inside to muck about in Jack's room. As they were looking at some of Jack's toys, a kitten entered the room and purred against Smiler's legs. With a huge smile the boy forgot the inanimate toys and began playing with the cat.

"Dad made a chaser for the cat!" Jack proudly announced.

He got it to show Smiler. It was just a piece of string but it had a small roll of newspaper on one end. Jack pulled it around the floor and immediately the cat became aware of it, he chased it frantically.

"Oh give us a go!" Piped up Smiler.

He was given a turn at it. The whole room shook with laughter as the cat chased the bait. Smiler would swing the paper around and around an easy chair in the room, with the feline getting frustrated because he was not let catch it. Eventually, Smiler tossed the bait out from the chair and then drew it in, as it got near the chair he would pull the string up and away; but the cat kept going and slid into the padded upright of the arm of the chair.

"Ah - don't be mean to my cat Smiler. Let him have it occasionally."

Smiler could see the sense in that and did so. The cat would play with the paper a little and then when he was on his back with the paper ball in his paws, Smiler would take his attention away from it by dropping one of Jack's Plastic figures just away from the cat. The cat would go to the plastic figure and Smiler would then steal the paper from the cat. Jack's mother came in and suggested that Smiler should go home now because Jack had to have his lunch.

The boy went home saying - "see you tomorrow Jack."

At home, little Kelvin was eager to have someone with whom to play, so Bryan relented and played with his little brother. Kelvin had an old copper-stick that their mother had discarded as she now had a new one; this stick was being used by the little bloke to push a cotton reel with.

"Ay, give us a go Kelv." Smiler stated.

Because he had not used the two items before, Smiler was a novice at it and Kelvin wanted to show him how it was done. Kelvin took the stick and expertly pushed the cotton reel a few yards.

"See, it's easy!" The cadet gloated with a smirk. Smiler tried again - unsuccessfully.

"Ah, you rotten little twerp, you have practised at it - anyway - that is only a kids game. Let's have a game of footy."

With that Smiler got their 'football' which was only a tightly rolled and folded newspaper, and they played 'end to end' kicking for the next fifteen minutes. Karen poked her head out of the back door and they were called in to have some lunch. A piece of bread and dripping with some peanut butter thinly spread was all each had. Finished off with a glass of water each - that was their lunch - but it was enough. There came a visitor to the house, it was the local preacher.

"Just thought I would pop in to see how you are coping."

The reverend said, by way of opening the conversation. Their mother fussed over him and offered to make a cup of tea. It was gratefully accepted.

"Now, I am thinking of beginning a choir at church of a Sunday morning before the eleven o'clock service. Would you like your two eldest to participate at all?" He asked, smiling at the two children.

Their shocked looks and stunned silence was quietly answered with - "We can not afford to buy them any new clothes." A worried mother stated.

"Oh no - no indeed, that will not be necessary, the church will supply the surplices needed if at all the children are good enough to be wanted for the choir. We will have to assess them first of course - er - are you willing to have them come next Sunday at nine, just to see if they have any ability for singing?" He eagerly awaited her decision.

She looked at her children, and then asked them.

"Well, what do you think, do you want to give it a go? It may do you some good, give you something to do so you will not be getting in my hair all of the time."

Smiler had no desire at all and was about to say so, when Karen said

"Won't hurt to try, anyway are any others going?"

Smiler looked keenly at the reverend for the answer.

"My word yes, there are already seven young people interested and perhaps that boy David at the back of your place; he said that he was very glad to try out."

Smiler begrudgingly acquiesced when he heard that his friend would be trying out. Came the Sunday morning and all were milling about the church grounds, keenly watching for reverend Mullins to call them in to choir practice. The reverend came out with a huge grin on his face and welcomed all to come into the hall, where choir practice was to be executed. There were twelve little hopefuls attending and each was instructed to sing the scales. Well, none of them knew just what the scales were and had to be coerced into giving voice. A terrible racket ensued. Eventually each had been assessed as to their ability with singing, none were outstanding and the reverend smiled with confidence that the good Lord would provide eventually. There were three or four hopefuls though, amongst these were Karen and Bryan, David, though rusty showed promise. Two were absolutely hopeless but the vicar thought it best to try and encourage them, to the disadvantage of the rest. Karen actually had a very melodious voice and in time, would prove to be the head chorister. Bryan - Smiler - had what could become a boy soprano voice and the reverend gentleman tried his utmost to keep the boy as a lead singer. Smiler had other ideas and it was only through the astute eyes of the vicar, who became to realise that to keep the boy interested, he would really have to get David to remain. The reverend gentleman tried something a little different with these two boys; he had them sing a duet.

This was a stroke of genius as the dulcet tones together had a remarkable effect. It was truly the sound of angels singing. The whole choir became instantly aware of what the correct coordination of voices could produce. They all became quite enthusiastic. Reverend Mullins had a grin from ear to ear, his wildest dreams appeared to be materialising. Not only that the choir the church so dearly needed was an apparent possibility but the initial choristers were of a greater quality than he ever realised was possible; coming from the impoverished families in his diocese. With regular training and exercises to produce the better results, the choir was beginning to sound reasonable. It still needed lots of practice though and reverend Mullins gave plenty of encouragement to keep his choristers interested and happy. It became a regular feature that after choir practice, Missus Jellop, who did the church flowers and general housework for the reverend, also got him cups of tea; was seconded into providing refreshments for the children. This too, was a stroke of genius. Most of the children were very glad to have these little extra luxuries and it held the choir together. The after-practice activities became a great draw-card for others to try out for the choir. Soon the reverend deemed it was appropriate timing for the children to give voice at one of the Sunday services.

Surplices were provided and although some thought they looked to much like girls to be dressed up in 'dresses', because all were similarly clad, well they submitted. Two weeks of crash courses in learning hymns etcetera, was a gamble that The Reverend Mullins took.

Many who did not usually attend church were suddenly parishioners as their children were to be centre stage. Gasps and 'oh's' were quietly heard as the children were noticed in the choir resplendent in their surplices and almost unrecognisable. Smiler, as ever the mischief maker, had managed to hang an old dusting rag he found, down the back of the chorister in front of him. The duster hung from the surplice and came down to her waist; it was unnoticed until the girl turned into her pew. Silent titters coming from the congregation made the vicar aware that something was amiss; he could not see what the titters were about, so continued with the service. When the first hymn was to be sung, all waited expectantly for the expected riot of noise from the untrained voices of this new choir. A rather pleasing aspect of it was that the choir did not forget the tune and followed the words in near perfect unison. There were only three hymns that were practised as that was the choir's total repertoire, it sufficed beautifully. Reverend Mullins was swamped with well-wishers after the service. Typical comments were:-

"Oh I was very pleased with my children's singing, I had no idea they were so good." And.

"Reverend Mullins, you did a marvellous job with those little b - blighters, did you have to use a whip?" The good man passed it off with a smile saying -

"The Lord helped me tremendously, quite pleasing for novices, wouldn't you say?"

In all, the exercise was a howling success. Smiler was pleased with his singing and was in the habit of singing bits of what he had learned, as he went about his daily mischief. David once again was the brunt of the younger boy's activities. It was after the school classes came out and Smiler saw David as he returned from his school. As the older boy was now in technical school, they were at different schools. The older boy had just got in his front gate when Smiler accosted him.

"Can I play with your racer Dave?" Was frowned upon.

"Nah, you will only break it!" David said as he went to the door.

"Please, I will look after it - true - ah go on, please; pretty please."

"Oh all right but you better not damage it, wait here and I will bring it out; Mum said you are not allowed in until the week-end." He popped out and passed the toy to Smiler, who said.

"Gee thanks Dave - I'll look after it true I will!"

The boy played on the footpath in front of David's house with the car for about ten minutes, when suddenly the toy jumped the nature strip and ran along the gutter. It disappeared down the storm water drain. Peering down the drain from the road level, Smiler could see the toy but it was just out of reach of his outstretched arm. Frustrated he gave vent to an oath. "Damn!" He looked about for a means by which he might retrieve it - there was nothing about - maybe a stick? Smiler was tugging at one of the shrubs in David's front garden when the lady of the house caught him.

"Oh you horrid boy, leave my hydrangeas alone, go on scoot!" Shamefacedly smiler scooted. The next day when David fronted Smiler again, he demanded his toy car back. His little mate told him what happened and the boy was berated severely for his misdemeanour. The pair of them hurried to the scene of the mishap, luckily it had not rained or else the toy would have been washed away.

With a huge effort, David retrieved his car - non-the-worse for its night in the storm water drain. Their friendship was not overly strained by this latest little glitch. David frowned.

"Gee you are a worry, everything you touch seems to go haywire; you must be more careful or I will not let you have any more of my cars."

Smiler showed a little penitence and was forgiven. Came the next choir practice when the Reverend Mullins was to teach his choir some new hymns, young Smiler was of course late as usual; the reverend smiled it off with a 'hrrrmmmpft'. Of the new hymns were - 'Onwards Christian Soldiers' and 'To be a Pilgrim' - were mentioned and Smiler innocently queried.

"Why would Christian Soldiers want to be Pilgrims, don't they have to fight?"

This of course made the children present giggle. So Reverend Mullins had cause to explain just what was meant by both titles.

"Decorum children, let us not be by-tracked at what we are about."

"What does decorum mean?" Smiler asked very innocently. "Dear me - do not change the subject - we have much learning to accomplish!" Reverend Mullins urged.

"Yes Reverend."

"Now then, I have explained the scales and you have practised them very well - the choir will sing 'Onwards Christian Soldiers' as a choir and we will try to harmonise 'To be a Pilgrim'. Now I want David and Bryan to come in as a duet on the line 'To be a Pilgrim' each time it comes around. Is that understood? All the rest of the choir will remain silent on that line."

A proportion of the assembly muttered about this as they were not sure about it. Reverend Mullins was waving his baton and quietly intoning.

"A one - a two - a three."

The children began to mouth the words in their hymn books. It was a riot of noise and mistakes. Reverend Mullins muttered 'Oh God help us' as he rapped his pulpit with the baton. He had the duo sing on their own and the rest just listened.

"Now" - the choir-master said - "the rest of you will not sing what David and Bryan sang - you will remain silent until the duet has been voiced. All together now!"

And so the choir practice continued. Eventually choir practice was over and the children were allowed that for which most of them came - the stuffing of themselves with the goodies provided for them. It was purely by accident that the soft drink Bryan had, inadvertently spilled over the leg of the boy next to him.

"Watch it!" The boy said as he brushed the offending liquid off.

Smiler tried to assist but in doing so, more of his drink slopped on the affected leg.

"Ah you did that on purpose." The victim accused.

"Did not." Smiler replied as he fended off a push from the boy.

"Steady now children, it was truly an accident, I saw it!"

Reverend Mullins stepped in to avert any misunderstanding. Smiler gave the reverend gentleman a huge grin as he replied.

"See, I told you so."

The children were encouraged to finish up as they needed to go home to their parents to be ready for the service that was soon to follow. David grabbed Smiler and hurried him off home, just in case the victim attempted to 'get even'. When the service was finished and as the parishioners were either going home or gathering about the Reverend Mullins to ask of their children, a rather important-looking man was demanding to have an audience with the reverend gentleman.

"I am the Director of the Children's Choir in the City, I made a special effort to come and hear your choir today as word has got to the city regarding some of your Choristers. Would you make time for an appointment with me please?" Reverend Mullins was flabbergasted.

"How wonderful - er - would now be a good time? I have an hour before lunch!"

It suited the director admirably and they adjourned to the presbytery. It turned out that the gentleman was quite impressed with Reverend Mullins three main choristers - Karen, David and Bryan. Now although Reverend Mullins was flattered that his work at bringing their voices out was recognised; the truth was that with those three gone there would be nothing left of what was showing the signs of becoming an excellent choir. He expressed as much to the director.

"Well now, perhaps you could bring some of the others to the fore or mayhap acquire even better voices in the future. The point is that I can improve these young people much more adequately in the city with the best training available. Think it over - the children will benefit enormously with the correct tutorage - now is the time for them. Before their voices get spoiled by those who are not quite singing in the right key!"

Reverend Mullins was absently nodding in approval for the director was right.

"We will leave it to the children and their parents, shall we?"

Within a week the arrangements had been made for the three choristers to attend the church choir in the city, for a try-out of their voices. It was a foregone conclusion when the respective parents had been made aware of the benefits - and the fact that a quite substantial fee would be advanced to them for their services - if in fact they were accepted. The three unwilling children were accompanied by their parents, who attempted to brighten the children up with intrigue as to what the future would bring. The choirmaster was organising his children for practice, when the director approached him with the three would-be singers. They and their parents were all agog with wonder at the large practice room where the choir practice was being held. Of course Bryan tripped over a step which he had not been aware was there, consequently the pile of hymn books that he dislodged when he grabbed for support, were scattered about the floor.

"Careful boy!" Called out the director as Bryan attempted to clean up the spillage.

"Tut, tut, never mind; the boys can straighten them later. Mister Blains, the awkward one is Bryan - he and the other boy make quite pleasant harmony - er, David is it?" He peered at the lad in doubt. "Yes and the little lady is the lead singer - Carmen is it?"

"No Sir, the name is Karen, spelled with a capital 'K'". That young lady explained. "Bryan is my little brother."

"Quite so - now meet Mister Blains - he is the choir master and pay particular attention when he instructs."

"Yes Sir." The three chorused in unison.

"Well now, that is a good start"

Introductions were made all round and the parents were asked to sit in the background and pretend they were not there. The director sat with them. Mister Blains held his baton high and nodded to his choristers.

"Just a scale of hums please." He brandished the baton and the voices rendered a scale of hums. Mister Blains turned to the three would-be choristers.

"Now just like that, all together." The baton was raised again.

A mediocre chorus of hums was given.

"Yes, well we will have to learn how to sing in tune won't we?"

He arranged the trio in a semblance of order with Karen ahead of the two boys.

"Now, one at a time please so that I can assess your individual pitch. Karen, you lead then the little one followed by the other - er - David."

And so the first hearing was begun, it lasted for but fifteen minutes; then the director took the visitors away so that the choir could begin practice in earnest. Outside the church the director was explaining the procedure required of all choristers.

"The choirmaster needs to have complete concentration from his choristers; they must not be distracted from the lessons by ogling back at parents you know. They have to concentrate their efforts in the time allotted to them; time is of the essence because practice is so coordinated for precision you know. They only have an hour at each session and there are thirty or so choristers to be tuned precisely. That is how the State choir is kept in CINC, the beautiful voices blending in complete harmony needs to be properly trained for the most beneficial results. Come, let us relax in the comfort of the presbytery and have a cuppa." He led the way.

And so Bryan (Smiler) began what was to become his settling down period for the future, which gave his life more substance and solidarity; he began learning how to behave as a growing youngster should. His was now the beginning of the age of maturity that would fashion him into manhood. Gone the foolish days of childhood and stupid pranks, his blossoming future beckoned with the good graces of the church and proper direction.

The End.

21 Rubber Legs A true story

There were many activities in the active life of 'rubber legs' that was one of the incidents whereby Bryan was nick-named. At first Bryan took objection to the nick-name but as the years drew on he became inured to it, as most people at the two ice rinks where Bryan showed his expertise automatically cottoned on to the somewhat degrading term. It was very annoying for the young man who had only been ice skating for six months, to indulge in this pastime which was very new to him. The term came about because Bryan was a perfectionist; in learning to skate he wished to do what most of the so called 'riff-raff' at the ice rink practised daily. In those early days of his skating career all of the common scallywags took to doing a routine called the chopsticks, this involved more or less dancing on the spot in a corner of the busy ice rink out of the way of those who wished to do nothing more than skate around with their friends and just converse. The riff-raff needed to do something more energetic and of course played the fool in the corners. As Bryan (Rubberlegs) became a better skater he learned more and more of those intricacies of skating, which were becoming less known these were mostly called 'trick' skating and because it was a most unusual form of skating; people had to stop and gawk at those who performed these feats. This caused a little congestion in the corners where it was being practised and the management of the ice rinks began to forbid the practices. Of course the said scallywags only had the ice to do this on and so they got to doing just a little at a time so as not to be so noticeable, Rubberlegs was one of these.

Over the years of skating Bryan learned all that he could in this art and eventually he ran out of tutors, so with determination things were practised that were unheard of at the ice rink; such things as were practised by the ice dancers became a new learning experience for this 'hooligan' who incorporated new moves and dare devil antics into his routines. By this time he was an avid ice hockey player and during rest periods in practice, every now and again Bryan would indulge in his pet pastime much to the annoyance of his coach because quite a few of the players would join him and often they came asunder because it was a new experience for them. Bryan was heavily chastised for bringing practice into disrepute and it was frowned upon at practice during the ice hockey. After thirteen years of ice hockey Bryan was advised upon medical grounds to desist playing as he had developed arthritis, through the medium of the cold in the ice rink and then the hot temperature outside. He did stop playing ice hockey but as his lady friend at that time was still very interested in ice dancing, Bryan accompanied her when ever she went. This did not stop him from skating however, by this time the new innovation of rollerblading had come from America, out of the cold and into the daily grind of rollerblading Bryan became obsessed with his cherished 'fancy skating' as he referred to it, mainly because there were no tricks involved. As Rubberlegs lived near St. Kilda and there were many rollerbladers skating along the foreshore on a good surface from Port Melbourne to Brighton, Bryan (Rubberlegs) got into the habit of holding up his hand signifying a stop sign whenever he noticed a well accomplished skater heading towards him. With a query on their face he would ask if they knew how to do a 'flip-turn', invariably they did not so Rubberlegs would demonstrate one for their benefit and upon most occasions the skater would like to learn more. At one stage Rubberlegs would have as may as four hundred pupils a week wishing to know more, usually they were office workers on their lunch break or holiday makers but his expertise grew and he became well-known in the area; people came in their droves after work on a week day and at week-ends for tutoring. Rubberlegs did not charge for his expertise and was satisfied to just teach. One day a father and his twelve-year-old son came along and the boy wanted to learn how to do a good jump, Rubberlegs taught them both to jump a rubbish bin successfully. The father was not as accomplished as the boy so Rubberlegs took him aside and tried to improve him a little so that his son would not 'rubbish' his father. The man always landed awkwardly and it would be an improvement if he could just master a straight foot upon landing. Imagine the surprise of the tutor to find that this man had a prosthetic leg. In the future Rubberlegs would always enquire if he was at all suspicious of an awkward skater. There were many things that Rubberlegs taught. Some examples:

The Grapevine: A combination of 'wows' crossovers a central spin and a 'sit spreadeagle, then the whole lot repeated upon the return.

Cross footing: There are various types of Cross Footing, forwards, backwards, in front and behind plus variations.

Crossovers: These are amongst the fundamentals of skating but Rubberlegs found many new ways in which to entertain himself with these basic exercises.

Chopsticks: Chopsticks comes in many forms and they are very tiring. Chopsticks is basically dancing upon the spot, with the legs moving in and out as a pair of chop sticks. These may be practised inwards, outwards, in a tight circle or a very large circle (Rubberlegs is the name given to this large circle variety) there is also an inwards/outwards type of chopsticks. Chopsticks can also be accomplished in a straight line left or right inwards or outwards.

Maltese Cross: This is another basic mundane thing to do which can be made to look spectacular with a toe or heel lift.

Wall Skating: Only very proficient skaters are advised to attempt this exercise, it involves skating in an arc then attacking a wall, preferably brick or concrete, where the wall is an extension of the floor.

Moon Walking: As copied from an American entertainer, it involves moving backwards while appearing to propel forwards, spectacular upon Rollerblades.

These are just a few of the capers Rubberlegs was involved in teaching, many other things such as one footed lay backs forwards and backwards, thirty or so jumps of one kind or another, sprays upon the ice only as it is detrimental to the compounds to attempt sprays on rollers, seven or eight different ways to stop, one wheel skating on the toes or the heels, train lines forwards and backwards, snakes, esses, corkscrew and varieties thereof, varieties of the wow which is mostly used for learners to gain control and all those things that I can not bring to mind. Oh I just remembered - there are many types of Spread eagle too.

When Rubberlegs was but a learner at chopsticks, he would often discover one of his mates standing behind him with one hand above his head; this hand was pretending to be holding a string upon which Rubberlegs was hanging like a puppet. Because the body was virtually motionless in so far as travelling was concerned, this action was quite believable, as the body rotated so the holder of the imaginary string would turn with the movement. As the chopsticks was being progressed Bryan got into the habit of placing a one shilling coin (10 cents) on the ice and performed around it, to his credit he never once came asunder by stepping on the coin. This gimmick was a great spectator sport as every person expected to see a fall. One very hard exercise for Rubberlegs was the Spread eagle, this can be performed in a variety of ways but Rubberlegs was not as agile as a good many others due to his ice hockey days. His legs became muscular and did not respond very well to the Spread eagle. This exercise is performed by skating sideways, that is, one foot facing forwards and the other facing backwards. One could actually skate around the entire ice rink sideways. With muscular legs this is quite an effort. By moving the forwards facing foot forwards and then drawing the backwards facing foot up to it one could propel them along. There are many variations which a proficient skater could accomplish doing this practice. One chap, who was rather slight of stature and stood barely five feet high with his skates on, nightly performed the spreadeagle all the way around the ice rink. Not only did he do this but he actually circumnavigated the rink leaning over backwards with his hair brushing the ice; in those days of the 1950's hair was worn very short. The Grapevine too has a few varieties, it may be performed in its natural style of north and south or in a triangle; even a square. There are many added varieties of this one too, one or two 'wows' a double or triple central spin and many different spreadeagle sits, toes up, toes down and even just a toes in stop before the return.

At this time of writing Bryan (Rubberlegs) is eighty years of age and still tutoring the arts of rollerblading, he is currently Coaching a thirty-eight-year-old and tutoring him to be an instructor so that Rubberlegs' sixty-three years of practice will not be wasted. The student, a Malaysian young man, is currently instructing a couple of his own students under the practised eyes of an expert. Both young ladies are progressing very well indeed.

When and if Rubberlegs does get another student he passes that student on to his instructor, this is because age and arthritis has affected the coach so badly that his movements are now dependent upon a mobile scooter. From the side, the coach now watches over his students; nothing escapes his eagle eyes. Bryan Howard Reede-Pelling (Rubberlegs) uses the last three quarters of his name as a nom-de-plume for he is also a prolific writer. He currently has 17 of his works published and another 20 are finished and awaiting publication. One of his most cherished works is an instructional manual of those tremendous exploits that are pertinent to skating, his baby as it were. Besides wall skating, the only other lessons to pass on to his instructor are the many and varied jumps and spins that are quite difficult to teach when one is unable to demonstrate those very prolific movements. There is yet time for his star pupil to come to grips with these as yet.

Acrobatics upon ice is only sometimes used in stage shows or reviews, there were not many performed when Rubberlegs was into ice skating. With his forays upon roller blades though, somersaults could be practised in park lands at bends in the pathways upon which the skaters were apt to glide along. Rubberlegs would skate flat out until he came to the bend in the pathway and then execute some of these highly dangerous somersaults as he went straight ahead instead of turning; a reasonably soft landing was some consolation for a mistimed stunt. He only came to grief when he attempted combinations of some of these jumps though.

Bryan used to teach swimming to under-privileged children for some fifty years of his life and of course diving was part of his routine, so of course were a few dives. Not being an exponent of diving and having never been instructed himself, he had limited experience at this activity and from a standing start or even upon the springboard; where a dive was usually a one-and-a-half it was stand upright and enter the water head first. It was different on the grass where the somersaults began in a standing position and had to end in a standing position; nonetheless Rubberlegs persevered and successfully completed many somersaults including with twists. These he has yet to pass on to his student instructor. To properly enjoy the art of skating be it upon ice, four cornered skates or roller-blades it is most desirable to be expertly instructed; not only for safety's sake but so that one does not learn bad habits. Skating correctly is a very enjoyable pastime and an excellent way to exercise.

(Bryan) Howard Reede-Pelling.

22 Bird Poems

Azure Kingfisher

Little kingfisher of regal stance,
Not often seen with casual glance.
Creamy white chest and blue azure back,
Looking for bugs or shrimps to attack.

It sits for hours upon a branch low,
One wonders when at last it will go.
But patience it has all the day long.
And only when flying sings a song.

Now it could be said or so I've heard,
Azure kingfisher, wonderful bird.
Large head and bill with tiny wee tail,
More colourful too, always the male.

Tiny swift elf it dives for a meal,
A flash of brightness, plenty of zeal.
To see nature true makes up my days,
Wonderful bird on our waterways.

@ Howard Reede-Pelling.

From the Bridge

A footbridge spans the Yarra where
I sit for hours, at birds I stare,
Those gentle doves that give a coo
And some, well gee, I wish I knew.

Rainbow Lorikeets pretty birds
And they are never lost for words,
They give a raucous strident screech
And hang about like any leech.

But small blue Wrens and tiny Tits
They always thrill me just to bits,
And Bell Birds with that ringing peal
Hide in the gums that do conceal.

Of course the common Sparrow too
It does abound as Mina's do,
And there are Wattle Birds galore
But I don't care I must see more.

Did I forget Magpies and Ducks?
The Mud lark which in mud it mucks,
It builds its nest as Swallows do
Rosellas, Starlings, Blackbirds too.

To idly while my time away
Look down at water so grey,
But up on high I see the birds
Peaceful, I have no need of words.

@ Howard Reede-Pelling.

Little Bird Song

Little bird, little bird, sing me a song.
Little bird, little bird, I'll tag along.
Whistle sweet, whistle sweet, your song is true.
Whistle sweet, whistle sweet, how I love you.

Colours bright, colours bright, sweet little bird.
Colours bright, colours bright, have you not heard.
Prancing gay, prancing gay, you won my heart.
Prancing gay, prancing gay, we will not part.

Little bird, little bird, we'll build our nest.
Little bird, little bird, make it the best.
Tiny eggs, tiny eggs, safe in a storm.
Tiny eggs, tiny eggs, we'll keep them warm.

Bill and coo, bill and coo, soon eggs will hatch.
Bill and coo, bill and coo, what a good match.
Little birds, little birds, break from the shell.
Little birds, little birds, looking so well.

@ Howard Reede-Pelling.

Coo!

Foolish Dove upon the road,
Pecking at the tar,
Your crop is full you have a load,
Look out, here comes a car!

Flutter madly leaden wings,
Fly the wrong way too,
Lead your mate into the things,
Not even time to coo!

Barely missed you that time,
Go back if you must,
Scratching in the grime,
Looking for a crust.

A senseless bird the Dove,
Never seems to learn,
That's a car above,
Just feathers left to burn!

@ Howard Reede-Pelling.

Graceful Giant

Slight the breeze that whisks on by as ever wafting in the sky,
Oh graceful giant of feathered wing who soars above ev'ry thing,
Use the wind so very well with majesty and pride do tell,
Far wings outspread this lovely bird, walks ungainly so I've heard.

Ah! Grace and poise so far above to watch it fly that I love,
Wheeling in a driving arc it keenly scans the Nature Park,
For there is a lagoon below, upon it is a mate, I know,
Harsh the call it screeches loud winging home a mate so proud.

Down amongst that multitude in bustling chatter oh! So rude,
Then taxi in on webbed feet settle smoothly very neat,
The mate was found unerringly, could we do it you and me?
No that is something birds do best prancing as it comes to rest.

Communicate in nature's way bills clashing what do they say?
Perhaps a hearty welcome home, stay with me here, do not roam,
They preen each other settling down amongst the weeds muddy brown,
Together forage in a band, lovely bird, the Pelican.

@ Howard Reede-Pelling.

My Swallows

Such glossy velvet almost black
The brilliant sheen upon her back,
With faded orange neck and face,
My Swallow wings at such a pace.

Sweet lively bird of tapered wing
A kindly elf, a pretty thing,
Lilt gently on the fickle breeze,
Seek insects as you brush the trees.

Replete she preens upon the wire
Chest whitish grey, I so admire,
My feathered agile little friend,
That stops to chatter without end.

No not to me her song is meant
For there, another does torment,
She did but answer a mating call,
And never sang to me at all.

The two are rapt in nature's way
That cock of course, has more to say,
Pursues his hen with wond'rous poise,
At last she weakens to his noise.

'Tis nesting time that part of year
Love blooms, my birds are very near,
They fly with sure majestic grace,
My Swallows wing at such a pace.

@ Howard Reede-Pelling.

Pidg'ns

O'm thirty miles fr'm 'ome jus' now
An' I come 'ere be car,
T' let me pidg'ins show me 'ow
T' git back, it ain't far.

They've all done it of'n enough
They knows th' way be heart,
An' even though th' flyin's rough
Th' leader's pretty smart.

E' circles 'roun' th' let go place
Until 'e sights th' way,
An' then 'e scoots orf at a pace
Th'others in th' fray.

They's 'awks an' winds an' all that stuff
Wot makes th' goin' 'ard,
But 'e don't care if it is rough
As 'e 'eads for me yard.

I finds 'im 'ome when I gits there
An' all th' others too,
They's struttin' 'roun' wivout a care
All sayin' bloody coo!

@ Howard Reede-Pelling.

Ah, they's a nuisance.

Them flamin' Galahs is took over agin'
They 'as eaten me crop t' th' groun',
O'l 'ave t' give 'em a good ol' mickey finn
T' git rid a' th' buggers fr'm town.

They ain't wot y'd call a real boon t' th' place
'cause they's alwuz eatin' th' new seed,
An' y' keep getting' all that egg on y' face
When they's 'angin' aroun' fer a feed.

Yer c'n shoot 'em an' swear an' frow fings at 'em
But it don't do no flamin' good,
I fink o'l 'ave ter git me ol' matey Lem
Ter 'elp me trap 'em ifn 'e would.

Now I know there is drugs wot knocks 'em right out
They gits drunk an' they looks real funny,
N' I can't feel sorry, they's worse than th' drought
It's worf it 'cause 'at saves me money.

@ Howard Reede-Pelling.

Pesky Maggies

I got this darn Magpie wot wakes me each day
'e's up at th' breakin' a' th' dawn,
Me missus allows it's more likely t' pay
If I frightens 'im orf wiv a horn.

But th' darn 'orn'll make more noise 'n 'e does
N' I gets a 'eadache real easy,
O'd rather git sumpin' that makes a real buzz
'er else make 'is perch real greasy.

Mind you, Maggies sing a won'erful ol' song
An' they ain't alwuz reely pesterin',
I s'pose they's nature n' we gits along
Excep' when th' buggers is nestin'.

Too right they's dang'rous an' 'its yer on th' scone
But tha's on'y t' protect th' young,
A coupla weeks an' th' nestin' time's gone
Maggies is good ter be out among.

@ Howard Reede-Pelling.

Somethin' t' crow about

We 'ad a storm las' Saturd'y night
Wiv' an 'owlin' wind wot ruined me shed,
Crikey it give us a rippin' fright
An' a darn picture fell an' 'it me 'ead.

Th' chook 'ouse ain't got a roof no more
'cos it blew orf inter our big dam'
They's a lotta cleanin' up f' sure
O'm gunna be workin' 'ard I am.

Me 'ens is strewn all over th' place
An' they ain't a crow in me rooster,
Sits aroun' a queer look on 'is face
'e don't chuck a chest like 'e useta.

Th' missus reckons they'll all come good
T'be in th' coop once agin,
But o'd swap places wiv' 'er I would
'stead 'a seachin' th' scrub f' an 'en.

@ Howard Reede-Pelling.

Printed in the United States
By Bookmasters